The Vagabond Stage

To Vanessa

Kell Cowley

From one theatrical
author to another.

Kell
Cowley

Odd Voice Out Publishing
Chester, UK
www.oddvoiceout.com
oddvoiceout@gmail.com

Ordering Information:
ISBN: 978-0-244-50095-5
Quantity sales. Special discounts are available on quantity
purchases by corporations, associations, and others. For
details, contact the publisher at the email address above.

Printed in the United Kingdom

For K.C. Finn, my partner in oddness and the theatre master of our own personal troupe. My novels might never have seen the light of day without you.

Prologue

To my crowd, whoever you might be.

It has taken time to find the words to tell this tale. Not just the time I spent mastering a quill, learning the sounds and strokes of every letter. It's easy enough to make the shape of a word, but the hardest thing of all to make those words speak. Especially for me and who I've been – a stuttering farm lad, afraid of his own voice. A boy who long kept his mouth shut and lived only in his head.

But I know the words now. I've collected enough words to tell the story of all I have become since I left that boy behind. All the roles I've taken on, each with their own voice and their own guise. And for the parts that I've played...their own dress.

My master says that to be a player is to live and die many times over. He's the one who wrote my girls into being. Those girls I became on his stage. My master writes stories to be said out loud. His scripts are filled with the hottest of words that must be raged, wailed or wept over when they are performed before a crowd.

I cannot write like he does. This isn't a story that I can shout over the drunken bellows of the inn yards we usually play. These are words that I want to pass on very softly. Words I want to whisper from this parchment to one listener at a time.

Are you listening? Then let me tell you.

Let me put down in words how my first life ended and how my many lives that followed began.

Act One
Scene One

The Dying Boy

The night I saw my first play was the night I burst into flames. It wasn't the first time I had feigned my own death, but I felt certain it would be my most horrifying attempt so far. I had sworn that this would be the death that stuck. The death that I never returned from. Leastways not to my family, who'd proved to be such a poor audience.

It'd once been my habit to snatch up my father's butchering knife, jab it beneath my arm and stagger to the ground, rattling out a scream as I fell. This rarely earned the response I was hoping for. I belonged to a farming family and slaughter was a part of our routine chores. Pa would sometimes jump at my shrieking displays, little flinches that filled me with mirth. But after booting me in the ribs and seeing no signs of bleeding, my dramatic turns would receive only gruff orders to put the knife down and get back to work. Pa had no use for my many and varied deaths. He kept saying I needed to grow out of them.

Everything needed to grow on the farm. I was forever in trouble for being the stunted member of the Child family. I was in the summer of my fifteenth year, but my spine had yet to stretch, my beard had not sprouted and my voice remained shamefully squeaky for a lad my age. But in spite of my weedy appearance, I was quietly mastering a skill. Even if it was only this secret craft of my own invention. Even if, in my family's eyes, I was just playing pretend. I felt certain I would one day use my sole talent to devastate them all.

I was ready now. I was rehearsed. This night, if all went to plan, I would give my family something they had never seen before and would never forget. They'd get a glimpse of everything that I might become. And then they would never have to see me again. Neither would I see them…which would be a relief for all concerned.

I stood in my room, staring down at my props. For months I'd been gathering materials to stage my own spontaneous combustion. I'd been polishing the chalky bones that were all that remained of our pigs once their meat was stripped and cured. I'd been pocketing fistfuls of ash from the hearth early each morning. Slowly I had crafted a burnt black skeleton. *My* burnt black skeleton that I had been hiding under the bed, waiting for the right moment to make it smoke.

I took a breath, my nerves rattling me. I wasn't ready to explode just yet. So, I slipped out from the bedroom, wanting a last look at my intended audience before I took my leave of them. I shrank against the wall as I tiptoed downstairs. I knew where all the creaks were in our floorboards. I'd practiced avoiding them so I could lull the old house into an unsuspecting silence. I was quiet as a shadow, a ghost haunting my own home. If I held my breath, then I could make-believe that I had disappeared from sight. I was especially good at this last charade. My family were always so willing to play along.

Pa and my brother Flannery did not see me as I peered into the kitchen to find them sitting beside the heap of turnips they'd unearthed that afternoon. They studied the roots vegetables like they were lumps gold, inspecting them for dirt in the fading light. It was dusky but not yet dark beyond the farmhouse windows, the sun reluctant to set on what had been a sweltering July day. It was a day I'd spent lurking in patches of shade, playing out my death scene in my mind and assessing it for possible pitfalls. Meanwhile, the other men of the Child family had been toiling in the fields, picking and preparing our crops for the market on the morrow.

Now they sat slumped in their chairs, their eyelids drooping and neither of them talking.

I was never close to my pa or brother, but it was hard to look away, knowing this would be the last time I saw them. My eyes lingered on Flan's face the longest, the face that I shared with him – the same wide green eyes and short snub noses. My brother's cheeks were fuller and his skin more sun-browned, lending him an altogether more comely appearance. The same features on my face were pinched and pale and seemed to bulge from my skull. Such was the result of me shying away from outdoor chores and consequently going without so many suppers. As we'd grown, Flan had gained the height and weight advantage and he always made me painfully aware of it.

He had a sense of timing Flan, I'd give him that. He always waited for just the right moment when our pa turned his back before lashing out with his feet or fists, bruising me for no better reason than that he could. I had only one fond memory of making Flan jump in return. It was the morning I suspended myself from the rafters in the barn. I'd coiled a rope loosely around my throat, but fastened it about my waist, hiding it beneath my shirt so it looked like I was strung up by my neck. I had dangled for almost an hour before Flan found me. His scream upon entering the barn had thrilled up my spine.

10

"You'll go to hell, you know that!" Flan had snapped, realizing my trick only after I had scuppered my illusion with a smile. "Why do you do these things, Timmy? What's it all for?!"

I'd shrugged, swinging on my rope harness.

"It's just something I'm working on."

"You never *work*," he'd sneered, before seizing my breeches and yanking them to my ankles, leaving me squirming and exposed.

I swallowed the memory down and turned my back, leaving Pa and Flan to nod off over their vegetables. I'd be getting their attention soon enough. And this time, there'd be no logistical difficulties, no trouble with timing or twitchy involuntary movements that gave me away. No more cords that snapped, blades that nicked or water that got up my nose. I'd leave them trembling in cold sweats. I would –

"What are you creeping for?" a voice sneered.

I froze in the doorway of my mother's room. Ma had already given up on the futile evening, though the moon was barely visible in the still blue sky. I twisted my neck to see her slumped in bed, her back thrust at me. She might have been talking in her sleep. It wouldn't be the first time I'd overheard her scolding me in her dreams.

I held my breath, willing her to drift off again.

"I can *tell* you're creeping," said Ma, her voice a slurred murmur. "Get back to your shadows, you morbid thing. Stop tiptoeing your cursed presence all over my house. May the Devil strike you down. May he turn you to ash and bone…"

This last happy thought was how my mother had bid me goodnight all my young life. It was me who'd prevented her having a larger brood of children, so many lost siblings that might have been of better use in the running of the farm. I'm told that after Flan came, Ma's body had been racked with birthing pains once more, pains so grievous she had screamed the house down and brought many townsfolk trudging uphill to what they'd assumed would be her deathbed. They say Ma begged a physician to take a knife and cut the *'Imp of Satan'* from her belly, but the man hadn't the skill or stomach for such an exorcism.

It was a full day later that I had finally emerged. The midwife had predicted I would be stillborn, but after my wailing proved her wrong, she persisted that I'd turn blue by the following winter. Somehow, I'd survived to grow into the scrawny whelp now darkening my mother's door. She'd never forgiven me for living this long. My hard birth had left her not only barren, but near crippled, rarely moving far from her bed. Though her hand still whipped out to wallop me whenever I was within reach. Ma liked to put tears in my eyes. She swore she'd never known a boy so quick to cry. She said if only I'd been born a girl, then they could've sold me off as a little wife to some lonely traveller.

Ma was the one I'd miss the most. Her superstitious ravings had fed my imagination more than anything else on the farm. If there was anyone in the Child family I took after, it was her. I waited until Ma's breath fell back into a steady rhythm of snores. I couldn't risk her stirring like that again. I had to act now. I stepped back into the room I shared with Flan. The single cot bed belonged to my brother, of course. I slept in an itchy nest of straw on the floor. Or at least I did on nights when I wasn't locked in the sty as punishment for my idleness. Since my own bed wasn't fit to serve as a stage, I spread my bundle of bones on my brother's sheets instead. My charred remains were tucked inside my single set of work clothes, the final costume for the corpse I would leave behind. As a last touch, I took a pinch of cinders in my fingers and sprinkled it over the mattress, like seasoning.

Everything was made ready. I climbed up onto the cot, stepping carefully around my mock skeleton and clutching my bag of ashes. I cleared my throat, ready to speak my last words. It was so rare that I used my own voice. I still didn't know enough words to string into a fitting speech and I had a lingering childhood lisp that always forced me to keep my sentences short. But there were a few fiery words I'd been holding in my memory. The curse words

13

that Ma spat at me every day…the only thing that she'd ever given me.

"May the Devil strike me down!" I cried at the top of my lungs. "May the Devil turn me to ash and bones!"

I threw up my arms, scattering ashes into the air around me. I stood in the black cloud that filled the room, letting its flakes rain down on my face. The noise of my eruption was still echoing off the walls as I leapt down from the cot, landing noiselessly on my toes. Panting for breath, I had to resist the urge to cough. I could already hear feet upon the stairs, feet rushing up to see. Without wasting another moment, I rushed to the window and jumped to the ground.

I could've done myself a mischief with this fall, but I had a lot of practice in leaping from high places. It's one of the few ways a restless farm boy can find release – the thrill of climbing to a precipice, then plummeting from it. I had suffered bruises and sprained ankles through most of my childhood, but now I was nimble enough to land like a cat. Even so, this particular fall caused my knees to crack at the joints. The soles of my feet were stunned by the ground and tingled numbly inside my shoes. My teeth cut into my lower lip and I was tasting blood on my tongue as I pressed my ear to the wall.

I had to clamp a hand over my mouth to muffle my own cackling laughter. I could hear Ma shrieking new curses, Pa stumbling on the stairs and Flan yelling from the landing to *'Come quick! Come see!'* The farmhouse had been thrown into chaos. I could picture my family huddled together, staring into the smoke that'd once been their lunatic son. The son who they had tried to starve and shun out of being. Now in place of that son they'd have a story to tell.

And it felt good to be leaving them that way.

Better to be a story than their boy.

Scene Two

A Tragedy of Blood

Our farm sat on the outskirts of a town called No End. Leastways that was how its name sounded when spoken in the local accent. And even if mispronounced on their part or misheard on mine, it was a name that suited it well. The town was a backwater thoroughfare for travellers journeying down from the Welsh lands or up from the southern ports. A ruddy little pit-stop on an old Roman road. A place to take lodgings and rest your bones, but no place to stay and make an ending. I had always sworn it wouldn't be the end of me.

Having turned the farm boy to dust, I'd gone into town in disguise, dressed in a ragged doublet stolen from our scarecrow. Its previous owner had been stabbed in a tavern brawl and Pa had been gifted the garment by the barkeep to settle a debt. He had put the jacket on the scarecrow, deeming it bad luck to wear the weeds of a murdered man. The doublet still stunk of old blood and it had been pecked full of holes by the birds. It was too long in the sleeves for me and hung low over my slops and stockings. But the costume still made me a new person. Made me something more than Timony Child.

This wasn't the first time I'd tried to run away from the farm. I'd been thrown off the backs of wagons before this night and learned from my bruised backside that nothing came for free in this world. If you want to go anywhere in these lands, you best have something to barter. And this night, for once, I hoped that I could sell myself. I was a little older than the usual prenticing age and Pa had failed to place me into a new trade at every past summer fayre. But none of those professions had been suited to my particular gifts.

Tonight, there were strange folk in town. *Players*, Pa had called them. He had called them many other names besides. Rogues, gypsies, sodomites, painted minstrels, confidence men and vagabonds. He had huffed about the house, saying these players were *'bringing blasphemy to our tavern'* and *'making queer scenes in our streets'*. Anything that made Pa huff caused me no end of curiosity.

Pa had vowed over breakfast that morning that neither he, nor any member of the Child family would give audience to this play. He said this looking smugly certain that the rest of the township would follow his pious example and shun the strolling theatre. But now as I made my way up the main street toward the market square, I found that every homestead I passed was dead quiet and seemingly deserted. It looked like this play, whatever a play might be, had brought every other person from the parish out of doors to bear witness.

Approaching the tavern, I could see its inn yard was crammed from entrance to rear. On any usual night when the alehouse was this packed it would also be raucous with voices. But this evening it was eerily hushed. Something was going on here and it was so rare for anything to happen in the town of No End. A local constable was stationed at the inn's arched entrance, but even he was proving a poor watchman. His back was turned away from the street, his eyes fixed upon whatever was taking place within the tavern walls. So, he took no notice as I slipped into the rear ranks of the crowd.

I was too small to see above the heads or through the huddling bodies in front of me. But the one advantage of my puny stature was that nobody minded if I snuck on ahead. I wouldn't be blocking any man's view and in my dark raiment I was like a little shadow flitting through the throng. The crowd's focus was held by something else. Or rather…someone. I could just about hear a voice from the far side of the yard. A fair speaker who had everyone hushed.

Their words began to reach my straining ears –

"Fire and slaughters now behind me, into these woods I'll fly.
At last I'll pray and see the day retreat from where I lie.
Oh, could it be I've finally found a place where I might die?"

It sounded like a girl. I could hardly believe it at first. She didn't talk like any maid I'd known from the village, nor had I ever seen a woman being given leave to speak at such a gathering. Her voice rang out clear as a bell, but was prettily undercut by her whimpering breaths. And for some strange reason, this girl spoke everything in rhyme. Her words created music in the air. Without yet having a glimpse of her, I imagined this girl must be a witch with a charmed tongue who'd cast a silencing spell over the mob, enchanting them.

The crowd was thicker the closer I drew to her voice. In the sweaty cram of arms and shoulders, I mouthed one of my mother's harsher curses and then sank to my knees to crawl through the maze of legs that now lay between me and the farthest wall. The people who stood over me hissed at the disturbance around their ankles, stamping on me as I snaked over the cobbles on my belly. I bit my lip, absorbing their kicks and trying not to make a sound as they winded me. A few fresh bruises later, I brushed aside a long-mottled skirt in my path and I finally came up for air. And that was the moment I saw her.

The girl on the stage wore a red dress, its skirts unfurled around her like the petals of a crushed flower. I had never seen clothing so red before. The rustic dyes of our local tailors would only yield the dullest brown and grey hues. And the dress wasn't all that made this girl beguiling. Her long black hair was thick as a horse's mane and her skin was so milk pale you would think she'd never stood a day beneath the sun. I would've called the girl pretty, but the word wasn't enough. She wasn't pretty like the freckled milkmaid who had been promised as a wife to my brother Flan on his sixteenth birthday. This girl was impish and peculiar. She was such a shock to my senses that I could only see her as beautiful and I was right away in love.

I let go a sigh as I stared. I'd always wondered what falling in love would feel like. In this town, love was another superstition that my pa spoke of with his customary peasant wariness – like it was a sickness that needed draining with leeches. In my usual habit of impudence, I'd secretly been looking for love in the face of every young maid in the parish. But I'd been searching for so long without feeling any of its supposed tingles I'd begun to think the condition must be a fanciful myth after all. Now I knew different. Now I felt it. My heart throbbed, my skin prickled and my loins stirred in a way my mother would have called damnable. There was just one problem.

The girl appeared to be dying.

"Water! A little water...or just the slightest fall of rain?
A little tear upon my eyelids that I'll not open up again."

Speaking this last couplet, the girl collapsed in a swoon. She turned her head skywards, lifting a trembling arm, her fingers outstretched as if she was grasping for the moon. I realized then that the girl was only pretending this death. And in all my days of dying on the farm, I had died shockingly, violently, disgustingly... but I'd never thought to make my deaths beautiful. I felt so thoroughly outdone. I couldn't tell if I was weeping in sadness or with envy, but my eyes filled and I was soon swiping at my cheeks. I was always so quick to cry. Ma had warned me that too many tears and I'd never grow a beard.

I glanced at the rest of the townsfolk, only to find them squinting and crinkling up their noses. I perceived that their silence was more disapproving than reverent, as if they had only chosen to mark this play so that they could properly scorn it afterward.

"Douse the little hussy, I say..."

This muttering came from a stony-faced crone who stood behind me. I was fighting the urge to turn around and bite her when her words sparked an idea in my mind. I glanced about me, my eyes falling on the crude tables that had been pushed to the edges of the yard. I focused on a tankard that seemed to be unguarded by its owner. The mug was filled with the tavern's own bitter brew and not the life preserving water that the lady had called for. But the ale would likely have a more rousing effect...if I could just persuade her to drink.

I crawled to the table and seized this improvised medicine. Rising to my feet, I braced myself to step on stage and become the hero this story required. Before I could, a hand caught me by my collar.

"Patience, dear heart," a velvety voice whispered. "I can't have an amateur blundering in before my tragedy reaches its close."

I froze, not daring to turn. The fellow's smooth speech and lofty language was enough to tell me he was high-born, well-schooled and my better. And he had claimed ownership of the play. He must be the very theatre master I'd come to offer my service to.

"Now, you may not be familiar with the customs of the modern stage..." the fellow went on, "...but this performance is not like one of your farmer's auctions where the crowd is encouraged to raise their voices and participate in the proceedings. There's plenty that our girl, Gwendolyn might be willing to sell you. But that manner of trading is usually left till the curtain has closed if you take my meaning. For now, the only water that she craves are your tears."

I flinched as the man scraped a knuckle over my wet cheeks. I kept my leaking eyes on the platform, unable to look away. It was then that a dark-skinned man in furs slipped out through the backcloth that was strung up behind the stage. I'd never seen a man so brown before. His skin had a tawnier tan than I imagined that any could catch from the sun in these parts. The dark man in furs had a towering stature and stood looming over the fallen maid. Slowly he sank onto all fours, snarling like a wolf and circling the girl as she lay panting for breath. Her hand reached towards him, as if beckoning him near.

With this last frail gesture, the wolf man pounced. His paws pinned the girl's shoulders and he buried his jaws in her breast. Her red dress disappeared behind a writhing mass of fur. The girl let loose a scream which was echoed by the startled crowd. Blood spilled over the boards in red rivulets, spreading from the girl and wolf and trickling towards the lip of the platform. And now the audience erupted with cries of *'murder!'* their eyes wide and mouths agape. As one sweaty mob they lurched forward for a closer look at the stage, their frothy drinks flowing over and mingling with the carnage.

The girl and the wolf remained frozen in their final positions as a third player stepped onto the platform, strumming a lute. This young minstrel had a handsome face, a trim beard and a tender smile that restored calm as much as his gentle music. I sniffled, my nose dripping, as I struggled to compose myself. The illusion was lifting now, but it'd left me wrung out and still weeping as the lute player sang a mournful lament for '*Gwendolyn*' and her woebegone fate.

The playwright spoke into my ear again.

"Believe it or not," he whispered to me. "These tragedies of blood are all the fashion in our cities. We must offer something to compete with the gory scenes of the punishment platform." He squeezed my shoulder. "Listen lad. Since you're so eager to play a part, might I ask you to lead this ungrateful mob in some applause?"

In a flourishing movement, the playwright lifted the tankard from my hand. Then he stepped from behind me, treating me to a little kick in the ankle as he mounted the stage. The young musician seeing him approach, ceased his song and lowered his lute.

"Your hands! Give us your hands!" he prompted the crowd. "Give cheer to our playwright! We'd all be lifeless puppets without his words to move us. If you please…Arthur Makaydees!"

Spurred into action, I began slapping my palms together until the crowd reluctantly joined the applause. The playwright planted his feet on the blood-soaked boards, ready to ingratiate himself whether his audience cared to receive him or not. He quaffed the ale and threw the mug over his shoulder, then reached down to raise the girl Gwendolyn to her feet. He twirled her under his arm, showing off how very far from dead she was. The man in furs and the minstrel joined them in a ragged line. They took hands and flopped into a bow.

"Hush, you are too kind!" Makaydees said to the crowd who had already fallen back into a bemused lull. "How I envy you who dwell in these quiet country towns, safe from the many rankles of the world. I imagine you'll die very old and very snug in your beds. And be sure to lock up your daughters, lest they suffer the same misadventures as our poor doomed maiden. For all its colours, the road beyond your parish is beset with scourges. Be thankful that we bring you but a taste of its horrors. And please...be *generous* in your thanks."

Standing at the playwright's side, Gwendolyn smiled and clasped her skirts, sinking into curtsy and making sure to give the crowd a flash of her slender white legs as she did so. And this sight of her waxy limbs, more so than the playwright's cajoling, had all the men present reaching for their coin purses. This suggestive peek beneath her dress had left my cheeks hot too and I was thankful for my low hanging doublet. Who was this devil girl in red? I had to know.

But at that moment, I found myself spun around on my heels and then yanked up onto my toes. Suddenly I was standing before the foul huffing breath of the tavern's own landlord.

"Hoy! Did you snatch that fellow's ale?"

The barkeep didn't wait for an answer, just drew back his fist. I shut my eyes, steeling myself for a blow. But it never struck. I cracked a lid to see the man's face brightening with recognition.

"Wait...wait, I know you, don't I? You're that farmer's lad from up on the hill, right?" He laughed, lowering me onto my heels. He waved to a woman that was walking by carrying a laden tray. "Mable, love! Pour us a half. Young Flannery is here!"

His wife began to grin too. It was only after squinting at me over her mugs that the smile turned sour on her lips.

"That boy's not Flan," she said. "Look at the curls in his hair. Look at his big ferrety eyes. He's that other one."

The barkeep frowned. "Which other one?"

"You know." She hushed her voice. "The afflicted one."

He nodded grimly. "Oh, I see. *That* one…"

He recoiled like I might be carrying the plague.

"The lad's never been right in the head, they say," Mable muttered. "That poor yeoman has had to live with the burden." She raised her voice, making her words slow and deliberate as if she was addressing a simpleton. "Why so far from home, boy? You best not have come to disturb the peace. We don't want you causing a scene."

These two witless barkeeps were now blocking my path to the players on the platform. I tried darting around the babbling obstacles, only to have them thrust me backwards.

"Oh no you don't!" the barkeep barked. "You'll be leaving the other way. Mable, take the little wretch back to the Child's farm. Be sure to demand a reward for fetching him home."

At the mere suggestion of being taken back up the hill, I opened my mouth and let rip a scream every bit as piercing as Gwendolyn's death rattle. The barkeep's wife threw up her tray of drinks with fright, soaking the jackets of those stood nearby. The crowd staggered back, parting to leave a clear path to the stage. Seizing my chance, I made a mad dash for the platform, hurrying up its steps and rushing across its boards. The players had already started slipping behind its back curtain. But Makaydees and Gwendolyn halted at the sound of my cry. The playwright and his damsel were just turning their heads when I slipped and fell sprawling in a puddle of blood and ale.

I spluttered, desperate to speak. But the air had been knocked from my lungs and my eyes were watering, so I couldn't even see the faces of those surrounding me, watching me in my toils. There was only one thing that I could think to do. I let out a trembling gasp and slumped on my back, stretching my fingers up to the sky. And it felt like dying. It felt like the whole world slipping away from me.

The next moment it did. A hand seized my leg, yanking me off the stage and into the barkeep's arms. A rough cloth was thrown over my head, like a curtain closing upon my escape.

Scene Three

The Miracle Doctor

The next morning, I stood shivering in the vegetable patch, waiting for the dawn. After the scene I'd caused at their inn, the two barkeeps had hauled me uphill, delivering me back to my family. My family who'd seemingly spent the last few hours since my flight in a state of turmoil. We found them huddling outside the

29

farmhouse, unwilling to step back inside for fear that the Devil was still prowling and might yet drag them into the same hellfire whence he'd taken me.

After the barkeeps bartered a handful of eggs for *'the safe return'* of their *'poor brain sickly son'*, Ma looked like she would like to gather some kindling and do the Devil's burning for him. But Flan had offered up another form of punishment. I was still dressed in the scarecrow's doublet, so my dear brother proposed that this should henceforth be my role on the farm. Ma and Pa agreed, neither willing to have me under their roof practising my *'dark sorcery'* any longer. So, I'd spent a chilly night on the hilltop, my hands tied and tethered like a puppet's strings to the crossbeam of the scarecrow's frame.

I waited for the sun to rise and offer the slightest warmth. I tugged at my bindings, but my struggling only tightened the rope's bite on my wrists. In those cold despairing hours, I could see my future stretching out before me. The scarecrow and I would be stuck on this hill for every day and every night we would ever know. We'd both be rooted in the ground – no hope of escape, other than in our minds.

I imagined the scarecrow thinking. So many thoughts stuffed into his straw head, pouring from his tattered mask and covering his stiff shoulders. Birds would swoop low, tug the straw loose and carry those thoughts away. Little bits of the scarecrow's brain scattering off to new places trapped in their beaks. I wondered what the scarecrow would do when his mind ran dry. When his head was left an empty sack.

As the sun rose, the birds came with it, circling over me, smelling the blood on my clothes. Gwendolyn's blood. I opened my mouth and I moaned – *"Gwendolyn, Gwendolyn, Gwendolyn."* I didn't stutter her name. Her perishing last night may have been playacted, but it would become real for me if I didn't escape soon. The players might linger at the market but most likely they would be moving on before the sun was low once more. If I missed them, if I couldn't catch up or *worse*, if they refused to take me with them, then that strange girl in red would just be a memory to mourn, all my dreams dying with her.

No sooner had the dawn's glow touched the hill than I could see the shadows of my family rising in the farmhouse, readying themselves for market. Well, not Ma. Due to the cramps in her hips, she only left her room to limp downhill to church. But she sat watching me from her window, the living scarecrow she'd made of her son. Pa meanwhile was bustling from the kitchen to the yard, filling his wheelbarrow and ignoring my presence altogether. Was this how they intended to treat me from now on? Like an untamable dog that they needed to tie up out of doors to keep me from running wild?

I had to wonder why they didn't just turn me loose. But there was at least one member of the Child family who still cherished having me around. This much I remembered as my brother Flan trudged over the field with a heap of vegetables in his arms. A cruel grin spread across his face. The face that I hated sharing with him.

"These are the rotten ones, not fit for selling," he said, taking an onion in his fist. With a shrug, he added, "Ma said I could."

I swallowed, my heart sinking. "Ma said?"

"She said you'd done enough to deserve the pillory. But as there's none in town we have to make one for ourselves."

He punctuated this sentence by hurling his onion very deliberately towards my crotch. With my hands tied, I could do nothing to shield the delicate parts between my legs. I twisted my waist just in time so the vegetable glanced off my hip. I had no time for relief as the next moment an egg cracked against the bridge of my nose. I heard Flan snort a laugh as its rancid yolk oozed into my eyes, leaving me blind and unable to dodge the rest of the projectiles that were flung in my direction. Never one for suffering in silence, I let out yelps at each stinging blow. Finally seeming to tire of targeting me from a distance, Flan strode close, scooped up a fistful of dirt and threw it in my face, smearing it with the yolk upon my cheeks.

"No more playing dead, Timmy," he cooed. He jabbed something pointed against my chest. A carrot I realized. Not anything he could actually run me through with, but my body still tensed up. "It's my turn to play now. You're going nowhere."

"*You're* going nowhere!" I shot back in frustration. When I lacked the words to win an argument, I'd resort to echoing the last words said to me. "You'll *never* go anywhere! You'll be rooted on this pig farm for all your days! You'll be *st-st-stu...*"

I didn't know if I was scolding Flan or myself with this speech. But either way my rant was halted by the plain old word '*stuck*'. I just couldn't force it through my lips. Then I gagged as Flan jammed his carrot hard between my teeth.

"Poor scarecrow! Can't even speak."

"Flan!" Pa's voice bellowed across the field. "*Flan*, peace! Cut the little fool down! We've a visitor come to our farm!"

The carrot was wrenched from my jaws. I heard my brother hissing curses as he tugged loose the knots tying my hands to the crossbeam. I collapsed to my knees, rasping for breath. My eyes were still covered in a syrupy mix of yolk and soil, so I could barely perceive the two men approaching in my mired vision. I trusted that the shorter of the figures was Pa. The stranger I did not dare to look at. Huddling forward, I hid my face behind my elbows and wished that I could bury myself in the ground. I had never felt uglier in all my life.

"So…this is the boy that caused the uproar in the tavern?" said the visitor, his accent bold and brassy like the city traders.

"Aye sir, he's our little cross to bear," I heard Pa mutter. I could tell he was already squirming. He hated having to explain my peculiar presence to guests. "Excuse the mess of him, doctor."

The word 'doctor' sent a shudder through me. Why would some travelling medicine man have come to our farm?

"I shall pardon him," said the doctor, his voice suddenly sounding a lot nearer. "For I believe he cannot help his compulsions. Now, if you'll let me take a closer look at the patient…"

Don't look at me, I thought. *Don't look because I am ugly and strange and shameful and I don't want you to see me.*

None of these thoughts made it to my lips. Suddenly my chin was grasped and tilted upright. A handkerchief wiped the filthy mulch from my cheeks. I winced against the glare of the rising sun, but as I blinked my eyes open, I was forced to stare into the face of the medicine man. Only then did I realize that he was no doctor at all.

It was the playwright. It was Arthur Makaydees.

34

My lips struggled to form a thousand questions. Why had he come to our farm? Why had he appeared to my family in the guise of a doctor? Why did he want to see me? Was it possible he'd come for *me*? I tried to ask all of this wordlessly through my straining eyes. But the playwright's face remained stony and critical.

"Clearly a desperate case. Perhaps incurable."

"What are you saying, sir?" asked Pa. "Does the boy suffer from some known sickness? How can you tell, sir?"

"I can tell because it is my profession to diagnose and treat such maladies," he asserted, rising to his feet. "I'll have you know that I'm a famed and respected miracle doctor in these parts. Mullarkey is my name. Humbug Mullarkey. Here, see my medical licence..."

Rummaging in his knapsack, Makaydees produced a crumpled scroll, unfurling it in his hands before my father's bewildered eyes. With my vision clearing, I took the chance to look at the playwright in the cold light of day. He was broad in the chest and wore an unusual blend of colours and fabrics – a threadbare green jerkin over patched russet doublet and a yellowing puff shirt. His long hair was slick and silvery. His eyes were conker brown and heavy-lidded. His face was painted white and trickles of perfumed sweat made him seem like a decorated candle that was dribbling wax.

"I hail from our country's capital where I worked in a little asylum by the name of Bethlehem Hospital, best known as Bedlam. I tended to the poor lunatics of that charitable house for many years. But I've since taken to the roads on a sort of pilgrimage, hoping to mend the wits of those who I find suffering in smaller parishes."

Pa and Flan were both still puzzling over the playwright's scroll, so they missed the moment when Makaydees turned his head and treated me to a sideways wink. And in that instant, I knew what this was. Another piece of theatre. The playwright had taken the role of a quack physician, flourishing his forged documents. It was a well-judged act too. While my father would never allow any son of his to leave the farm in the company of actors, there was every chance he'd agree to have me committed to a madhouse.

"Yes, well...this all seems to be in order," Pa rewound the scroll, not wanting to confess to his illiteracy. "So, it's our Timmy's health that you've come calling about then?"

"No, not his health," said Makaydees. "I have come here for your boy's extraordinary mania. I was not present for the play at the tavern yester eve, but I've heard tell that your lad hurling himself onto the bloodied stage rather stole the show. This morning I found a trail of red footprints leading this way out of town. So, I have come to assess his unwieldy distemper for myself." He looked to the ropes dangling from the crossbeam. "I see you already have methods for treating your son's ills? Have you found them to be remotely effective?"

Pa shuffled his feet, sheepishly. "Sir, you mustn't think us heartless folk. For many years we had pity for his ravings. But we have been brought to our wits end. Never a day's work out of the little knave, yet we'll be lumbered with him to the end of ours!"

"My dear fellow, you need not explain yourself," Makaydees said cheerily. "Believe me, your practices are a good deal gentler than many I witnessed at the asylum. Kill or cure, that's our motto! I do not come to judge. Instead I hope to relieve your burden."

Pa's frown deepened. "Sorry sir, I don't..."

Makaydees grimaced a smile. "I can see that I must be plain, not tantalising. A specimen such as your son would be of great value to me in my work. It is so rare that one sees such an impassioned imbalance of the humours. I should like to take him on the road with me and make a study of his madness. I may even find ways to heal it."

"Heal?" Pa murmured, slow to understand his offer. "I...I've heard that bleedings help. Will you be bleeding him, doctor?"

"Indeed sir," the playwright enthused. "I find a good bloodletting is the best thing to release the bile. I bleed the patients in my charge at least once a day. Twice if we've the crowd for it."

Pa blinked rapidly. "Crowds, sir?"

"Yes. You'd scarcely believe the audiences we used to entertain back at Bedlam. The playhouses could hardly compete with us! I would demonstrate my little medicine show for you now were it not that I've left my blades and leeches back at camp with my fellow surgeons. But if you'll entrust your deranged son to my care then..."

"He's lying, Pa!" Flan burst out suddenly, his cheeks full of hot air. "Don't believe his fancy words! Our Timmy's never been mad. He just likes to play pretend. Like this quack is playing us right now. We should never have let this queer fellow on our land. Look at his painted face and his gypsy clothes. He's no doctor."

Panic shot through me as I realized my brother could still rob me of this chance for escape. He could keep me on the farm so as not to be deprived of his favourite victim. I had kept silent thus far, trusting in Makaydees to seal a bargain. But now I met the playwright's stare and held it. I read the quiet command in his gaze.

This was my audition. I knew it. And I don't know what possessed me, but I opened my mouth...and I barked.

"Ruff! Ruff! Ruff!" Through barred teeth I added, *"Grrrr."*

"What's gotten into him now?!" Pa spluttered.

"Calm yourself. Tis but a common delusion," said Makaydees with a sage nod. "Really, what did you expect? If you leave this

38

insane boy tied up like a dog, then in his fanciful mind he will start believing that he has been transformed – fur, fleas and all."

Flan stamped in frustration. "He's pretending!"

My brother marched over to me, raising his foot, as if hoping to kick the drama right out of me. But I'd already taken too many bruises. I wouldn't stand for one more. So, I reached out and caught Flan by his boot before it could strike. And then with a pounce, I bit him hard in the leg, just below the hem of his breeches.

"AGH!" Flan screamed. "Get him off me!"

"Yes, and I'd be quick about that," said Makaydees, watching our family fray with his arms folded, perfectly at ease. "If his teeth break the skin there is every chance of infection. I've known this manner of brain fever to be quite contagious. It would grieve me to see you lose both sons to its thrall. Best to keep them separate."

Pa lunged forward to pry Flan free from my jaws. As my brother staggered back, I caught sight of the raised red tooth marks that I'd left in his calf and I panted with a sickly satisfaction.

"Never fear! I have tonic that should bring the lad out of this fit," Makaydees insisted, taking a wineskin from his pack.

The playwright knelt once more and tipped a hefty mouthful of mead down my throat. I began to gag as the burning liquor set my eyes watering again. I let the tears streak the dirt on my cheeks, not wiping them away this time but allowing them to hang prettily on my chin. The wineskin was pulled back and I lay panting and staring up at the little circle gathered around me. My first audience.

"W-what happened, Pa?" I gasped, all trembling innocence, like a child who's been shocked out of a bad dream. "What did I do to Flan's leg? Oh God in heaven...what's *wrong* with me?"

Pa held my stare and I saw a hint of paternal compassion in his eyes. I'd finally got a reaction. I'd managed to move him.

"Timmy, get to the house and pack your things," he said. "Don't fret. This man's going to make you well at last."

Scene four

The Changeling

It didn't take long to realize I had no things to pack. There was little need for me to linger in my first and only home, especially as it was market day, and I would only make Pa late setting up his stall. There was no sense of ceremony as I left the farm, no kind or words shared. Just a curt nod from Pa and a last scowl from Dar before I was sent to bid some manner of farewell to my mother.

Ma was still sitting by the window, staring at the bare crossbeams of the scarecrow. From this position, she'd plainly been looking down on the little show I'd put on in the vegetable patch.

I squirmed in her doorway. "Ma, I'm—"

"I heard," she said, cutting me short.

She turned to face me, clutching her bible to her chest. Unlike the rest of the Child family, Ma knew how to read. She'd been taught by the parish priest during the months she'd spent bedridden after my bad birth. Most of what she read was religious scripture, but I'd once smelled a book of fables hidden in her blankets. It seemed I wasn't the only one creating the farm in my mind. No

Scene Four

The Changeling

It didn't take long to realize I had no things to pack. There was little need for me to linger in my first and only home, especially as it was market day and I would only make Pa late setting up his stall. There was no sense of ceremony as I left the farm, no hugs or kisses shared. Just a curt nod from Pa and a last scowl from Flan before I was sent to bid some manner of farewell to my mother.

Ma was still sitting by the window, staring at the bare crossbeams of the scarecrow. From this position, she'd plainly been looking down on the little show I'd put on in the vegetable patch.

I squirmed in her doorway. "Ma, I'm…"

"I heard," she said, cutting me short.

She turned to face me, clutching her bible to her chest. Unlike the rest of the Child family, Ma knew how to read. She'd been taught by the parish priest during the months she'd spent bedridden after my hard birth. Most of what she read was religious scripture, but I'd once found a book of folktales hidden in her blankets. It seemed I wasn't the only one escaping the farm in my mind. Ma crossed the floor towards me, gripping her cane and gritting her teeth against the pains in her pelvis. The pains that she'd suffered with since bringing me into the world and that would likely trouble her till her dying day.

"Look here," she hissed, her voice hushed. "I don't believe for a moment that swaggering peacock of a man is any kind of doctor. But it's clear from his vain speeches he's a fellow of learning. He may come to school you if you stick by him. That is, if you're not lost to the sin and perils, he is sure to draw you into. Whatever his wicked business may be, tis best you go with him. There's no place for you here. Never has been. I still curse that you were ever born."

Ma hardly needed to remind me of this, but it seemed she could never say it enough. As a parting gesture, she smacked her holy book against my ear. Maybe it was because of the dirt in my eyes. Maybe it was because it was hard saying goodbye even to a mother who loathed me. Maybe it was just because Ma's blows always really stung. But I found myself bursting into a fresh bout of tears.

"Enough of that!" Ma snapped with a second whack of her bible to turn my other ear pink. "Quit playing the woman, Timmy. Take it from me...it'll get you nowhere in this world."

I nodded, swallowing the last of my sobs.

Then all in a blur, I was out of the farmhouse door and following the playwright down the slope. Once I was on my way, I did not turn to look back at the little house on the hill. The house that up until this morning had trapped and trammelled my entire life. Now it sat like a box of salt on a shelf beyond my reach. And I knew that I would not be missed. I knew that by nightfall my family would fall back into their tired old routines. Flan would be mucking out the pig sty and chicken coops. Ma would be preaching sermons from the landing and Pa would be cringing on the stairs below. I would vanish very quickly from this picture. I had never truly been a part of it.

"What did they call you, lad?" asked Makaydees.

"It's T-T-Timony, sir," I stuttered out.

This wasn't my real name, but my lisp could never get passed the '*Th*' sound in the middle of Timothy and so I softened it to an N sound when speaking it aloud. The playwright nodded.

"Dainty little name," he remarked. "In my troupe, you may go by whatever you please. Just so long as you're prepared to trade your name at will for the many others, I will give you." He treated me to a sidelong glance. "I trust that you understand the nature of your new trade, farm boy? You realize that the roles I'll expect you to take on in my theatre will require you to do more than just barking?"

"More I can do, s-s-sir," I said, faltering.

"Don't start bragging yet," he cautioned. "You still have a clumsy peasant's tongue and you'd do well to keep it silent till you've cured its slurs and stammering. Save your breath for the march, lad. It's a fair stretch to the forest where my fellows have made camp. Come now! They'll be fretting over what's become of me."

I snapped my jaw shut and did not question him further. My new master kept his own mouth busy slugging from his wineskin and I couldn't have spoken even if I'd wanted to. My heart had leapt into my throat at the mention of the larger company of players. Only now had the realisation struck me. I was on my way to see the girl.

My face flushed at the thought of meeting Gwendolyn. I played out the scene in my mind, planning my actions. Might I take her hand? Should I bow down and call her *my lady*? I scratched the dirt clinging to my cheeks, then smoothed my doublet and straightened my spine, dearly hoping the girl would not stand taller than me.

After hour's tramping over fields and meadows, we came to the outskirts of the Forest of Dean. I had always been curious about these woods, knowing they would be my first threshold if I ever escaped the farm. Ma had told me the forest was infested with tricksy fairies who stole human babies and swapped them for evil imps who would burn crops and curdle milk. She had once been convinced that I must be one of these changeling fairy brats. She'd ordered Pa to drag me to the edge of the woods and there beat me with a switch till my cries summoned my *real* family to come and collect me. Pa had duly warmed my jacket until sunset. But no matter how loud I'd wailed, no fairy clan had ever emerged. No human had cared to save me either.

But the playwright had come. He'd seen something in me at the tavern and he'd come. Now he might be leading me to a family I could at last belong to. I smelled the player's camp before I saw it, an alluring scent of broth and burning logs that caught in my throat as I was drawn into a tight circle of trees. Along with the smell there was a cloud of red smoke. *Red smoke* rising up from the player's campfire. I had no notion of how such a thing had been conjured and suddenly feared I'd fallen in with the Devil's henchmen after all.

The crimson midst shrouded the forest clearing and made shadow puppets of the three figures within its space. The first of these strangers to step forward was the burly brown fellow who had played the wolf that had eaten out Gwendolyn's heart. The man had a high bald head and bulky arms painted with green symbols. Beaded necklaces hung from his throat and coloured scarves were gathered up at his belt. I remembered Pa's mutterings about wandering Egyptians with skin as dusky as the sand lands from whence they'd sprung. I had never seen a gypsy with my own eyes before. I stared at the man a little too hard, my jaw lolling open. The fellow stared right back, scanning me up and down. Then he let out a jaded sigh.

"Adding a new face to our theatre already, Mak?" the gypsy said. "Hope that you're ready for the row this'll cause."

"Oh hush, Wally," said Makaydees. "I won't stand for hysterics before breakfast. There's roots for the pottage."

The playwright threw down the sack of turnips and onion that he had been given by my father as a form of payment for my future care at the mad house. The gypsy snatched the vegetables up eagerly and returned to the bubbling pot over the campfire. I shifted my stare to the other two players in the clearing, who seemed equally startled by my presence at their camp. The younger and taller of the men, I recognized as the lute player who'd sung Gwendolyn's lament. The shorter fellow was a greying old man with ruddy red cheeks and twinkling blue eyes. He was the only one who smiled when he saw me.

"Makaydees!" the young minstrel began, throwing up his arms in a fluster. "You didn't tell us where you were…we didn't know if you had…where in God's name *were* you, Mak?!"

"Peace, my dear Lavern," said Makaydees, his voice mellow from the mead he'd drunk down. "I just took a stroll up to that farm on the hill. Our nest was looking rather empty this morning, so I thought I'd venture out early and catch us a few worms."

"You've brought back more than grubs!"

Lavern waved a hand in my face. I didn't flinch at the gesture. I was used to being treated like an object nobody knew where to place.

"I mean *honestly*," he continued in exasperation. "Don't you think that it's a little soon to be hiring a new apprentice?"

"Too soon?" Makaydees interrupted him. "Too soon to teach him his moves, learn him his lines, curve his spine, grow out his hair and sweeten his voice? Lavern, you know as well as I do that it'll take weeks to break him in and months to polish him."

I wasn't fully listening to the two men's argument. My attention had been snared by a garment hanging on a washing line between two trees. A red dress with its skirts fluttering in the breeze and its sleeves billowing as if a ghostly maiden were hovering inside. The spirit of Gwendolyn. Curiously, the girl herself was nowhere to be seen. I could not help wondering why the men were cooking and laundering. Surely if there was a woman among them, she should be the one who took these chores. My eyes swept the camp once more.

The only other things occupying the clearing were a tumbrel cart and a small horse tethered to a tree. I supposed that Gwendolyn might be off collecting firewood or some other chore too menial for the men. I opened my mouth to ask after her whereabouts, but Makaydees and Lavern were still busy with their bickering.

"Have a heart, Mak," Lavern implored. "After what happened last night you could've allowed a little time for *recovery*."

Saying this, Lavern flung his arm towards the cart behind him. It was only then I noticed a pair of bare feet protruding from the straw. I peered closer and realised that these feet were attached to a slender body and a wave of wild black hair spread among the hay. My eyes widened as I stepped forward and saw a strip of cloth bound tightly across the sleeper's face. A cloth that looked alarmingly like a gag or a blindfold. And that wasn't even the worst part. This cloth was stained with blood. This was the girl. She was here and she was hurt. My mouth opened and found that I couldn't help myself.

"*Gwendolyn!*" I rushed to the cart, the sight of the wounded maid overwhelming my sense. "W-w-hat have they…?"

A low moaning arose from the hay, stopping me in my tracks. I'd thought I was rushing to the aid of a suffering damsel, beaten senseless by her brutish companions. But there was nothing frail or delicate about the gruff noises she was making as she stirred.

"Now you've done it," Wally muttered.

The groaning girl clambered up from the straw and clawed back the long tangles of her hair. She coughed and retched, scratching her armpit and baring her teeth. Standing this close, I realised...I wasn't looking at a girl at all. This was a boy, hardly any older than me. A boy dressed in a vest and breaches with a bloodied bandage tied round his nose and his cheeks. This boy, who last night had been Gwendolyn, peeled back his lids and glared at us with raw irritated eyes. The other players fell silent, watching him with breathless foreboding. He looked like a fresh corpse risen up from the grave.

"How now, Rum?" asked the old man, lowering his laundry pegs and approaching their bilious companion.

The boy called Rum did not answer. He gripped the edges of the cart and dropped onto a set of legs that trembled at the knees. He clung to a wheel for support, then took a few tentative steps toward the fire before collapsing onto his hands. Lavern rushed to his side, placing an arm around his shoulders. Rum only snarled, clasping his head in his hands. A strangled voice tore from his throat.

"*Cowards*!!" he raged. "Those filthy whoreson bastards! A plague of cankerous boils upon them! They've *ruined* me! I can still feel their blades! My head is *splitting*! Make it stop!"

His cries caused the birds to flee from the branches above. I backed up against the cartwheel, my mouth falling open. I thought of my own outbursts and how wild I could be when a temper was in me. Rum made me feel like I'd been holding back all these years.

Makaydees barely blinked at the tantrum. "The pain in your head will lessen if you cease in this piteous wailing. You drank rather more ale last night than your constitution can temper, little Rumpus. You seem to forget the calamities that it drives you into. *What* – if anything – do you remember of the previous evening?"

Rum's eyes became glassy and confused.

"I was lying on stage…I was coming to the end of the death scene. Not a cough or murmur from the crowd. They couldn't take their eyes off me. So, I spoke my last words, I gave my last breath, let my hand fall…and…when I rose up they were cheering! Stamping their feet. Chanting my name. Coins raining over the boards!"

"You enchanted them, lad," Lavern commended him.

"Such a performance," the old man chimed in.

Rum nodded, lapping up their praises, before slumping back in Lavern's arms as if he were dying all over again.

"Well, your memory of the crowd's adoration of you is cockeyed enough," Makaydees snorted. "Dare I ask if there is anything else that you can recall from your evening in that tavern?

Rum shook his head. It seemed he didn't want to remember.

"Let me refresh you..." Makaydees paced the clearing, taking up the tale. "After shedding your costume, you were given monies to buy yourself a light supper. The rest of us retired to our room to share a pipe so we remained oblivious to your exploits on the floor below. We have since heard accounts from witnesses who saw the bloody scene with their own eyes. Rather than feeding up your raw bones, you took your purse to the gamblers den and bet it on a game of dice. You played until you were so plied with ale you became clumsy in your attempts to cheat. When accused, you turned over the tables, inciting a brawl that spilled into the common room. The barkeep called to the constable at his door. This lawman took one look at your pretty mug and contrived to teach you a sharp lesson. He dragged you out into the street where his sword stole two kisses from your cheeks..."

As this retelling drew to its close, Rum threw off Lavern's hands and began storming about the camp, kicking up twigs and scratching at the bark of trees while the other players in turn made nervous attempts to restrain him. I scurried over to stand by Makaydees, seeking my new master's protection from this volatile ruffian.

"He...he saw the play!" Rum howled. "This injury was meant to destroy me! To end my career!!" He blanched, a realisation dawning on his face. "But I'll heal Makaydees," he insisted with a tone of forced optimism. "He didn't cut me deep. The marks will soon fade. A brush of powder will be enough to cover these scratches!"

Makaydees looked doubtful. He raised a hand and gently uncoiled the bandage from Rum's face. I winced as I saw the slits in the boy's cheeks, two thick gashes carved into his soft skin. The longer cut ran from the corner of his eye to the edge of his lip. A shorter gash lined his other cheek, pointing to his nostril. Rum was close to tears as his scabs started to bleed afresh, but he set his jaw firm, refusing to cry, more out of obstinacy than courage it seemed.

"Francis," said Makaydees, turning to the old man. "Take out your needle and thread. These cuts will need stitching."

Rum's eyes widened in fear and disbelief. "No! It can't be as bad as all that. Please, Mak! Fetch a looking glass!"

"No mirrors!" the playwright told him sternly. "I warn you, lad. Your vanity will not take well to this new reflection. But we must tend to your wounds lest they become infected."

Before Rum could protest any further, Makaydees tipped his head at Lavern. Understanding the signal, he grabbed Rum from behind, pinning his arms to his sides. Rum hissed and struggled like I'd seen farm kittens struggle when they are held down in buckets filled with water. Lavern dragged the writhing boy across the clearing and sat him with his back braced against a tree. Then Francis knelt before him, his needle threaded and ready to stitch. Rum wailed and pleaded, his head thrashing to avoid the needle's bite. His long dark hair whipped against the old man's face like knotted cords of leather.

"Easy lad!" Francis soothed. "It's for your own good! Lavern, tie his hair back, else it'll get tangled with my thread."

"Cut it off," said Makaydees, his face solemn and resigned. "Cut his hair short. He won't be needing it anymore."

Hearing this instruction, Rum went limp and seemed to fall into a numb despair. Makaydees turned his back, ushering me over to the fire where Wally was chopping vegetables. I stared into the smouldering wood and tried to block out the snapping sheers and Rum's hiccupping sobs. I couldn't look. I knew what was happening by that tree. They were killing Gwendolyn. She wouldn't rise from her death this time. There would only be that foul boy left in her place.

After a long moment of silence, Makaydees clapped a hand to my back. "This is the player's life, lad. That rickety cart yonder carries the costumes and properties of our theatre. We travel the land in search of crowds wherever we may gather them – in barns, taverns, markets and fayres. Any place we may transform through our spectacles. And in any play we perform, there are certain roles that must be filled." He nodded over to where Rum was whimpering through the last of his stitches. "He has just lost his role. You are inheriting it."

I sat there blinking, not knowing how to react, my mind turning numb. On the far side of the clearing, Rum's ordeal drew to a merciful close. After a last tug of the needle, Francis and Lavern took him by the arms and raised him to his feet. Rum wiped his eyes and shrugged off their cleaving hands, attempting some semblance of dignity. He strode towards the fire, his stare finally falling on me.

I wasn't sure if this was the first time Rum noticed me or just the first time he was choosing to acknowledge my presence. I raised the corners of my lips in what I hoped was a sympathetic smile and not a grimace of horror. Rum might not be beautiful or a girl anymore, but we were close in years. We might yet be friends.

It was that moment that Rum pounced. He hurled himself on me, gripping my collar and slamming me onto the forest floor. I lay gasping on my back, dazzled by the sun overhead. Rum's fingernails swiped at my face and I squeezed my eyes shut before he could scratch them out. Then just as suddenly I felt his weight leaving me. Wally had coiled an arm around Rum's chest, lifting him off his feet and tossing him aside as though he were as light as a handful of hay.

"None of that, Rum!" Makaydees scolded. "Keep your claws out of him or we'll blunt them too. Do you hear?"

Rum glared at Makaydees and Wally who stood shielding me from any further assaults. Rather than trying to maul me again, he marched over to the washing line and tore the dress from its pegs. He threw the garment toward me like he was spitting at my feet.

"*There*!" Rum sneered in bruised defiance. "It's yours now. You can live in it, you can work in it and you can *die* in it!"

Scene Five

The Elixir of Life

Francis was the first to approach the dress. He lifted it from the ground and laid it across a log. The other players huddled round like mourners at a funeral. Rum was the only one who stood apart. He snatched up a blanket, stamped over to the treeline and threw himself down in a patch of shade beside the cart horse. With my attacker at a distance I could breathe again, but couldn't bear to look at the costume I'd just inherited. So instead I stared down into the campfire where tendrils of red smoke were still curling from the smouldering embers.

"How do you make it red?" I asked.

"Madder root," said Francis, stroking a liver-spotted hand over the skirts. "Twas Wally and his people that taught me the trick of it. Those eastern dyes have given us leading ladies in every hue."

"Sorry...I meant the smoke," I clarified.

"Oh, that! Best ask the big fellow himself."

Wally tapped his nose. "Let me keep some mystery, Francis. I'm still mastering this bit of sorcery. Once the powder's mixed right we'll be able to conjure up a Hellmouth on our stage."

A thrill of excitement raced up my spine. I thought of my own attempt at going up in smoke. How I craved to learn the craft of a more astonishing spectacle. Makaydees, however, gave Wally a withering glance before stamping out the dwindling flames.

"I told you not send up your fantastical smoke signals when we're camping in these woods," he scolded. "We've had enough drama this morning. Let us eat before the next ordeal."

Wally nodded, then in mute movements began serving up bowls of pottage with clumps of acorn bread and cups of rainwater. The gypsy fellow was a fine cook considering that most of what had gone into his broth looked to have been scraped from the forest floor. Even so I ate his stew slowly, my belly still a knot of nerves.

"Not been properly introduced yet, have we?" said the old man sitting to my left. "All this hullaballoo has us forgetting our manners." He treated me to a friendly nudge. "Francis Winter at your service, lad. Don't look so timid. The rest of us don't bite."

Francis shot a chiding look at the rest of the players, who shared a wince and then each leaned towards me in their turn.

"Lavern Garland," said the minstrel, offering a handshake.

"Wallace Farr," said the gypsy with a nod.

"Timony," I replied, careful not to stutter it this time. I left out my last name. I wasn't a Child anymore, in more ways than one.

"Arthur Makaydees," said the playwright, who sat with his back propped against a tree, not moving for anyone. "Humbug Mullarkey is merely an alias I use when dealing with especially gullible peasants." He waved a finger at the far side of the clearing. "And that little storm cloud on legs over there is Rufus Murphy. Better known as Rumpus or Punchdrunk to those who've had the displeasure of carousing with him in alehouses or gambling pits. We call him Rum for short. Excuse his foul temperament. It's the Irish blood in him."

"Go easy on the boy, Mak," said Francis. "He's every right to feel heartsick over what happened last night."

"That ruined face is entirely self-inflicted. We warned him that his after-show activities would land him in trouble erelong."

"Then why didn't we stop him?" asked Lavern. "I always said we should tie Rum to his bed when we're boarding at taverns."

"We never kept him from the gambling tables because oftentimes he came back with winnings," said Wally. "Even among my old tribe, I never saw one so quick with their fingers. And it helped that he was playing against men who had already fallen in love with his heroines. His pale pretty face drove them all to distraction."

Makaydees smirked. "His Gwendolyn had much the same effect on young Timony here. He came close to improvising his own entrance last night. He fancied playing the hero and reviving our girl before her breath gave out. I was forced to hold him back."

The players broke into giddy laughter.

"If only Rum had known he had a rescuer in the wings!" Francis chuckled. "You should've let the scene to play out, Mak. I always said Wally's wolf needs a hero to fight in the last act."

My face grew hot and I fell to stammering.

"I-I wasn't trying to be a hero..." I said. "I just...I didn't want the play to end that way. That is, I didn't want the lady to die so soon. And I didn't realise that she was...I mean, *he* was a..."

Lavern snorted. "Hush. You're not the first bumpkin in these parts who's been unaware of the conventions of the modern theatre. We can't put a real woman on the stage. There's laws against that sort of thing. It would incite men to lust, tis said. Though we find that many men still fall to drooling over our skirted boys instead."

"Aye, Lavern would know," said Wally. "He was our first heroine. He held the role for four years till he grew too tall for it and his beard crept in. But in his time, he had to fend off marriage proposals and other less wholesome solicitations after curtains."

Lavern shuddered at the memory. "It's not a role I was sorry to lose." He sighed. "But Rum will miss it terribly."

The players glanced across the clearing to where Rum lay coiled in his blanket. Only the cart horse stood over him, its shadow shielding him from the sun, its head bowed as if in concern.

"We are all sorry to have lost his girls," said Makaydees, a note of melancholy creeping into his tone. The playwright shook himself, as if wishing to throw off unwanted sentimentality. "But no matter. Our fair maidens will live again in our new apprentice."

"Yes, but we may well starve in the months it will take this lad to be as good as Rum was," Lavern said bitterly.

"His training will take time, yes," said Makaydees. "But whilst we are striving for perfection, we still have plays to put on. Lest you have forgotten we have a show scheduled in just two days from now. Don't think for a moment that we're missing it."

Lavern, Wally and Francis blinked at Makaydees in dismay. I was every bit as flustered. Had he just said *two days*?

"The Bristol show?" Lavern spluttered. "Mak...you can't possibly be serious! I know that it was important to you. I know it'll hurt your pride to break your word, but...but two days, Mak? We'll never have a play ready in two days. Not without Rum! We..."

"We can and we will, dear heart," Makaydees insisted. "Master Wallace, collect up our gear and get our invalid on his feet. We'll be journeying by daylight to avoid highwaymen and we'll make time to rehearse in the cool airs of evening. Come now, all of you! Harness up Rosalie and let's follow the salty air to the harbour."

Lavern still had his feet planted in protest.

"How can you even be considering putting this witless farm boy on stage in just two days? Are you expecting him to have mastered his lines in that time? I trust you've noticed he lisps."

I hadn't spoken more than a handful of words to Lavern yet already he'd noted my speech impediment. But rather than flush with shame, I felt suddenly determined to prove him wrong.

"Yes Lavern," Makaydees sneered, tugging at one of his earlobes. "I have these fine fleshy trumpets attached to my head, see. Marvellous devices that have told me all I need to know about the flaws in our new apprentice's elocution. I am not saying that my script won't have to be adapted to his limitations, but I'm telling you that —"

"I can do it," I blurted, stumbling to my feet.

Makaydees and Lavern ceased their squabbling and turned to stare at me. They had no idea of the apprentice they had found. They did not know I'd been in training long before I saw their play. Long before I even knew what an actor was. I had no notion yet of how I was to become a girl, but I forced myself to look at the log. Gwendolyn's dress was still stretched out there, waiting to be filled. And if this was the role they needed me for, then I would take it.

"First thing a player needs is a bit of nerve, I say," said Francis, his apple cheeks ripening into a smile. "Keep it up, lad!"

Lavern looked chastened but still not convinced, while Makaydees looked like he had fresh plots forming in his mind. But before he could voice them, Wally crossed back over the clearing.

"I can't get Rum to move," he muttered. "He's in a bad way, Mak. Says he has a fever. He's refusing any food that I try to put to him. He's just lying there, babbling in his old Gaelic tongue. It's like he's making a deathbed out of that blanket. He won't even lift his head for Rosalie and he loves that old mare. Never ignores her."

Makaydees sighed. "Is this sickness real or pretend?"

"Most likely the latter," Wally conceded. "But you know how it is. Even when Rum's putting it on, he's always convincing."

The playwright nodded and then motioned for us come together in a tight huddle. He slipped a hand inside his jacket.

"Gentlemen…it seems our little invalid believes in his elaborate mind that he may be dying. I suspect that his fit is a false one too, but we'll need a suitable device to put an end to the act."

"Let's stick a couple of leeches on his hide," Wally suggested in hushed tones. "They'll have him on his feet sharpish."

"No, this calls for a more subtle remedy. Let us look to the folk plays of the latter century." He settled his sly gaze on me. "You see, boy, after the final battle it was traditionally the role of a quack doctor to provide a potion to revive a stricken hero. I've one such hearty tonic here in my pocket. One of the best from Humbug Mullarkey's medicine show. I call it the *Elixir of Life*. It'll purge Rum of his bile in an instant. All we need is an appropriate nursemaid to administer it."

Makaydees produced a small bottle from his jerkin and palmed it to me. The other players shared devious smirks.

"How will I get him to take it?" I spluttered.

"Charm him. Disarm him. Believe me, lad, you'll have tougher crowds to face going forwards. You best learn how to win them over. Lavern, you be his teacher in this little exercise."

The players were all watching me now, waiting to see what I could deliver. I crossed the clearing and sank to my knees beside the heap of blankets that Rum lay bundled up beneath.

"R-r-rum..." I began, flustering over his name. It was the first time I'd dared speak it. "I've medicine for you."

Rum kept the covers pulled over his face. I was close enough now to sense that he was pretending. This was a charade I was familiar with. There were many mornings on the farm I'd doused my face with cold water and worked myself into a feverish distemper. I would writhe in my straw bed until my skin broke out in ugly red rashes. With a good measure of moaning and retching, I could convince Pa to let me off working a day in the fields. I had an urge to yank off the blanket and force the tonic down Rum's neck. But I knew this game would be more satisfying if I could trap him in his own lie.

"Rum," I persisted. "Did you hear?"

"That you Lavern?" he croaked through the cloth.

"Yes, I'm here," said Lavern, falling into a crouch beside me. "Our new apprentice has a remedy for you, lad."

"I want nothing from that little wart!" he fumed. "I'd rather die in these woods than take his stinking peasant medicine! I'll die here like Gwendolyn, forsaken by the whole rotten world."

Rum kicked one of his legs outside of his blanket, but his foot missed me by several inches. I steeled myself against his harsh words and intended blows. There was nothing he could say that hadn't been spat at me already by members of my family.

"Tis a tonic my mother swears by," I said, pressing on with my mock doctoring. "A cure-all of her own inventing."

Lavern nodded at me in approval. Then he reached a hand beneath the blankets, his fingers feeling for Rum's brow.

"Alas…your fever is hotter than I feared," he cried. "Those cuts in your cheeks may've become infected after all. This medicine could be our last hope. Won't you spare us our heartbreak, Rum? Won't you offer some hope to lowly vagabonds such as we?"

At these words, Rum tentatively uncovered his face. Not only did he seem flattered by Lavern's speech, he also appeared unsettled by the assessment that he might truly be nearing his end. It seemed he wasn't as prepared for death as he'd boasted. His eyes were suddenly filled with quailing tears. His breath came in airy tremors. And not even his scars could hide it. He was Gwendolyn again.

"Please…we just wish to make you well again," I told him, the words tumbling from my mouth before they were fully formed in my mind. "Unless it's on stage…I shouldn't wish to see you die."

Rum frowned at me. I could've told a hundred lies to unsettle him, but instead I had opted to tell him the truth. I watched his face slacken, its girlishness slipping to reveal a brash boy who would drink from a privy if it would spare his friends from grief.

"So…what's this medicine then?" he asked.

I didn't answer him. Instead I seized the moment. I uncorked the tonic, grasped Rum by the chin and tipped the bottle, pouring it straight down his throat. Rum jerked back, slapping a hand over his mouth. His eyes widened and his chest gave a heave. He shoved me aside, rushing for the bushes where he vomited profusely.

"It...it's a miracle!" gasped Makaydees in feigned wonder. "Why before the boy could not even lift his head. But now he dashes like a spooked hare!" He clung to Wally's arm, pretending to steady himself. "How I marvel at these rustic remedies!"

Rum wheeled around, his eyes blazing.

"What *was* that bottled horse piss?!"

Makaydees reeled again, clutching his chest. "Now the boy has his voice back too! He's bellowing at full pitch. His hands are making fists and there's colour beneath those scabs. What a startling recovery! It's almost as if there were nothing wrong with him at all."

Rum glowered at the amused faces surrounding him. He marched over to the cart, seizing a pack from the heaped luggage.

"Laugh the day away, Makaydees," he snapped. "I'm leaving. Do you hear me, you old cackler? I'm leaving! I've no role in your theatre anymore. You've been and replaced me! You've taken my dress and you've cut off my hair. Clearly I'm no use to you, except as a jester. Well, no more I say! I'm done with you all!"

Rum slung a bag from the cart over this shoulder, but Makaydees caught his arm and brought a halt to his dramatic exit. He put a finger beneath Rum's chin, gently lifting up his face and then regarding those deep rifts in his cheeks with a fresh contemplation.

"They give you character," Makaydees assured, his lips softening into a smile. "We'll always have use for *that* in our theatre."

Rum lowered his pack, his chest deflating as the last of the hot air leaked out of him. He let himself be tugged into the playwright's chest, burying his wounded face against his jacket. I exhaled at the sight too, happy to have played some part in mending this feud rather than being the cause of it. I slumped against the nearest tree.

An arrow struck the bark, inches from my head.

I stood rooted, not sure I believed what had just happened, even with the arrow's feathers so close to my cheek. Lavern seized my wrist and yanked me to the ground, a heartbeat before a second arrow was fired over us, burying itself in the throat of the player's cart horse. I saw Rum opening his mouth to yell before Makaydees clamped a palm to his mouth. Wally hurried over to the treeline.

"*Huntsmen!*" he told us breathlessly.

Makaydees nodded, not wasting another moment.

"Grab everything you can carry," he urged us. "Grab it all up, lads! And then run like the Devil is chasing you."

Scene Six

The Pirate Bride

I never knew how much my legs could hurt till I was running for my life. After the arrows were fired into our camp, we fled the clearing in a blur of panicked breaths and the whinnies of the dying cart horse. Rosalie slumped to the ground with far less ceremony than the maidens of Makaydees stage. And without a beast of burden we were forced to carry all the theatre's properties ourselves.

Lavern and Rum hefted the costume trunk between them while Makaydees and Francis threw baggage over their backs. I snatched up the cooking gear and Wally, being the strongman of the company, took the heaviest load – hoisting the long wooden arms of the tumbrel and dragging its wheels through the forest himself.

Despite not being built for a cross country sprint, it was Makaydees who led our flight, barking orders for us all to keep up. But not long into our run, old Francis was lagging behind, trembling at the knees, a hand clutched at his chest. Wally halted the cart and lifted him onto its rear before resuming his position at the reigns.

I don't know how long we ran like this, leaping over logs and roots in search of a place to take cover. Unlike my fellows, I couldn't resist looking back. There was nobody in pursuit and if my lungs hadn't been on fire, I would've told the others it seemed safe to slow down. But I had the feeling they wouldn't have listened. I had the feeling they were accustomed to making these desperate escapes. But what fate were they fleeing from? And what'd they done to deserve it?

There was no time to ask. My sole focus was keeping pace with my fellows while my blood throbbed and the strain of exertion stabbed at my sides. After what felt like hours of this purgatory, Makaydees brought us to an abrupt halt on the lip of a woodland dell. The rest of us almost staggered into his back before we stared down to see a cave mouth a little way beyond a shallow stream.

"There," Makaydees rasped. "Stow the cart there…"

None of us argued as we heaped the gear back in the cart, then built a small bridge of stepping stones to help Wally get the tumbrel over the brook and into the cave. Only once this was done were we able to throw ourselves down and moan. Kicking off our boots, we sprawled beside the stream, our blistered feet in its lapping waters.

Rum was the only one of us to remain standing.

"We shouldn't have fled," he gasped out.

"I beg pardon?" Makaydees asked in umbrage. "Did you want us to hold our ground and pick a fight with a royal hunt? Challenge them with the wooden swords from our properties sack?"

"It was no Queen's hunter that shot at us! They would have been on horseback and would've overtaken us in a few gallops. Those arrows came from a common poacher. He must've spied us through the trees and spooked us into abandoning our horse." Rum kicked up the dirt in frustration. "We shouldn't have left her! We should have chased that rotten prigger and turned his own crossbow on him!"

"I wasn't going to risk our necks on avenging a cart horse," said Makaydees. "I'm not the gambling man that you are, Rum. And for that reason we shall all live longer and be thankful that those stray arrows did not strike any member of our company."

"Rosalie *was* one of us!" Rum protested.

Makaydees pinched his temples. "Well, if you must lay blame for her loss, I'll remind you it was Lavern who insisted we cut through the forest. I would've happily kept to the roads."

Lavern sat upright at this affront. "It's a market day! I thought that all hunters would've gone into town to trade."

"And not for the first time, you thought wrong. Which has cost us both time and a trusty steed. I must be warier of your council, Lavern. Personally, I'd rather face a lowly highwayman than a hunting party. Better to tangle with our fellow outlaws than a company of armoured lordlings who could string us up on sight."

"Did you say...*fellow* outlaws?"

This last question came from me and the players all fell silent at it, exchanging furtive looks. None of them offered me an answer. Instead it was Francis who spoke next. The old man knelt down beside Wally, who lay on his back, his huge chest heaving, his long arms laying like deadwood on the ground. Francis took a cloth from his pack, soaked it in the stream and pressed it to Wally's brow.

"Peace, boys..." Francis chided with a sudden world weariness, talking like the rest of the troupe were insolent children to him. "You best save your breath for the explaining we need to do. It's time we let our new apprentice know what a life he's in for."

These explanations that Francis spoke of took over the rest of the afternoon. After we'd crawled into our cavern hideaway and slumped against its cool stone walls, Makaydees took a deep breath and began telling me why their company so often found themselves fleeing from the last town they performed in. Why each of them had false names and carried counterfeit licenses in a variety of trades.

It was because of something called the Vagabond Act, a law which deemed that strolling players without patronage were no better than rogues and sturdy beggars. The players counted on small-town peasants being unaware of this decree, for an inn keeper would not offer a stage to common criminals, but most made the misassumption that such an eloquent and scholarly gentleman as Makaydees must be touring some production from the London playhouses, well known to be protected and frequented by good Queen Bess herself.

My master reassured me that due to her majesty taking pleasure in the arts, the laws against unlicensed players had been somewhat eased during the past two years. For example, it was now rather less likely that an unauthorized actor would be burned through the ear and whipped through the streets just for putting on a play. But they were vagabonds all the same. And as such they had to keep moving, never lingering for too long in any town and practicing such conceits that would hide their true craft from the local authorities.

"Have no fear," Makaydees assured. "I've studied the Poor Laws and the worst we face is being sent to the correction house and forced into some mundane labour, like the work you endured on that farm. Not that it will come to that even! I swear it to you now, lad, I will always craft a better ending for my troupe."

"Would that you could simply find us a patron," Lavern muttered. "Then we'd have no need to run ourselves ragged, living with the threat of arrest – or worse – hanging over our heads."

"Don't start, Lav," said Wally. "You know…"

"I *know* that licensed actors in London are considered artists and visionaries, not idle ruffians! Right now, in the capital, tis said they're building a new theatre, south of the river. And the players who'll tread its boards won't just be safe from gaol and the lash, but spared from military service – never having to fear being shipped off to fight the Spaniards." He let out a wistful sigh. "What a life!"

"What hogwash!" Makaydees scoffed. "You know that those city companies are all at the mercy of the Privy Council and must censor their scripts so as not to upset Puritan sensibilities. What artist wants to live like that? The best playwrights of our age have been lost to murder, prison and the rack. And the latest news from the city is that they have banned satires. They are burning books in the streets! I tell you…it's only on these roads that our theatre can speak freely."

Lavern slumped against the cavern wall, not seeming convinced, but looking too weary for dispute. My eyelids were drooping too and I could scarcely take in their rivalling words. The rest of the troupe were similarly spent and Makaydees treated us to a pitying smile before he permitted us to lay down and rest our aching bones.

We were woken before we'd recovered by rough shakes and loud claps in our ears. I opened my eyes to find the deep shadows of evening had crept into the cavern. The space where we had slept was now lit by rush lights and Makaydees stood in the centre of their flickering glow, an armful of parchments clasped to his chest.

"Gentleman! I trust you're ready for a night of rehearsals? We still have that play to put on in two days after all."

"You...you still want to go to Bristol?" Lavern groaned, rubbing his eyes. "If it be so, let it be noted that I am in no way responsible for making *this* horrible decision for our troupe..."

Makaydees didn't honour Lavern with a retort, but simply thrust a skullcap into his hands. Lavern was tasked with threading the remains of Rum's hair into a wig to be fixed to my head like a tangled crown. Francis, who served as the troupe's chief costumer, beckoned me forth to take my measurements, so I stood with my arms outstretched and my legs clamped together, back in the scarecrow's pose.

"We call this one Mirabelle," said Francis, his eyes gleaming as he unfolded a pale blue dress, cradling it like a maiden who had swooned his arms. "Mirabelle, the Pirate Bride...another tragic heroine in our collection. I dare say she'll take some adjusting before she fits you, but if you wear her well, she'll let you tell her story."

"After a number of tweaks to my script, she will," said Makaydees. He sat with his parchment in his lap and an inked feather in hand. The quill wasn't moving yet, but his eyes were glazed as if the spectacle was unfolding in his mind. "For starters...I will be cutting every one of Mirabelle's lines. For this debut performance, our new apprentice will be playing the maiden mute. She'll be a young nun who has taken a vow of silence. Lavern and Wallace, you will learn your parts anew, taking longer speeches to cover his lost lines."

Lavern and Wally shared a mutinous look, neither taking it as a compliment that our master trusted them to learn a fresh script in so short a time. Reluctantly they reached for the new pages, careful not to smear the ink that had scarcely begun to dry.

"What part will I take?" asked Rum.

"Well...you've the perfect countenance for a villain's role now," said Makaydees. "But I don't want you upstaging Wally's Pirate King. No Rum, this time around I will require you to take an off-stage role –simulating the storm, handling the swords and..."

"Props?!" he blasted. "You're putting me on *props*?"

"I'll write you a part in time! But till those scabs have fallen away, your face will only act as an unwanted distraction."

Rum's jaw tightened, his cheeks flushing beneath his stitches. He got to his feet and marched out into the night.

"Yes, *stand watch!*" Makaydees called after him. "Make yourself useful and let us focus on our preparations."

Rum did not answer and a hush fell over the cavern. The tension in the air began to ease as Wally and Lavern concentrated on their lines and Francis busied himself with sewing. I'd avoided adding my voice to the player's squabbles, but now it was quieter I took my chance to query what the troupe had yet to explain to me.

"What's so important about this Bristol show?"

"Tis Arthur's birthday," said Francis. "No matter how old he gets he still must have his way when it comes around."

"That is not the *sole* reason, as well you know," said Makaydees, his head snapping up. "This show marks a long-awaited homecoming for me, lad. I spent the happiest days of my youth in that harbour town. I began my theatre career treading the boards of a tavern belonging to my oldest friend – Sam Barrentine. Let me tell you, no crowd ever wept so hard over my tragedies as that common room full of sailors. They always returned to shore with salt in their eyes and a homesickness in their bellies. I could've happily recited my poems and staged my plays in Bristol till the curtain fell on my own time."

"Why didn't you s-s-stay?" I lisped out.

He avoided my eyes. "Too many reasons why. Chief among them my desire to bring my plays to new audiences, recruit new actors and take inspiration from the road. My friend Sam begged me not to go. He swore if I went off to live as a roaming player, I would be dead or gaoled before I turned thirty. He bet me a share of his life savings upon it." He flung his arms wide. "Well, that was ten years ago and my thirtieth year is almost upon us! I've long intended to celebrate it back in Barrentine's inn, performing one of my plays before I claim my winnings. I wouldn't miss settling this wager for the world. Wouldn't miss the look on Sam's face when he sees I have lived to be an old man."

"Well, you're still returning as an outlaw, Mak," Wally pointed out. "I remember how you used to boast that we'd be riding into Bristol in a golden pageant wagon with the Queen's own seal of approval. How old will you be when that day comes, hey?"

"It is better I return this way," Makaydees shrugged. "Outlaws are the true heroes of our age. We see handbills bearing their names and likenesses on every door we pass. That is fame, lads! That is legend! Men dream at night of living like rogues while women dream of being carried off by them. I can't account for such tastes, but as a playwright I must do my best to satisfy them. And with *Mirabelle* we'll be offering the nautical variety of these popular villains. It will go down a storm among the seafarers, explorers and privateers. I know that crowd well. They're all as one barnacled body in Bristol."

"Just remember Mak," said Lavern. "We've a young apprentice yet to be trained. He'll be scared out of his wits if we put him on stage in front of a rabble of leering seadogs. Not to mention we risk our own arrests in that low company. I say again…we'd be better taking another tour of the quiet midland towns I've mapped out..."

"And I say we shall not keep retreating in our own footsteps! You worry too much, Lavern. Have I told you this?"

Lavern rolled his eyes. "Ceaselessly."

"Enough fretting. Look to your scripts!"

"W-w-hat of my part, sir?" I asked.

Makaydees frowned a moment, considering.

"I think it best you know little of your role. It'll allow you to be spontaneous and get caught up in the act. If you need to prepare in some manner why not get acquainted with your costume?"

He nodded to the dress that Francis had hung upon the cartwheel. I rose to my feet and reached a tentative hand towards it.

"Don't put it on here!" Francis blurted, flapping his hands. "I don't want to see our new Mirabelle before the show."

Wally chuckled. "Excuse him. He's like a superstitious father who won't see his daughter before her wedding day."

"Tis bad luck, I tell you!" Francis protested.

"Take a walk, boy," said Makaydees, gesturing for me to leave the cave. "We need to be free of interruptions here."

At first, I felt spurned as I bundled the dress called Mirabelle under my arm and slipped away. But soon I was glad to be out in the cool evening air. I was still barefoot as I waded downstream, my eyes raised to the gleaming moon and my ears drinking in the forest's twittering night noises. It wasn't long before I came to a deep pool in a woodland clearing, its waters silvery pale under the starlight.

This pool was a peasant's mirror. I could see myself in costume, I realized. I could see myself as a girl. I shook off my doublet and shirt, then held the dress pinched at arm's length. I was still struggling over how I should feel about it. When Francis had taken my measurements, looping his tape round my body and marking its span, it'd felt like the tailor was trussing me up like a yuletide goose. Like this frock might be another rope being knotted around me. In the past I'd dreamt up my own roles. This female part wasn't my choice. It was something being woven around me. I was a fly caught in its web.

Francis had told me that every boy actor must suffer the skirts first before they can grow into the men's roles. But even so, I couldn't help imagining how hard my brother Flan would have laughed to see what a mockery had been made of my effeminate ways. *Playing the woman will get you nowhere.* Isn't that what Ma told me? But maybe she was wrong. Maybe I could be the woman that she couldn't dream of being herself. A woman of the road, wedded to rogues. Seeing this girl in my mind, I slipped the blue dress over my head.

I pulled the skirts down until they flattened over my stomach and flared over my limbs. I slipped off my stockings and wriggled my bare knees in the airy pocket of my petticoat. Then I stepped up to the bank and I gazed down into the water to see the reflection of Mirabelle in its ripples. The girl had the same squirrelly eyes as me, the same upturned nose and pointed chin. But while these features looked peculiar on me as a boy, they seemed to soften and prettify now that I had put on this frock. And I couldn't help myself. I tittered a laugh and tipped my head to the side, reaching up a finger to tease my curls.

A shadow fell over the water, darkening my view.

I hadn't heard any footsteps approaching, so I let out a shriek and spun around on my heels, bunching up my fists.

The shadow only laughed at me.

"You certainly scream like a girl," it said.

"Rum?" I rasped, fear shuddering out of me.

"Who else?" he retorted. "And screaming won't do you any good. You're too far from the camp. The others are deep in rehearsals."

I stiffened. That sounded rather like a threat.

I swallowed. "W-w-what do you want?"

He didn't answer. He was taking in the sight of me in the frock, a dress he had no doubt worn himself. He snorted.

"You know, I should be thanking you..." he said. "They put you in skirts and grow your hair long and a female madness comes over you. Suddenly there's a singsong in your voice, your eyes are forever weeping and you find yourself wanting to fall into the arms of every sturdy fellow who smiles at you. I was in those dresses for too long. I should be pleased I can call myself a man again."

Rum planted his hands upon his hips and thrust out his pelvis. I suddenly got the feeling that he hadn't be standing guard at the treeline so much as reaching down his breeches and reclaiming his manhood in quite another way. And I didn't want to look at him. He still looked like the walking corpse of Gwendolyn, risen up from the grave to haunt me, her beauty marred by more than just those scars.

"What do you *want*?" I asked him again.

"To even our scores. My stomach's still in knots after your trick with the medicine. You deserve payback for that."

I looked Rum up and down. He was barely any taller than me, but it didn't make him less intimidating. Rum's fey coquettish gestures had left him. Back in his boy's clothes, he'd become a surly little braggart, spoiling for a fight. I'd suffered enough blows from Flan to know it was better to take the bruises than let myself be bullied.

I widened my stance. "What are you waiting for?"

Rum shook his head. "Not when you're dressed as one of our girls. It'd break the old tailor's heart if I put a mark on her."

"Last night you died in a pool of blood."

"A pig's bladder under my bodice," Rum explained with a shrug. "It doubles up as a bosom. The blood trickles out from a hole under my armpit. If you lie at the right angle, the dress won't stain."

"You'll have to teach me the trick of it."

"Mirabelle doesn't bleed. She drowns."

I thrust out my chin. "I can drown."

With this oath, I lifted my skirts, pulling the frock over my head and hanging it neatly on a nearby branch. I stood in naught but my skin, still ready for a scrap if Rum wanted one.

"Well, Mak won't want me bruising up your face either," he said, evasively. "You look better as a girl than I thought you would. I'd say the shadows must be doing you a few favours."

"I'm not a girl though. So, if you want to..."

"You're a *scold*," Rum sneered, taking two quick strides towards me. "Your first day as a woman and you're already the worst kind of wench. The ducking stool is what you deserve."

It was at this point I realized Rum was slowly backing me towards the pool. I had heard of the practice of plunging unruly girls underwater till they learned their place but I had never seen the punishment being carried out. Now Rum edged towards me with his hands raised, looking ready to demonstrate a ducking without the chair or crane. I stepped back until my heels teetered upon the bank.

"Come," said Rum, reaching out to seize me. "I won't hold you under long. Just enough to wash off the stink of pig shit."

I screwed up my nerve, not willing to give him the pleasure. Before Rum could pounce, I turned and threw myself into the pool head first. I felt the cold slap of water against my cheek. I held my lips tight and did not let go of my breath. I had practice in holding it. There had been many mornings that I had dunked my head into the drinking trough just to see how long I could keep it there. I had been hoping that one day I might feign a drowning in the river beyond the hill.

Drowning was a death I could do well. I sank like a stone, letting my body go limp in the slippery embrace of the water. There were no sounds down here, nothing but the quailing echoes of my soul. Fear coursed through my veins, but was numbed by the chill. It would be peaceful to die this way, like returning to the womb. The shadows of the pool curled around me and I snuggled them.

A hefty splash brought me out of my trance. I felt hands fishing for me in the water, like a frantic midwife trying to pull me out into the world. Suddenly those hands were beneath me, hooking under my arms and knees, hoisting me into the air. I panted for breath against Rum's chest, his skin now just as bare and soaked as my own.

"I thought you might've drowned yourself!" he spluttered.

"I thought you might've let me," I wheezed in reply.

Suddenly I felt shy of my nakedness. I'd braced myself for a fight with Rum but not for this. Whatever *this* was. I clung to Rum's neck as he carried me back to the bank. By the time we had clambered from the water onto a lip of stone, we were helpless with laughter. We lay on our backs, braying up at the moon. As our hysteria settled, Rum twisted his neck to face me. He nudged me in my ribs.

"You can drown when you're Mirabelle," he said.

Scene Seven

The Traveller's Toll

We set off for Bristol not long after first light. Although Makaydees estimated that we were only a seven-hour tramp away, the heat of the day slowed us down and stretched our journey. Lavern was still keeping us off the roads, leading us along country byways and often over bumpy terrain. Without a steed, we were tasked with pushing the cart between us. Sweat trickled into our eyes as our feet baked and blistered inside our shoes. We barely spoke, though Wally and Lavern could be heard murmuring their new lines under their breath, memorizing the latest script revisions for *Mirabelle, the Pirate Bride*.

I had no speeches of my own, of course, and Makaydees was still insisting I would only require a walk through to block my moves. He wanted to keep the play's action unfamiliar to me so my performance would be raw and authentic. I was still desperate for even the smallest amount of preparation, so I felt appalled when we pulled the cart into a small brace of trees and Makaydees ordered us to bed down for a few hours' sleep. He said our last rehearsals would commence only after we had rested our bones and cooled our boiling heads.

I couldn't so much as shut my eyes. While the others slumbered beside me in the cart, I lay on my back, staring up at the sky, restless with anticipation. So, I was still awake to see the shadows of evening creep in and just as the stars began to twinkle, I felt the tumbrel wheels slowly starting to turn. Peering through the struts of our vehicle, I saw that Wally had looped the bridal around his own burly shoulders and he was ever so gently drawing our carriage. The gypsy strongman was supposed to be standing guard for us, but it looked like he had seen fit to get us further on our way towards the harbour town. The others did not so much as stir at the sudden motion. I did my best not to disturb their drowsing as I eased myself down from the rear of the cart. Then I scurried round to join our driver at the reins.

"Need help?" I whispered to Wally.

I pressed my palm to the one of the tumbrel arms, making the best pretence I could of bearing some of its weight. Wally's lips hitched in a smirk. He seemed to appreciate my token contribution. Really, I just wanted to spend time in his company. Wally was the quietest and most mysterious of my new companions. Makaydees had deliberately kept a distance between us. After all, it was Wally who would be playing the role of the pirate captain to my kidnapped maiden. I was meant to fear him, not befriend him. I tried to imagine Wally dragging me around the stage, throwing me to my knees or whatever other menacing treatment Makaydees script had in store for my heroine.

With his hulking stature and swarthy skin, Wally did look the part of a brutish captor. His high domed head was currently wrapped up in a turban, so there was no mistaking his gypsy heritage. I supposed that Makaydees must be playing on people's fear of the foreign when he wrote his villains. Pa would've been terrified just to stand in the same room as Wallace Farr. But right now, Wally was smiling. A smile that softened his face and made a gentle giant of him.

"Why are you pulling the cart alone?" I asked.

The gypsy driver glanced back toward the tumbrel where our four fellows lay slugabed. If they were aware the cart was moving, they must be too weary to lift their heads to acknowledge it.

"Mak had a word in my ear. Asked if I'd steer us back toward the main road so we can make our way swifter to Bristol on the morrow. Don't tell Lavern we said so, but he's led us in a muddled route through the wilds. He hasn't got the strongest sense of direction, bless him. But me? I could walk us to the ocean blindfolded."

"I…I've never seen it before."

90

"Oh, wait till you see! It goes on forever. And some of the beaches down south from here have waves that rise up big as a monster's maw, threatening to swallow you whole. And there's the secret coves where you can camp in the shade and feast on crabs all day long. I used to spend whole summers there with my old tribe. "

"Your tribe? What do you…?"

"Tribe's just the word we use for family. Whether we're related by shared blood, shared race or just our shared journeys."

I didn't know a thing about gypsy life but I caught the wistful look passing over Wally's face and I sensed he'd had a harder time parting with his tribe than I'd had in leaving the farm.

"Where are your tribe now?" I asked.

"Around this time, they should be travelling south to trade at the summer fayres. Mayhap this will be the year I'll cross paths with them again? I want to show them that I've finally mastered a skill. You see, the Farr clan specializes in palmistry and fortune telling. But I never had any knack for it. Then I met Makaydees at market and he offered to train me as an actor. He said I could learn to be a pretend prophet at least. So, I left my people, telling them I would serve my apprenticeship, then find my way home." Wally's smile tensed a little, but did not fall. "A fair few summers have passed since I made that oath…I suppose this theatre's my family now. Here's hoping it'll become one for you too, Timony. I think

91

you'll fit in with us, lad. I think you'll find we're all people who've never really fit anywhere else."

My mouth fell open, my lower lip quivering. The gypsy kept his eyes on the road ahead and didn't seem to notice me struggling to make some manner of reply. He didn't seem to realize that his own words were quite the kindest thing that anyone had ever said to me. I took a breath, suddenly feeling like I might be able to speak without stuttering. Without fearing any slaps or scorn if I said the wrong thing. I was just opening my mouth to ask Wally a thousand questions when he raised his hand, hushing me with a sharp hiss.

"What?" I asked, startling. "What is it?"

He narrowed his stare. "I'm trying to listen."

I frowned. "Listen for *what*?"

"For whatever's coming up the road."

Wally murmured this so low it was more like he mouthed it. But somehow his apprehension reached Makaydees's ears. Our master was suddenly on his feet in the tumbrel, looking to his driver.

"Master Wallace?" the playwright prompted.

Wally halted the cart and stood tensed in readiness.

"You best wake the others," he urged.

Makaydees didn't question his instincts but sank to his haunches and gave each of the players a rough shake. They rubbed their eyes and rose nervously to their feet, staring off in different directions as they peered over the struts of the cart. For a moment it seemed like a false alarm. Like nothing but silence surrounded us.

I crept forward, squinting into the gloom and then...

...an arrow struck the dirt road before my feet.

I staggered back into Wally who coiled an arm round me, bracing me to his chest. Following the arrow, there was a crunch of booted feet and a rustling in the roadside bushes. We looked around us frantically, unsure where these footfalls were coming from.

Orange light flickered through the trees. Then suddenly, a pair of hooded figures emerged on either side of the road, each clutching a flaming brand. A third cloaked stranger stepped out onto the highway before the tumbrel, a crossbow slung over his shoulder. Then finally a voice spoke from somewhere toward our rear.

"Halt and pay the toll!" the voice demanded.

I slipped out of Wally's protective hold, rushing round the cart to see this assailant who'd crept up behind us. At first, he looked nothing like a man at all. Within his cowl, he had bright green skin, bugged-out eyes and a curling snaggle-toothed smile.

"Make no attempt to fight or flee!" he continued. "You are at the mercy of Robin Candle and his Goblin tribe. Pay the toll or we shall burn this cart to cinders! We'll melt your gold and then drink it from your purses! *Pay up!*"

The stranger calling himself Candle threw back his hood, revealing pointed ears and a nose and chin that jutted at ugly angles. A ragged ruff burst from his neckline and a daunting black codpiece protruded from his trunk hose. But the most worrying part of his elaborate apparel was the sword and scabbard hanging from his belt. My skin prickled in fright. I knew the constable from my old parish carried a rapier and I'd heard tell of some of the rougher townsmen concealing daggers. But this was the first time I'd stood so close to a lawless man armed with a blade. Lavern, Francis and Rum huddled closer in the cart. Makaydees was the only one to retain his composure. He sighed and brought his palms together in a slow patronising applause.

"Thank you, squire. Many thanks for that diverting little caper. It reminded me of the old mystery plays I enjoyed at country pageants in my youth. A little lacking in subtlety, but it still served as an amusing roadside curiosity. Take that absurd mask off, highwayman. Your voice will carry far better without its muffling. I count myself an expert in such matters. I'm a theatre master after all."

Candle seized the chin of his mask, whipping it over his head and revealing a broad face to match his burly arms.

"So, *you're* the players!" he jeered. He shared a grin with his three henchmen who surrounded our cart. "We've caught up, lads! We spied you fellows back in the forest. We'd hope to make your acquaintance then…but you left in such a hurry. Not even stopping to share the feast of horse meat that we enjoyed at your camp."

My stomach turned over. I glanced back at the cart where Lavern now had his hand clamped tight to Rum's shoulder, holding him back. So, it had not been a royal hunt that had shot Rosalie. But Makaydees hadn't been wrong to flee. While our company outnumbered Candle's gang, that didn't count for much when the highwayman and his rufflers were bearing blades, crossbows and torches.

Candle drew his sword now while barking orders to his men. "Get them out of the cart! Empty their purses! And as they be players watch that they don't palm us any counterfeit coins."

"We cannot offer you coins of any sort," said Makaydees evenly. "You would be better off stealing from a grave."

"We can make corpses of you yet," Candle sneered. "But when it comes to actors there's no telling if you'll spring up after perishing. If we killed you, we'd have to kill you thoroughly."

I stood clinging to the cartwheel, wondering when exactly it would be appropriate to start having loud hysterics over Candle's unabashed plans to murder us all. My master was still firmly planted in the cart, refusing to be rattled by the bandit's threats.

"The best I could offer is a drink at the next tavern we play. But as I stand before you now even my wineskin has run dry."

Candle twirled his sword handle in his palm.

"In that case, we shall not kill you outright," he announced as if wishing to play fair. "If you lads prove to be honest in your thirst and destitution then we will neither rob you, nor harm you. So, take a step back, Moon man. Be fearless if you are honest."

This last command was directed at Wally who stood silent on the other side of the cart from me. Candle raised his hand and dropped it as if he was trying to persuade the towering gypsy to sit like an obedient dog. But Wally held his ground, allowing his shadow to stretch over the highwayman. Candle's smile began to waver.

"Come now!" he continued with forced pleasantry. "If I deem you trustworthy then we'll ride into Bristol together. Outlaw brothers, side by side! But first, I must play the villain's role, if only to impress your cynical theatre master here with my talent."

Candle nodded to the two rufflers at his sides and they planted their torches in the ground, rolling up their sleeves and approaching our cart. The third man kept his crossbow trained on us.

"Step down!" Candle barked. "Let me see all you in the light. I'm afraid you'll have to play my hostages first."

Lavern was the first to move. He dismounted the cart and then with astounding nerve, turned his back on the highwayman and his sword, lifting a hand to help Francis to the ground. Once the old tailor was set on his feet one of Candle's thugs stepped forward to seize his collar, seeming intent on throwing him to his knees.

Lavern shoved the man hard in the chest.

"Keep your hands off him!" he snapped.

The rufflers bristled, closing around Lavern and raising their fists for a beating. Their leader stepped between them.

"This must be your hero player!" said Candle, still addressing all his words to Makaydees. "Has this young lionheart been knighted yet? The Goblin King can make it so! Come, sir, and kneel."

Candle tapped the dirt road with his sword.

"Humour the man, Lavern," Makaydees said coolly. "If you refuse to take your role, I fear we'll be here all night."

Lavern reluctantly sank to his knees. Candle smiled, taking sinister pleasure in this mock ceremony. As he tapped Lavern's shoulders with the flat of his sword, I saw the blade brushing his neck, a tentative graze suggesting that he would love to swipe his sword across Lavern's throat and paint the cartwheels with his blood.

"*Don't!*" I blurted out, rushing forward.

Candle retracted his sword and extended his free hand to knock me to the ground. Lavern made to stand while Candle's back was turned, trying to seize upon my clumsy diversion.

"Stay, Sir Knight!" Candle insisted, reversing his stance before Lavern could find his footing. "We must see if you are a true knight before you can rise up and claim your title."

Lavern scowled, remaining on his knees. Francis, who had been forgotten during this feud, crouched by Lavern's side and put an arm around his shoulder; a show of mute solidarity.

Candle snorted, then turned towards Rum.

"Well, will you look at these *scars*!" he exclaimed, tugging Rum down and drawing him into the light. He clasped Rum's chin to exhibit his wounds to his men. "If I had a face like this knave, I'd have no need of a mask. How came you by these cuts, boy?"

Rum stood stiff in his grasp. "In a tavern brawl. Some crossbiter tried to cheat me over a wager and we came to blows."

Candle held Rum's hard stare, seeming to welcome it. "Given the fire in your eyes, I dread to think how your rival fared! Eyeballs on his plate and his tongue in his flagon, I'll wager!" He treated Rum to a slap on the cheek, knocking his eyes out of their staring match and causing him to stagger. "I suppose we cannot take you as one of our hostages, lad. We must cast you in another role. Grit your teeth and stand over there with my men. Show the rascals how it's done."

Beads of blood slipped through Rum's ruptured stitches where the highwayman's slap had reopened his scabs. Still glaring Rum shuffled over to stand beside the henchman who was holding the crossbow, the one who had most likely shot the arrow into Rosalie's throat. I couldn't read Rum's thoughts, but I imagined if any violence flared between our gangs, he'd want to fight the horse killer first.

I was feeling relieved to have thus far escaped the highwayman's attention. But just as I was shuffling over to join Lavern and Francis in the mud, Candle caught me by the scruff of my neck, jerking my head back and bearing my throat above my collar.

"Don't think I've forgotten you, little one," he cooed. "I must keep an eye on you. You move so quiet and furtive. I think it best that you serve as my assistant. Now for the plunder!"

Candle lifted me under one arm and then mounted the cart himself. Once I was set on my feet I was prodded in the back until I bent down to open the trunk and spill out our knapsacks. Candle gestured for me hold each item aloft so that he could examine it in the light. He had the scrutiny of a jeweller with a keen eye for value.

"Such colours! My compliments to your costumer, he has a gift for his dyes. These garments would fetch a price…"

"You weren't asking for clothes, but coins," Makaydees reminded him. "And you've found none in your search."

Candle let out a hiss and yanked me back to my feet, tugging my collar so hard that I was hoisted onto my tiptoes.

"I've yet to search *you*, theatre master! Does your chest really fill your coat? What is it you're hiding there, man?"

Candle gave my neck a quick shake, causing me to squeak like a pinched mouse. Makaydees rolled his eyes as if bored by these trifling threats. With a sigh, he opened up his jacket and as he did so, two long lengths of knotted handkerchiefs unfurled from his chest. I blinked in surprise at this ragged padding used to lend him a plumper appearance. Without his stuffing, Makaydees was as lean as the rest of his troupe. But Candle paid no mind to the trick of his garments. Instead his eyes fixed on a bottle peeping from my master's jerkin.

"What's this that you keep so close to your heart? You've played falsely, sir! This liquor would've paid your toll."

Candle seemed delighted to have caught Makaydees in a betrayal, as if he'd only put our troupe on trial for the pleasure of condemning us. I felt his fingers tightening around my throat. Glancing behind me, I saw the ruffians flexing their legs, looking ready to deliver kicks to the *'hostages'* still kneeling and at their mercy. Makaydees shrugged, producing the little bottle and removing its cork.

"This?" He sniffed the air and then shuddered in revulsion. "Bilge water, sir. I swear…you could not hold it down."

"And I say it's the finest honeyed mead in the land!"

"You think this is an act? The proof is in the tasting."

Candle beamed at the challenge. "For what wager?"

"If I speak true then you will cease all harassments of my troupe and be our humble passengers on the road to Bristol."

"Agreed man! And if you're lying to me again then I will slice off this lad's ear and wear it as a broach upon my tunic."

He seized my ear and then placed his blade beneath its lobe. To my dismay, Makaydees did not so much as wince over this bargain. He just tilted his head and then asked in a casual tone –

"Is there nothing you'd prefer to his ear?"

"No sir! I have worn ears before. Fingers and tongues too. I could even cut off those parts that make him a little man and leave you with a eunuch. I've heard that they sing beautifully."

I was close to tears now, but Makaydees took no notice. He passed his bottle to the highwayman threatening me.

"Drink then! A toast to mindless brutality."

Candle sheathed his sword, keeping a grip on me as he raised the bottle to his lips. I expected the highwayman to back down, refuse the dare or at least insist Makaydees took the first sip. The theatre master might have handed him poison. The moment Candle sipped I knew he must mad. He had no care for his own safety, never mind anyone else's. And that was when I realized just what it was he was swallowing. It was that same foul medicine I'd given to Rum. The *Elixir of Life*. The tonic that Makaydees told me he had bought from an apothecary to expel the black bile from his worst hangovers.

After drinking a mouthful, Candle held Makaydees stare, keeping his expression cool. I felt a shudder pass through him. His eyes watered and a trail of spittle slipped from his lips.

"It has a kick to it," he conceded. "But I've stronger constitutions than most. Hold still, lad! Let's take this ear off cleanly..."

He pushed me back, bracing me against the struts of the cart and wrenching my chin to the side. I waited for my master to call off their bet or offer a less gruesome prize. But Makaydees only halted him to polish his blade with one of his many handkerchiefs.

"Stay your hand a moment, sir. Let's not risk infection on the poor boy. I pray you...take your time with this surgery."

"Mak!" Lavern objected from where he knelt in the dirt.

"What? We cannot deny he can hold his liquor."

Makaydees treated Candle to a clap on the back. And this smack, along with his stalling, finally settled their wager. The highwayman's chest gave a hitch and then vomit spewed from his lips, spraying over my doublet. I had never felt so relieved to be drenched in sick. Candle released my throbbing lobe. Then to my surprise, his heaving turned to laughter. He threw up his arms in merry surrender.

"At last!" he exclaimed, returning his sword to its scabbard. "At last, good sir...a fellow outlaw whom I can trust."

Scene Eight

Walking the Plank

A harsh red dawn rose over Bristol. I narrowed my gaze on the horizon, struggling to distinguish where the blue of the sea ended and the blue of the sky began. I'd always dreamt of seeing the ocean. Now the sight of it stung my eyes, filling them with sun-dazzled tears. Tears I had to wipe away fast, lest Candle and his gang see my cheeks were wet and accuse me of weeping like a silly little maid.

The highwaymen were still in our company as we rode towards the harbour, unwelcome passengers weighing down our carriage. The three thugs who served as Candle's muscle hadn't offered us their names, but they had seen fit to spend most of the morning's journey spitting at us over the sides of the tumbrel, making a jolly game of trying to land their phlegm in our hair. We did our best to duck and avoid this rain of saliva, but I noticed Wally and Rum shooting dark looks at Makaydees. If our master just gave the order, we would turn the cart upside-down and beat our captors senseless with its broken pieces.

But Makaydees was keeping up a cheerful banter with Candle. So, we held our peace as we rode into town together. A silent wave of relief swept over us all when Candle called for a halt, declaring that he and his lads planned to catch crabs for their breakfast and spend the daylight hours hiding out beneath the ship landings.

"Then we'll be stealing a boat and making for the New World!" he bragged. "You boys should join us. We'll take your theatre to the other side of the globe. Teach those filthy savages they've found over there a thing or two about English culture."

"One stage at a time," Makaydees replied evasively. "For now, our focus must be upon bringing our pirate tragedy to *The Drunken Boat*. Will you and your boys be attending, Candle?"

"Oh, we'll be there, playwright," he said as he hopped down from the cart. "Watch for our lanterns in your crowd."

Candle treated us to a sly wink, then disappeared into a side alley between the ramshackle buildings. The moment he was out of earshot, Lavern let out a lungful of shuddering breath.

"*Makaydees!*" he hissed. "I pray you! Let us find other lodgings and avoid another meeting with those barbarous men. Nay let us turn the cart around and quit this town altogether!"

Wally and Francis nodded in frantic agreement while Rum's eyes blazed, his knuckles twitching by his sides like he'd rather chase the highwaymen down than flee from them. I chewed my lip and fidgeted. Stains of Candle's vomit still smeared my doublet and I was desperate to wash his stink off me. But I sensed that I was still too new to the company to be allowed a vote in this matter.

"Patience, my friends," said Makaydees. "When you've hooked a big catch, it's no time to let go of the fishing line."

"What's that supposed to mean?" asked Rum.

Our master beckoned us over to the tumbrel where our luggage lay strewn about the hay following Candle's fleecing. After sifting through a bundle of papers, Makaydees held aloft a handbill. The other players huddled close, reading the pamphlet's message.

"What?" I pestered. "What does it say?"

The other players left me to stew in my illiteracy a moment longer before letting me know the handbill warned of a highway thief named Robert Chandler, only son to a humble London candle-maker. During his time in the city, young Rob had been a notorious rogue, regularly in trouble for *'lewdness, rabblerousing and making a most appalling spectacle of himself'* in local taverns. Such incidents had led his father to arrange for his conscription so that he might learn some soldierly discipline. But after being sent west for a ship bound for the Irish war, this Robert Chandler was still violently averse to following orders. It was not long after receiving his first lesson in swordsmanship that he ran his commanding officer through the guts and turned deserter. He took to a life in the wilderness, robbing travellers after dark and making a folk legend of himself under his new name.

"…Robin Candle," I said swallowing.

"The very same," said Makaydees, rolling the scroll and slipping it into the folds of his jerkin. "He is quite the rising star it seems. One who fancies himself a Robin Hood or Francis Drake, though really, he's just a stripling mutineer. But he has a hefty reward on his head. Now do you see the confidence trick that I have been playing all night? The hunted have become the hunters, dear hearts."

"Mak…" Wally began, "…it does no good for lowly vagrants to turn in a more famed outlaw. The justice won't hand the likes of us any reward. They'll just clear more room in their cells."

"Then I should say it's a good thing I'm a close personal friend of Samuel Barrentine, the proprietor of this town's finest inn. Now, if old Sam is a little sore about me winning our long-held wager today, then I can easily compensate the man by offering him a share of the bounty when I allow *him* to be the one to turn Candle over to the law. Our part will be to draw the villain to his tavern, to act as bait for the trap. Candle and his gang will be snatched up by the Watch as soon as the curtain's closed. We may slip away quietly having doubled our fortunes. After one night, our purses will be fat enough for us to take the rest of the summer off and train our new apprentice proper." Makaydees slapped his palms together, brimming with triumph. "What say you, my lucky lads? Didn't I tell you I'd always craft us the best endings? Rum, my little gambler – would you call this a sound bet?"

Rum's brows were still knitted in a scowl, but he nodded his head in agreement. "For Rosalie. Let's see him hanged."

"I could get behind that," Wally concurred.

Lavern looked desperately to Francis, who offered only a hopeless shrug. Nobody even bothered seeking my support or approval. I stood forgotten in the player's circle, fingering the cut below my ear. Finding himself outvoted, Lavern let his shoulders slump.

"On your head be it, Mak…" he muttered.

"Do not look so grimly on our every venture, my dearest doom merchant," said Makaydees, patting Lavern on his cheek. "Have a little faith. The sun is shining and we're soon to be rich men. And you boys realize that you've yet to bid me a happy birthday?"

This was true. Due to the chaos of the night, our master's hard won thirtieth year had been passed over. He batted aside our belated well wishes and nodded for us to continue on the road into Bristol. In the early morn the only people out on the streets were the market traders, erecting their stalls and setting out their wares, their tables crammed with the foreign riches – soaps and spices, teas and tobaccos. Grocers clasped exotic fruits in their palms. Fishmongers spooned jellied eels into large clay bowls. Makaydees broke away from our cart to swap pleasantries with these merchants as we rode past, letting them know there was to be a play on this evening and the inn where it would be performed. Wally told me we would count on these chattering peddlers to spread the news of our coming. As unlicensed players, we could not distribute pamphlets without risking our arrest.

Drawing closer to the harbour, we often had to swerve to avoid the groggy sailors who were stumbling home drunk and debauched after a long night spent in the taverns and gambling dens. Some denizens were huddling in the shade of alleyways, lacking the strength to even finish the walk home to their beds. Some lay sprawled in sunlit roads, soaking in their own sweat and dribble, looking like bloated slugs that had drowned in the trail of their own mucus. A little further through the winding lanes and we came to the sea front, bustling with mariners unloading boxes of cargo whilst the fishermen hauled in nets of their stinking catch. The ship masts stretched skywards, sails bound tight to their poles like the pale skirts of kidnapped maidens.

Finally, we halted outside *The Drunken Boat*, a long red bricked building with a stretch of sunburnt yellow grass before it.

The tavern's sign bore a painting of a galleon slowly sinking into a mug of dark ale. On the threshold of this establishment, a man was shooing the birds from the window ledges and sweeping away the dry mud that caked the doorstep. He was large and butter-haired with flabby cheeks and tanned skin, which made me think of pastry that'd been overdone in the stove. Catching his first glance of this portly fellow, Makaydees jumped down from our cart, his arms spread for a reunion.

"Sam!" he exclaimed. "Sam, you old devil!"

The innkeeper startled, then shielded his eyes against the sun's glare. The man took a slow step closer to our tumbrel, though not near enough to welcome an embrace from our master.

"Art?" said Sam, raising his broom and acting like he were seeing a ghost rather than a long-lost friend. "That you?"

"I promised I'd return this day, did I not? I said I'd bring a play to the favourite of my past haunts. Did you ever doubt it, old friend? Did you think me long in my grave? Happy I am to prove you wrong and be here to settle our wager. I made it, Sam! Ten years a strolling player and thirty breathing the filthy air of this world."

"And I told you you'd get thin, didn't I?"

Makaydees tensed up. After our encounter with Candle, he had yet to put the stuffing back into his garments. His clothes hung

110

loosely over his frame and his hair fell into the hollows of his cheeks. For all of his elevated speeches, our master was a beggar off the road. Barrentine was a plump proprietor with his own roof and a stage he could easily turn us away from. I could see there was a far greater distance between these two men than the long years they'd spent apart.

"I suppose you best come in then," said Sam, rather begrudgingly. "No plays till evening time and I keep half the takings on the door. But I'll do you a free supper if it goes down well."

Following this curt address, the fat innkeeper turned his back and retreated into his tavern. Makaydees was left staring at the door that'd been shut upon us, seeming unable to look around and face us again. The wagers and rewards that had been our stake in coming to Bristol in the first place now seemed far from sure bets.

But we still had a show to put on. All my thoughts were focused on the promised play and what I'd need to do in it. I was still utterly in the dark about my role. Candle holding up our cart had robbed us of our planned rehearsal. In the little time we had left, my fellows hadn't the energy to give me even the barest bit of training. Makaydees was busy shadowing Barrentine as he went about his chores, still hoping to hatch a bargain with his former friend regarding Candle's capture. Our master had tasked the rest of his troupe with the play preparations. But Wally was exhausted from dragging the cart and Lavern was still a bag of nerves. Francis ordered them both to rest in the tumbrel, else they wouldn't be fit to stand upright, let alone perform.

Rum, meanwhile, had fallen into one of his black moods brought on by the mirrors hanging on the barroom walls, a cruel reminder of his ruined looks. He sullenly rigged up our backdrop curtain, but beyond that service he was unwilling to even be around us. It fell to Francis to give me some manner of direction. The tailor took a cluster of script pages and then sat me down beneath a tree in the tavern's rear garden. He said at the very least he could read the play aloud to me, so I'd be familiar with its story. I nodded frantically and thanked him with all my heart. But Francis barely got through the prologue before our heads nodded onto our chests and we fell dead asleep.

By the time we woke, slumped against the tree trunk, the tavern was already bustling and we were all out of time. I was rushed behind the back curtain to be frocked, wigged and powdered. Francis stuck pins into my skirt hem so it wouldn't trip me and tightened my bodice strings to give me false hips. I had a wimple to keep Rum's hair from falling into my face, though in all honestly, now this moment had come, I was desperate for any way to hide. No hope of that. Once Francis had finished adjusting my garments and painting my face, he grasped me by the shoulders, inspecting me at arm's length.

"There she is..." he whispered.

I swallowed, scared of what I had become. My skin felt suffocated under my make-up. I wanted to scratch it all off.

"Can I see her?" I asked, lifting my fingers to my cheeks. A little more forcefully I added; *"Please*, I need to see."

Francis just batted my hand away. "None of that! We've already got Rum sulking over his new reflection. I don't want you fretting for the same reason. Just try to see Mirabelle here." He tapped a finger to my brow. "It's *feeling* the girl that matters now."

I bunched up my skirts in my fists. The way I felt as this girl was just the problem. I felt ugly, strange and shameful. I couldn't believe that anyone would ever care to kidnap me.

"How do you feel, lad?" Francis prompted.

Before my mouth could find the words, my stomach answered for me. It made a deep rumbling sound loud enough to catch the attentions of Lavern and Wally who stood in a separate corner, running through their barely learnt lines. Wally snorted a laugh.

"Hunger will get us through tonight's play if nothing else!" Wally reasoned. "Just think of the supper we stand to earn."

Supper was indeed the one bribe that could get me to step outside the curtain. We hadn't eaten all day and the smell of the salty fried food being served up in the common room was wafting backstage. They had potatoes in Bristol, those big starchy spuds brought over from the New World that looked like they could fill a man's belly for a week. Maybe this was how you learned your trade as a vagabond player? You found your stagecraft just to keep yourself from starving.

"Harken, my lads," said Makaydees, slipping backstage to join us. "Here's the plan. The highwayman is out there in the crowd right now. Our play needs to hold his attention till the Watch comes to snatch him. Barrentine says that he'll hide us in his chambers till he's collected the reward. Then we will split the bounty between us. Should all go well, we'll be counting coins by nightfall." He slapped each of our backs in assurance. "To your positions! You know what to do."

"I don't," I muttered beneath my breath.

I didn't think my hushed complaint would reach my master's ears, but his hand shot out, snatching hold of my arm.

"I'll tell you what you must do, boy," said Makaydees. He gave a nod towards the awaiting crowd beyond our backcloth. "Think of this as your execution. Imagine your sentence has been passed and you're surrounded by so many guards that you've no hope of escape. All you have left is your last moment on stage. So, you best make it count. You best make sure that all watching remember you."

The playwright made this speech seeming oddly assured it would be just the thing to cure my stage fright. Francis offered a rueful smile, while Lavern, Wally and Rum had already picked up their instruments and were taking their places. The music started up, the jangling sounds of a lute, flute and tabor mingling in the close air of the tavern, hushing its throng. Makaydees gave my wrist a squeeze then steered me round the curtain, standing me at the edge of a crude stage erected from stacks of lumber loaned from a nearby ship yard.

The tavern itself looked much like the inside of a boat. Its common room was so crammed with stewed sailors that it seemed to lurch like the creakiest of old galleons. I imagined this inn was meant to offer a homeliness to men on shore leave and estranged from living on dry land. A sordid crew, they were – swaying on their feet or slumping in their chairs with paunches bursting from their breeches. Barmaids with wild hair and yellow teeth moved among them, carrying slopping jugs of ale. The sailors reached out to clasp these oily hags about their waist, forcing them into their laps and slurring into their ears. The floorboards seemed to buckle beneath their tables, looking like they could collapse at any moment and plunge them down into the ale cellar where they'd be happily entombed among the beer barrels.

The music ceased and there was no more time to watch the crowd as they all turned their heads to stare at us instead. Lavern mounted the stage first and began speaking his prologue.

"Every morning fair Mirabelle sits and dotes upon the sea,
As though its waves and rushes could teach her to be free..."

Lavern beckoned me to make my entrance. Once I was in place, he gently shoved me to my knees. Doing my best to improvise, I clasped my palms together in prayer. And I really felt the need to beg someone for my salvation right now. Being trapped and wordless on the stage, I could only look to our crowd. This crowd who were all gaping as one large slavering mouth ready to swallow me whole.

"*Ha*! I should've made a eunuch of you after all!"

My heart seized and my eyes darted to my left. Sure enough there was Candle and his gang. They sat at a table lit by a rusted lantern that was breathing a sickly smell of tallow over the room. Candle looked younger in its glow. He might be the same age as Lavern, somewhere close to twenty. His face was neither handsome, nor ugly, but rather a face that blends easily into a crowd to be carelessly forgotten by those who have seen him only once. It was his voice that you'd remember. A cooing cackling voice intent on making you squirm.

Lavern pressed on with his opening speech, but Candle was busy with his own show of yawning and waving his hand before his nose as if to say Lavern's acting was stinking up the room. Candle's henchmen were quick to join in the chorus of derision, rising from their chairs to perform prissy imitations of our narrator's voice and gestures. Lavern must have faced mobs like this before, for he just strummed his lute all the harder, shouting out his lines above their jeers.

"Enough of this dribble!" yelled Candle, rising to his feet now and refusing to be silenced. "Makaydees? When will your pirate hero be arriving to dispatch this tedious minstrel?"

Makaydees stood with Barrentine behind the bar, watching us with sympathy, while gesturing for us to ignore Candle's interference. It made little difference. The highwayman got the drunks in the back of the room banging on the tables and chanting for Lavern's death. Wally, seeming confused over whether he had missed his entrance, hurried on stage in his pirate garb and jabbed his wooden sword under Lavern's arm – a killing that seemed unscripted as Lavern rolled his eyes before staggering to the floor, dying with as much dignity as he could muster. Candle applauded like a villain had been slain.

"*Now* it begins!" he cheered, licking his lips.

The sailors looked upon us like we were a cornered army after a lost battle. Makaydees had been right to call this an execution. The crowd were relishing watching us die. Playing the mute heroine of this bungled tragedy, I could neither speak, nor move. As Wally launched into his first soliloquy, I stood clutching a loop of rope about my wrists and biting a strip of cloth between my teeth. I felt like a girl trapped in a painting; a picture of pretty helplessness.

"Come my dear mistress, let me bring you aboard
You'll be the loveliest treasure in all of my hoard.
In my brig I shall keep thee...caged and adored..."

Wally paced the stage, throwing out what lines he could remember as my pirate captor. But it was painfully clear to all present that it was Candle who was holding us prisoner. The highwayman had abandoned his table now. He strode up to the lip of our stage.

"I don't think much of this pirate king either," he sneered, waving the lantern in his hand so its wax dripped over the floor. "If he can't command the respect of this crowd then what hope does he have of leading his crew in their scourges? You boy! The lad with cracks in his cheeks. Let's mutiny against this dull captain!"

Rum blinked at the sudden address. He'd been standing offstage, taking no role in the play, but simply serving as our stagehand. Upon hearing Candle's demand and perhaps boldly attempting to salvage our play, Rum set his jaw and stepped onto the platform. Opening our sack of props, Rum produced a small wooden cutlass. He lashed out wildly at Wally who for a moment did nothing but stare blankly, blinking at the dagger in Rum's hand. The pirate king wasn't supposed to die, but after Rum barred his teeth and hissed, Wally gave a comprehending nod and then belatedly collapsed onto the floor.

Rum took a breath and turned his weapon on me.

"This ship was doomed the moment you set foot on its decks!" he raged, giving up on poetic verses and improvising. "Any seafaring man knows that tis bad luck bringing a woman aboard. My captain knew it before you bewitched him. No more, I say! You'll walk the plank and step into the drink, else I shall cut out your heart!"

Rum clasped my arm, thrusting me forwards. Lavern and Francis were now positioned at either side of the stage, gripping the ends of a long blue cloth that passed for the sea. They shook it, sending ripples through its fabric. This was my signal to move towards the edge of the platform so their waves could rise above my head.

"Hoy!" Candle hollered. "Why is there no sea wind to blow up her skirts? Let's see some leg before she is drowned!"

With these words, Candle bounded onto the stage and the crowd laughed as the highwayman seized my skirt hem, intent on hoisting up my dress and exposing me as a boy. Our much-mocked performance would end with me as the punchline. And this felt like drowning. It felt like the trapdoor of a gallows was opening up from under me. My wig itched, my bodice was too tight, the tallow reeked from the lantern and I couldn't breathe. I couldn't even *breathe.*

A scream bubbled up in my throat, filling my mouth like foam. I spat the gag from my jaws and let the cry burst from my lips. Dropping the rope from my hands, I lashed out with my fists, striking Candle hard in his codpiece. A combination of the blow and my shrill wail sent the highwayman staggering off the edge of the stage where his feet were swiftly tangled in the blue cloth of our sea. He kept falling, his head smacking hard against a nearby table. With this blow, Candle's lantern slipped out of his hand, its flame still burning.

It caught the blue cloth and quickly began to a blaze.

This sudden fire in such a tight space created a chaos of stamping feet. Thankful for the diversion, I bounded off the stage, seeking my nearest exit. A hand came out of nowhere and seized me by the arm, dragging me to a backdoor. I looked up to see that it was Makaydees who had taken charge of my evacuation. He stared me hard in the eye and gave me my first direction of the evening.

"*Flee!*" he hissed, shoving me out into the night.

Scene Nine

The Mermaids

I was lost to the crowds, sinking fast and struggling not to drown in this town. In the dark blue swell of early evening, sailors and their wenches seemed like triple-headed monsters, their legs a confusion of skirts and breeches. I fled into the side alleys where there were fewer people but denser shadows. In this maze of knotted side streets, I groped along the slippery walls, knowing I had to keep moving.

If the highwayman caught up with me in these darkened passes, then the other players would be lucky to find my corpse in one piece come the morning. I was running so fast from this fearful fate that I was not even watching my footing. Another step and my heel landed on the back of a large grimy rat that snarled beneath my sole. A shriek leapt into my mouth as the rodent slipped away. I wanted to climb the walls but knew I had to keep going. I turned another corner into an opening that tapered between the close clustered buildings.

I was just emerging from this alley when I finally took a tumble. Pain shot through my knees and the skin of my hands tore against the gravelled ground. I stilled for a moment, down on all fours, dazed from my fall. I lifted my hands to my eyes, my fingers trembling as the blood welled around the tiny stones embedded in my palms. For a moment, I forgot about being chased down by a murderous outlaw. I just sat there and shivered like a bird that had been knocked from the sky and was now huddling in a heap of its own feathers.

"Hoy there!" said a voice behind me. "Best get off your knees, girl. They'll trample you into the ground in this town."

I turned my head to see a stranger bending over me, clothed in the mantle of a man with a heavy grey cloak and heeled leather boots. But the voice that spoke to me belonged to a young girl. A girl most unlike any maid I had ever seen before. Her skin was Moorish brown, a shade darker than Wally's, while her teeth gleamed white as she smiled down at me. Most striking of all were the girl's amber eyes, like two beads of tree nectar in the smooth bark of her face.

The girl waited for me to stand on my own, then rolled her eyes, took my arm and yanked me to my feet. She snatched the wimple from my head, almost pulling my wig away with it. She tore its white cloth in two halves and dabbed at the bloodied grit

124

from my palms. Then she grabbed my skirts and hoisted them up above my grazed knees. I froze, praying she wouldn't explore further up my legs.

"Look at those poor meatless stems! You're going to wake up with two dirty great scabs on those knees tomorrow. But if you're a Bristol lass, no doubt you're used to worse bruisings."

I winced at being mistook for a maid, but choose not to correct her. I'd made a mess of my first performance as a woman. If I could pass as a girl in the street that was some small consolation.

"Haven't seen your sorry little face out on these streets before," the girl continued, eyeing me curiously. "I bet that your father keeps a pretty thing like you shut up indoors, saving you for a rich merchant to make his wife. What is it they call you, pet?"

"M-M-Mirabelle," I squeaked out.

She frowned at me. "Is that French or something? You look like you could be French. Or Flemish maybe. Yes, a little Flanders girl! You come to this harbour on a ship? You fleeing from all of those Spanish wars? Can you speak the language here at all?"

I nodded and shook my head at her in rapid succession. I couldn't have spoken even if I'd wanted to. The girl babbled on at such a pace, scarcely leaving time for her to gulp down air, let alone give me any chance to answer her many gushing questions.

"To look at me...you'd think I had some fancy foreign name too, huh? Something exotic and hard to say without stuttering. But no, it's Doll they call me. That's Doll, short of Dorothy, with no family name to follow. I was a foundling in this town, you see. No Ma and Pa that I ever knew, though the ladies I live with do fill my head with stories. They say that with the colour of my skin and the glint in my eyes, I'm sure to be the bastard daughter of Barbary pirates. May even an heir of the Moroccan Pirate Queen, Sayyida al-Hurra herself. Now there's a name for you. Try saying *that* without a stutter!"

I continued to say nothing at all. It seemed my safest option. Doll tipped her head and reached out to cup my cheek.

"One thing's for sure...you're no woman, are you?"

My heart was plummeting before she added –

"...what I mean is you're just a young girl! Painting yourself older than your years so they'll let you in at that tavern, right?"

Doll laughed and tapped me on my powdered nose.

"Never fear! We've caught each other at the same game. I snuck out tonight to see the actors at *The Drunken Boat* too. You know, they say in London, playhouses are one of the few places a lady can go on her own? You've just got to be sure you can pass for a grown woman is all." She beckoned me near and whispered; "Bit of advice...don't dress yourself like a nun. Try putting a flower

126

in those rattails of your hair. A flower or ribbon maybe. Something bold that catches the eye. I like to string myself necklaces of seashells, but…I suppose you don't want to be drawing attention to a bosom so flat."

I flinched and crossed my arms over my chest.

"Oh, you are something precious!" She laughed and linked arms with me. "Enough gabbling, little miss. We best hurry along or the play will be over by the time we reach the tavern."

I strained against her tug, wondering if I should tell Doll that the play was most assuredly over and that I'd left the tavern in an uproar, if not burning to the ground. My heart seized once more as I thought of my troupe. Makaydees had ordered me to flee, but would he seek me out later? Or was he abandoning me to these streets?

I didn't have to struggle with Doll for long. That moment that we stepped onto the road, we were startled by a band of men, brandishing torches and clubs, storming into the marketplace.

"The Watch!" Doll hissed, pulling me back into the alley.

Out in the square, the watchmen halted outside a low building, humming with voices. They pounded its door, proclaiming that they were hunting for a highwayman by the name of Robert Chandler. When they were not granted swift admission, they battered down the door and began dragging revellers out by their throats.

Doll slung a protective arm around me.

"Looks like they're out to catch a big fish tonight. Small shrimps like us would be wise not to get trapped in their nets. You stick with me, little mirror girl. I don't know how far you are from your home, but I can take you to the safest lodgings in town."

With this oath, Doll led me back into the side lanes. A sudden rain shower began falling into the dark crevices between buildings, which offered some relief from the stink of piss and rotten fish that seemed to breathe from every corner of the harbour. Beyond the shielding walls, we could still hear the Watch raising the hue and cry. My mind was awhirl. Had Candle not been captured? Was he still at large somewhere in the night? Was there still a reward to claim?

A few more turns and Doll stopped us at the door to a little shop with shuttered windows. I guessed this must be the safe haven she had promised me. In my present peril, I wasn't going to refuse a hideaway. The salt rain had soaked me through and my dress was clinging to me like a second skin. If I didn't get indoors soon the frock could become transparent and my girlish charade would melt away. Doll treated me to a wink, then knocked five times on the door, two solid bangs with her fists and three sharp raps with her knuckles.

The door was thrown wide and the first thing to greet us was a spiked cudgel. The large girl who wielded it, swung it upright, pointing it out into the road. I almost bolted, but Doll caught hold of my arm and raised her other hand in flustering surrender.

"Put the club down, Greta! It's Dolly!"

The big girl in the doorway exhaled. "You forgot the secret knock again. Why must you give me turns like this when the Watch are out?" Before Doll could answer her, Greta shifted her footing and shook her club in my direction. "Who's the waif?"

"I found her snivelling in the gutter, the poor mouse," Doll cooed, petting my wet head so furiously I feared she'd pull my wig off. "I don't think she'd have survived the night if I hadn't stumbled on her. Now move your great arse and let us in, will you Grets!"

Greta muttered a curse, stowing her cudgel by the door, seeming disappointed that she'd not been given reason to use it. I stepped over the threshold and followed the girls down a passage lined with hooks on either wall. Doll snatched a plush green cape from one of these pegs, stroked an appraising hand over its material and then wrapped it round my quaking shoulders. Beyond the cloakroom there lay a snug chamber crammed with tables. A little

129

iron kettle was whistling over a fireplace and minty steam filled the close air of the room.

"Tea's just brewed," said Greta. "But don't go giving that urchin a taste!" she added, jabbing a finger at me as she filled two cups with the steaming brew. "I don't want her begging at our door every time she's thirsty. The Madame won't want her hanging round here either. She'd be as much use as that three-legged cat you rescued last week. The one we told you to tie up in a sack and drop in the ocean."

"Don't be cruel!" said Doll, handing me her cup in defiance. "She looked pretty before her paints smeared in the rain."

Doll sat me beside the fire, appraising me in its light. She rubbed the smudges under my eyes and pinched my cheeks to bring their colour back. A frown passed over her face and I feared she'd seen through my disguise. But just as suddenly she smiled again.

"Yes, she's got a sweet little mug on her! And I couldn't just leave her shivering in the road, the poor oyster."

"Dolly Daydream!" Greta sighed. "Your heart's in the right place, but your fool head is always up in the clouds. What were you doing walking the streets after dark, anyway? You know that the Madame doesn't like you venturing out at this hour."

Doll huffed. "Yes, the Madame mustn't lose the rarest treasure in her hoard. Honestly, Grets. I'm eighteen! I can't stay home to comb my hair every night. Most girls are wedded and with child by my age. Just because I'm the ward here, it doesn't mean I'm the child of this house. As if I could keep my innocence in this place!"

While the two of them bickered, I looked about my surroundings, beginning to wonder what manner of place this was. My eyes settled on a painting that hung above the fireplace, a peeling picture of a fair maiden with a long fish tail, hair spilling over her bosom and her finger curling in a gesture of enticement. My ma had spoken of mermaids once, calling them hussies of the sea that could summon up tempests and would tempt shipwrecked men into drowning.

"What you nosing around for?" Greta snapped, seeing me staring. "Doll, this thin dribble of gruel here best not be a spy!"

"I'm sure she's just curious," Doll reasoned.

"Well, if she was raised in this town she ought to have heard of our tearoom. No finer guesthouse in the harbour. Just a few quiet rooms where tired travellers can enjoy a brew, a sup and a soak in the company of our ladies. No harm in that! You got anything to say about it, miss? Can the girl even speak, Doll? Is she some sort of simpleton?"

"She's French," said Doll by way of explanation.

Greta gave up on my interrogation and took a savouring sip from her cup. I brought the steaming drink under my own nose. Its smell alone freshened and sharpened my senses. It was some potion of leaves and spices that did wonders in reviving me.

"It wakes up the noggin, don't it?" said Doll. "The sailors bring it over from the east. It is said to be all the fashion in Europe, but the drink still hasn't quite caught on in English cities yet. We get the first taste of everything in this harbour town."

"She'll get her first taste of something else should the Watch beat down our door," Greta warned. "You know what they're like when the passion is in them. We best barricade ourselves in until this storm has passed. Get your little friend upstairs."

Doll nodded, taking me by the wrist and leading me to a curtained corner of the sitting room. Beyond this curtain lay a stairway that took us to the upper level of the house. As I stepped through the drapes on the landing, my senses were overwhelmed by a second wave of smells and sensations. We stepped into a rush-lit room where around a dozen women were slouching on cot beds, most of them sparsely clothed in petticoats and corsets. These girls had bodies of every shape, with hair and skin in all shades, almost as though they had been chosen for their variety. Some girls sat with their skirts hitched over their knees, their feet soaking in basins, scrubbing their toes with cakes of black soap. Other girls nibbled at the sweetmeats on their sideboards, scooping up handfuls of sugared nuts and dried berries.

What *was* this place? I couldn't believe my luck. I'd discovered a group of women living in their own sumptuous feminine realm. What better place to learn my role? To practice the delicate movements and manners I would need in my performances. And just as I was thinking this, there came a loud belch from the far corner.

"You picked up another stray, Dolly?"

The question and the burp came from a red-haired girl with a face smeared in brown paste. She sat lounging in a wooden tub filled with milky water that barely covered her freckled breasts.

"What are you doing, Ruth?!" Doll gasped at her. "You shouldn't be using the water and mud unless we have guests!"

Ruth scratched at her navel where it bulged from the water like a small dimpled island. "I drew this bath for a fancy feller visiting from the city. But the silly bugger's hiding." She nodded to the cupboard against the wall. "He reckons the law will be beating our door down at any moment. *Which is true enough, I suppose!*" she added, raising her voice. "We don't take kindly to fly-by-night philanderers in this town! Bloody tourists! They're nought but trouble."

There came an indignant huff from inside the wardrobe which the girls collectively ignored. Doll meanwhile marched me over to a chair that was plumped with cushions and sat me on her lap, displaying me to them all like I was a newly patched quilt.

"This is Mirabelle," said Doll, coddling me to her chest. "I found her out in the street. She was running away from something, I think. Or someone. She hasn't told me yet. I don't think she speaks any English. She's probably a stowaway, fresh off the ships."

Ruth frowned. "She didn't ride into town with the highwayman, did she? The one they're turning the town over for?"

I shuddered at the mention of Candle, a flinch that Doll surely must have felt, though she did not draw attention to it.

"What highwayman?" she asked.

"It sounds like it's that Chandler fellow from the handbills," said Ruth. "That's the name we hear them yelling. We've been watching all the drama out of the window. First it was the smoke rising from Sam's tavern. His roof went up like a bonfire, but the rain looks to have put out the worst of it. Now they're just rounding up those responsible. I tell you, once they're found – every man of them will be chained to the rocks and left for high tide to drown them."

My stomach flipped over as I bolted from Doll's lap and rushed to the window. Sure enough, there was a cloud of smoke over the tavern, illuminated by flashes of lightning. Smoke from the fire I started. Well, no…it was Candle's doing really. But our play could easily be blamed instead. I needed to find my fellows and free them if they had already been caught. I had to *think*. But thinking was a hard task when my ears were full with women all chattering at once.

"What if the highwayman comes here?! What if he finds out our house while he is searching for his child bride?"

"If he's handsome, I'll hide him under my sheets!"

"Only if he takes a bath first. I'm telling you, those highwaymen stink worse than a peat bog during a hot spell."

"Ladies, enough of your haggling!" said Ruth, raising a scrubbing brush like a judge calling for order. "Greta won't be admitting any more outsiders unless the Watch come with their clubs. If this highwayman does show up on our door, then we'll either have to give him what he wants or let his lost pearl escape the back way."

The cupboard door gave a sudden creak. The flushed face of the man hiding inside poked out through its gape.

"Excuse me!" the man began in irate tones. "Did you say there's a rear entrance to this establishment? Why didn't you say so before! Hand me my clothes, you insolent harlot! And send a message to your Madame that I'll require a full refund. I didn't hand over that purse so that an ill-mannered trull could enjoy my bath!"

"It was you that chose to leave your soak. I'm not getting out while the water's warm. Not for you. Not for no man."

Just as Ruth said this, there was a pounding of feet on the stairs followed by Greta's voice making flustering pleas.

"I beg you, sirs. I swear you're mistaken..."

"*Enough*! We know he's hiding here!"

This second speaker had the booming voice of a militia man. There was a wave of gasps as the girls sprang to their feet, bracing themselves for a raid from the city watch. Greta rushed into the room ahead of the hollering men. She gave a quick curious wink to the other girls and then turned back to the doorway, stretching her arms out wide to block the men's path. Doll pushed me to my feet and started throwing off her man's garb. Ruth sat up in her tub, snatching a towel from the nearby rack, but true to her word, she didn't leave her soak.

"Please, sirs!" Greta cried in a voice far frailer than the one she'd used when wielding her cudgel. "Please spare our modesties! Tis late at night and most of us are not fully dressed!"

"Stand aside, strumpet! We'll search you to your skin if we need to and don't pretend you wouldn't enjoy it!"

Greta was caught by her wrists and then shoved to the floor as two watchmen burst into the upstairs room. Several girls sank to their knees and made unsuccessful attempts to crawl under their beds, like rabbits burrowing into the earth. The two men laughed and aimed slaps at their upturned rears. I couldn't comprehend this sudden change in the girls. They were whimpering and cowering in fits of terror. I realised too late that I was the only one still standing. The taller of the men approached me, holding up a pair of leather long boots.

"We found these in your entrance hall!" he barked, then reached out to seize the cloak that Doll had put around my shoulders, shaking it before my eyes. "And *this* looks to me like a gentleman's cape!" The man turned to address the whole room. "Listen, sweet ladies. We like your house. We don't begrudge you your little side-lines. However, if we find you're harbouring outlaws, we'll have you all whipped at the cart's arse and see it's the end of your business! So, tell me, my pretty punks...is there a man here we don't know about?"

I found myself lacing my hands over my stomach, just a little way above my crotch, fearing that if they were hunting for a man, they'd not make an exception for a boy in a dress. I was so eager to divert attention away from myself that I aimed a very deliberate glance at the wardrobe. The watchmen followed my look and smiled.

"Hiding in the cupboard, is he?"

Ruth reared upright in her bathwater.

"*Please sirs*, it is my husband!" she protested. "He came in from shore leave this morning. First time I've seen him in months! Please allow him some dignity, sirs. He is not well. His mouth is rancid with scurvy and he has a rash all down his left side."

"Now you've new lies growing upon old lies!" said the taller man, reaching for the cupboard door. "*Enough, I say!*"

"Enough indeed!" a new voice retorted.

My head whipped round to the entrance curtain. Through it stepped a woman a few years older than the other girls. Crow's feet pinched her eyes and her powders couldn't hide the pock scars on her cheeks. But she still had a vigorous sheen to her complexion and a curvaceous body like the figureheads I'd seen gracing the ship bows.

"M-Madame," the watchman faltered. "I..."

"Kit Makepiece and Ned Sterling, isn't it?" said the Madame. "I'd expected better manners from you, lads. We've always been polite to you when you've visited us. Even on nights when you've been drunk out of your skulls and poor company for my girls. So, I'll not have you bullying them and ransacking our rooms while

138

you think I'm napping and unawares. Yes, I am sure you'd be well rewarded if you were to bring this highwayman to the gaol house. But he is not hiding here. If you wish to question the fellow in our wardrobe then you'll have come back here at some civilised hour in the morning."

"How do we know you won't let him flee?" asked Kit, his tone meeker than before, looking like a scolded schoolboy.

"Take his raiment. He can't leave in his skin."

The watchmen brightened at the prospect of confiscating the man's clothes. Ned held the long boots close to his feet, trying to guess if they would fit him. Without further argument, they bundled up the other fine garments strewn around the room and left without another word. Once they'd left the Madame turned to the wardrobe.

"*Out!*" she sneered, tapping her foot.

The frumpy little man in the cupboard emerged with his head bowed and his hands folded over the private parts between his legs. He wore nothing now but the rings upon his fingers.

One of them looked to be a wedding band.

"Oh, bless you, dear lady!" the foppish man mewled. "Thank you for shielding me. Now I beg you, one more favour. Lend me some clothes and let me flee before they return tomorrow!"

"And break our bargain? Did you not hear the threats made against my business? Do you think it would be fair for my girls to be whipped through the streets in place of a jellyfish like you?"

"Yes…no…but surely these wenches are accustomed to beatings? And I…I could compensate them for their pains!"

The Madame held out her hand, nodding to the jewellery gracing his fingers. The fop sighed, slipping off his rings and dropping all but his marital one into her awaiting palm. Once this was done, he offered the Madame a simpering smile till she handed him a ragged nightshirt from their wardrobe. After tugging this flimsy garment over his head, he shuffled barefoot towards the curtained doorway.

"My humblest thanks, ladies!" he said, addressing them as one, a hand over his heart, almost moved to tears by this rescue. "You are the truly noblest women I've ever encountered. I'll recommend your house to every traveller that I meet upon the road."

He made a flourishing bow and then scurried off downstairs. All was silent a moment. The girls bit down on their lips. Once they heard the door slamming, their hush was broken by Ruth, who burst into a fit of laughter, sending up splashes from her tub.

"Oh Grets, you outdid yourself! *Spare our modesties, sirs!* What a lark! I don't know how the lads contained themselves."

Greta was doubled over too, clapping her hands.

"Kit and Ned just stopped by to get out of the rain. I told them about that fop we had hiding upstairs and they said that they'd help us pull off a scam if they could just keep the man's boots. Between us we have stripped the rich little fool to his skin!"

I stood staring at them all in dismay. So...so those two watchmen were friends and accomplices of the girls? And they had plotted to rob their guest of his every garment and possession. It was horrible. It was despicable. It was...really rather impressive. I turned to Doll, who'd fallen into a chair, helpless with her own giggles.

"You...you played him!" I blurted out. "*Yes.* I see the trick of it. You girls put on a show of being women too!"

With this realisation, I began to laugh too. My new role suddenly made sense to me. Doll meanwhile sat blinking at me, her smile frozen on her lips. The Madame crossed her arms and asked —

"Why is there a boy in my brothel?"

Scene Ten

Fly by Nights

"Nice head of hair, lad," said Greta, ripping off my dark tangled wig. "I reckon I'll make myself a new merkin."

I had no notion of what a merkin was. I was puzzling over the word brothel too, but this didn't seem the best time to ask questions. After the Madame had exposed me, I had been hauled downstairs and seated by the hearth again. I had the heat from the fire on my cheeks and the blazing stare of Greta hanging over me. She flung the wig down on the floor and snatched up a poker from the fire.

"Grets!" Doll protested. "Don't harm him!"

"Depends how swift he is at explaining himself. It could be that he's a spy sent here by Justice Long to sniff around our house and get the dirt on us!" Greta held the brand an inch from my nose. "What do you mean by coming here in disguise, boy?"

My mouth hung open, my tongue tied up in knots. Frantically, I tried to think up some confession which wouldn't result in my face being burnt and blistered. I'd seen in Rum's scars how merciless people could be to a boy in a dress. But I was scared of saying too much. My troupe were in danger. I didn't want to risk any more trouble to them than I'd already wrought this terrible night.

Doll stepped forward, speaking for me.

"Spare the poor lad his blushes," she said softly. "Isn't it plain why he's come here? Why, he's just a shy virgin boy who's wanting his first look at ladies in their under things."

"*Yes!*" I enthused, nodding vigorously. "Yes, that's it! That's what I was doing here!" The Madame was still glowering at me in distaste, so I quickly added – "That is to say…sorry."

"Well, I don't believe him," said Greta, her smouldering weapon still raised. "And even if it's true, what if he tells of what he witnessed upstairs? You know the justice won't tolerate us stealing from tourists! This boy could see us all gaoled and ruined!"

"He would never!" Doll insisted. "You should've seen him out in the streets, Greta. He was like a little angel that had been knocked from its cloud. He was even wearing a wimple!"

"That makes it even worse! It could be he's working for the clergy or those puritan folk who would like to see us burned at the stake as devil women!" Greta looked to the Madame for support. "We've got to protect our business first, like the Queen has protected her crown all these years. By putting her enemies to torture!"

"Honestly, Grets," said Doll. "Are you having your monthly blood or are you just sore no man has taken you upstairs in weeks?"

Greta's eyes widened with fury. She dropped her poker in the fire and lunged at Doll, her fingernails reaching into those rare amber eyes. I leapt to my feet, intending to shield Doll just as she had protected me. But the Madame got there first. She sent Greta staggered back with a red handprint on her cheek while Doll let out a squeal as the Madame grabbed a fistful of her explosive black hair.

"I'll not stand for catfights! Doll, I'll be washing that sharp tongue of yours with soap before the night is out. Now get to the kitchen! It's long past your turn to wash the teacups. And you, my scrappy warden," she said to Greta. "There's no need to resort to brandings. I can guess where this little mock maid has come from. I'm surprised you silly girls haven't worked it out. You're the ones who were babbling about that play. The play I expressly forbade you from seeing!"

Doll looked to me, wide-eyed. "You're a player?!"

"To the pots, girl!" the Madame scolded.

144

Flinching at her mistress's tone, Doll slipped out of the room. The Madame turned to where I sat before the fireplace.

"I may regret asking this, little actor," she began with a sigh. "But tell me...what is the name of your theatre master?"

She said this like she was already bracing herself for the answer. Before I could speak there was a knock at the door.

"Was...was that our secret knock?" asked Greta, bewildered. "But all of us are here. Who else is it that knows...?"

The Madame held up a hand for silence, marching to open the door herself and not bothering to pick up the cudgel on her way. Greta and I followed and watched her slide back the bolts.

Makaydees stood drenched on her doorstep.

"Arthur," the Madame said tersely.

"Bess," he panted. "Gods Blood, Bess! Can it have been ten years? How time has failed to weather your beau..."

"Flattery will get you nowhere. Especially if it's composed of lies. I wasn't this tired old bawd in our youth, Art."

He spread his arms defensively.

"Can't a gentleman offer a –?"

"Show me gentleman at my door and we'll see," she countered. "But you don't need to waste your time with pleasantries. And I know why you've come. I have what you're missing."

Makaydees sagged at the waist, pressing a hand to his chest. There was a little cluster of shadows behind him who let out bursts of relieved laughter. My heart swelled up, fluttering against my ribs. My troupe had come seeking me. They'd *cared* to find me.

The Madame ushered the players into her shadowed entrance hall with a lazy wave of her hand. In the darkened passage, it appeared my fellows had yet to notice my presence. But once we had spilled into the fire-lit common room, it seemed more like they were too exhausted for a reunion. Lavern and Francis staggered in first, clutching instruments in their trembling arms and promptly collapsed in the nearest chairs. Lavern was coughing up a storm and sat doubled over, tears streaming his cheeks. Wally came through next, hauling our costume trunk and stooping his back, too tall for the low-ceilinged teashop. And after the Madame took in the gypsy's towering stature, she promptly banished him back to stand at the door, saying she could use a big lug like him guarding her house in case the highwayman did come knocking. Wally nodded his assent, leaving without argument.

Makaydees entered the common room last, the props sack slung over his back, his long hair in rattails and dripping from the rain. Seeing my master, I made a point of stepping into his path, wanting to be sure he had noted my presence. When my master's stare fell on me, he gave a curt nod, but his eyes didn't linger for long.

"Where's Rum?" Makaydees asked, glancing around. "Don't tell me he's upstairs carrying on with those girls?"

"Rum?" I blinked. "He's not with you?"

Makaydees stare snapped back to me. And yes, it seemed that Rum was in neither of our companies. My stomach sank a little then, as I realized it must have been Rum and not me that my fellows had been hoping to find in the Madame's guest house.

"I...I was trying to tell you, Mak..." Lavern rasped out, between coughs. "When I ran back into the tavern for the rest of our gear, I saw Rum through the smoke. I saw him climbing out of a window. And Candle escaping the tavern right alongside him..."

"But why would Rum leave us to follow after that raving ruffian?!" Makaydees ranted. "Talk your usual sense, Lavern!"

"You know what he's like, Mak! Likely he still wants revenge over Rosalie. But if Rum's out there in Candle's company then it's more than likely he'll be mistaken for one of his band!"

"That sounds right enough," Greta nodded, slipping into the seat at Lavern's side. "Kit and Ned said the watchmen rounded up most of those highway thugs over by the docks. They were on the lookout for players too. The word is that your troupe were the ones who brought the highwayman to town, stowing him in your cart."

Lavern shared a panicked look with Makaydees and then dissolved into another coughing fit, clearly having breathed in too much smoke. Greta ran her fingers through his wet hair.

"Don't you fret over it, handsome," she soothed, pressing herself closer to Lavern's arm. "How about some tea to settle your nerves? How about you let me draw you a nice salty bath?"

The Madame's mouth quirked into a smile.

"This business or pleasure, Greta?"

"Well...this one sure is the pick of this litter," said Greta, tickling Lavern's chin as he sat wheezing against her bosom.

Makaydees bristled. "Excuse me, can we put your sordid desires aside for a moment?! A valued member of my troupe may have been arrested as a highwayman." He turned back to the Madame. "Bess, I'll need you to go down to that gaol house and..."

"And what, Art? Am I the only friend you have left in this town? You've realized my brother is now a joyless old miser?"

I looked from Makaydees to the Madame, realizing she must be another former friend from my master's youth, the sister of the tavern landlord. Through the heat of their stares, I sensed their shared history in this town wasn't an altogether happy one. But it was an old tie still strong enough to keep her from shutting him out.

"I thought that Sam might be angry with me because I never made an honest woman of you," Makaydees said haughtily.

"Because I never saved you from becoming this...mistress of vice!"

She laughed again. "I'd have never taken you for a husband, even if you'd had nerve to ask for my hand. You think I care to be your constant spectator? No Art...there's no place for women on your stage. Not real women at least. Just these delicate boy players you dress up in your miserable notions of romance. We're both selling dreams of love to lonely men. But I'm the one who's prospered for it. I'm the one who's got a roof over my head. I keep my girls safe, I keep them clean and make sure they stay out of the cells. What have your precious little vanity shows done for you and your lads, Art?" She shook her head at him, then softened a little. "I remember when you first came to this town. A runaway rich boy with your head in the clouds. What's become of your fat purse and your grand plans since?"

Makaydees cringed and lowered his gaze.

"The years have worn them both thin."

She plumped her lips. "You can't survive on dreams. Tis a wonder that you've lived this long. Happy Birthday, Art."

His head jerked up. "You remembered?"

"Oh, I remember. You and your sentimental promises. There's still trees outside this town with your awful poems carved into their bark. Yes, I remember you. Sometimes I even remember you fondly..." She allowed herself a sigh before straightening her spine and hardening her jaw. "If this friend of yours is in the gaol house, I'll not let him swing. I'll go in the morning and offer bail or a bribe for his release. I have influence in this town. Enough influence to call Justice Long himself to heel if I whisper the right words in his ear. But if I do this, Art, then tonight, you and your theatre are at my disposal. After all, we trade in favours in this house. Nothing comes for free." She marched over to the costume trunk and nudged it with her foot. "Open it up. Let's see which of your garments might fit my girls."

Francis blanched at this threat to his beloved frocks. Makaydees reached out and took the Madame by the hand.

"What if there were *other* favours I could offer you this night?" he said, bowing low and pressing a kiss to her knuckles.

The Madame raised an eyebrow, seeming a little affronted but no less enticed. She glanced over to Greta and winked.

"Why Arthur...we really are in the same profession, aren't we?" The Madame kept hold of his hand, teasing him towards the stairs as Greta coiled her arm around Lavern, leading him in the same direction. The Madame turned back only once, waving her finger at Francis and me. "I'll be sending Ruthie down, so don't even think about pocketing any of our tea leaves! And you, lady boy. Go make yourself useful. Go and help Dolly in the kitchen with those dishes."

With this last lazy demand, the two women disappeared behind the curtain, taking my master and Lavern with them. I glanced at Francis where he sat with nervous hand pressed to the lid of the costume trunk. Then I stared into the hallway to where Wally slumped against the wall, making a limp effort of guarding the door. Neither of them would look back at me. They seemed to be weighed down by either exhaustion or the shame of what our troupe had been reduced to. With nobody else to turn to, I marched into the kitchen to find Doll crouching by the door. She'd clearly been listening in this whole time.

"Thunder and lightning, highwaymen and house fires!" Doll exclaimed. "And we're stuck here doing dishes." She turned to the stacked crockery. "So, what do you want to do first?"

I swallowed. "I want...I want to make myself useful."

"Oh really? Sounds like a serious business."

"I want to find him. I want to find Rum right now. That girl in the bath tub...she said that you had a backdoor?"

Doll nodded. "Over there by the mops."

I turned to the shadowy rear of the shambolic kitchen, narrowing my eyes on the exit. I had to move fast before Ruth came downstairs to watch us. So, I darted around Doll, pushing through the door and out onto the streets once more. The rain had thinned and a hush had fallen over Bristol, the sort of hush that suggested its dwellers were hidden and holding their breath. The air itself felt hostile. A few hurried paces and I was already stumbling over my skirts.

"Did nobody teach you how to run in a dress?" a voice called after me. I turned to see Doll rushing up behind, her own frock bunched in her fists. "Also, you might try *thinking* before you go rushing off. Do you even know the way to the gaol in this town?"

"Rum might not have been caught."

"No, but it's still the best place to start looking and you'd be better off trying to spring him with a Mermaid girl. If we can just catch up with Kit and Ned, I could persuade them into leaving a cell door open. Kit's mother's a close friend of the Madame's and Ned has been sweet on me for years. What was *your* plan exactly?"

I stood squirming, making it plain I had none.

"Just running blindly into the night for some boy?" Doll teased. "You *are* getting carried away with playing the girl."

"It was my fault!" I snapped back at her. "It was me who made the highwayman mad. It was me who started that fire."

Doll raised a finger and shushed me.

"Hey! Don't shout that so loudly. Let's keep our wits about us, little mirror boy. Stick by me and stay out of sight."

Doll took my hand, pulling me close to the walls and leading me into those dark narrow lanes she knew so well.

"It's past midnight," she whispered. "Anyone still out in this town will be someone with wickedness on their mind. But hey...if it wasn't for mischief, we'd have nothing but chores."

A nervous smile sprang onto my lips. I still wasn't so far from the farm on the hill where I'd so often sought out my own misadventures just to relieve the boredom of my days. At last I had found a partner in them. Doll was in high spirits and seemed to believe she could steal the whole night into her pocket. I followed her lead, until a few turns later, when she halted our steps, squeezing my hand.

"You hear that?" she said, leaning into the bricks.

I listened. And yes...I could hear voices.

It was two men's voices up ahead, hissing at each other like cats scrapping at the end of the alley. Voices I knew.

"Don't lie!" said the first one, slow and menacing. "You followed me here! You haven't been able to keep your stormy little eyes off me. Did you come looking for a fight? No, surely not. So, what is it that you want from me? Don't dare lie to me, lad. You may be the best actor in your troupe, but I can smell a lie like plague breath and I will cut the tongue from any mouth that speaks falsely to me."

It was Candle's voice. Still bullying for the truth.

I eased myself ahead of Doll, peering round our next bend, to take in the scene out in the main street. The moon hung like a glaring eyeball over the road, illuminating the shapes of two men. The taller of them had his sword drawn, the tip of its blade resting under the chin of the smaller one, forcing him up onto his toes.

"You think I'm the best of my troupe?"

This was Rum's voice unmistakably, but without the cocky bluster I'd come to expect from it. Now he seemed to be struggling to keep the tremors out of his speech and the tears from his eyes as he held Candle's stare. It was only a few nights since Rum's last taste of a sword. Hardly time for his cuts to heal, let alone his nerve.

Candle's blade tapped the underside of Rum's jaw, a gesture that might have been affectionate if he'd been doing it with a hand and not a deadly weapon. He wheezed out a laugh.

"Why what was your theatre master thinking?! Why did he let that lumbering gypsy, that pious narrator and that little skirted eunuch lead his play while you were standing in the wings?"

"He...he gave my role away," said Rum.

"Then let me offer you a new one," said Candle, looming closer. "I've lost my gang to the cells. They were too slow to slip the clutches of those watchmen. They lack my talent for vanishing into a crowd. But you, lad? I saw you running quick as a jack rabbit, darting down one alley and then doubling back, leading them all a merry dance. You're just the henchman I need. What you lack in size, you more than make up in your speed and wits. How would you like to be the first mate to a new pirate king? With those scars you're best suited to play the villain now. Come! The time is ripe to steal a sea vessel..."

"How? How can we get our own ship?"

I frowned at Rum's tone, which was suddenly so conspiratorial, like he truly wanted to be in cahoots with this highwayman. Like he was an aspiring pirate after all. I wanted to say Rum was acting, but I feared I might be wrong. Had I really pushed him out of the troupe? Had he followed Candle seeking a new master?

"We may have throats to slit before we sail," said Candle. "But as you've seen...they all fall with a single stroke."

Suddenly Doll had hold of my hand again and was tugging for us to leave. She took a pace back and almost tripped before I caught her by the arm. And it wasn't her skirts that she'd stumbled on. There was some thick blunt obstacle lying at our feet. I would have thought it was a log but we weren't out in the woods here. Slowly I sank down to the ground and then stretched out my trembling hand. And suddenly my breath would only come in short snapping rasps.

I was touching the still cheek of a new corpse.

"*Hush!*" Doll hissed, slapping her hand over my mouth. "It's just some drunkard who's collapsed on his way home."

I wanted to believe her. But I felt no breath against my knuckles. My hand crawled over the slack face. Reaching the neck, I found ripped flesh at its throat, blood still oozing and slicking my palms. I froze, my body numb and my mind floating from my skull.

It was Doll who recovered her voice first.

"Ned?" she whimpered. "Oh, my poor Ned!"

Ned Stirling. One of the two watchmen from the tearooms. Little more than an hour ago this man had been walking on his legs, talking through his lips, *alive*. Now his arms were lolling in the puddles, his chest no longer rising. And as my eyes adjusted to the gloom, I could see another body lying close by. The fresh cadaver of Kit Makepiece. Turning to Doll I could see she knew it too. Her brown eyes were like dams fit to burst, struggling to hold back a flood.

"They...they were my friends," she panted. Her face hardened. "That's the one thing you should never dare steal..."

Doll spat upon the blood-soaked street, then dragged herself to her feet. She charged at Candle from behind. The highwayman had no time to wheel around. He was so startled that he nearly lost his grip on his sword, as Doll leapt upon his back, locking one arm around his throat and then clawing at his eyes with the nails of her free hand. Candle arched his spine and tried throw her off. He looked like an animal caught in a trap, fighting savagely for its freedom.

"He's here!" Doll screamed. "The highwayman's *here!*"

Her cry was enough for me to summon my own courage. I rushed from the shadows of the alley, intent on helping her to anchor Candle until the nearest search party came to surround him. But before I could reach her, I found myself tackled by Rum. He broke away from the fray and then wrapped his arms around me, pushing me back towards the alley. When I would not come easy, he sank low and seized me about my knees, slinging me over his shoulder and then carrying me off like the kidnapped damsel I was still dressed up as.

"Rum!" I protested, breathlessly. "*Wait!*"

He didn't stop or even slow his pace. For his small stature, Rum had a wiry strength I could not overpower. My legs kicked uselessly as he bore me far from Doll's screaming. The salt sting of the ocean air must've crept into my eyes, because my face was streaming with tears again. Either that or the frock truly had unmanned me.

"*Please*...we can't leave her...she's just a..."

"Did you not hear the watchmen rushing towards her cries?" said Rum. "They will help her to take the highwayman down. And if she survives her scrap with him, then she'll be the one to collect that reward on his head. Good for her if she lives to take the prize. I was attempting the same gamble before he got the drop on me..."

Rum lowered me back onto my feet. My legs threatened to buckle beneath me but I was ready to go running back.

Rum caught me by the arms, shaking me hard.

"We can't go back. We're outlaws too, remember?"

"But she's my friend," I gasped. "And she's just a girl!"

"Right," Rum sneered. "She's just a girl."

Interval

Tis a wonder that I survived the night.

The first curtain I stood before went up in flames and my audience fled screaming. Not the sort of debut a new player hopes for. But that was the type of players we were – acting for our lives, speaking each line like it could be our last. As my master taught me long ago...you must look on every stage as your gallows.

That was the way of it. That was our road. I knew by then I would never go home again. All things considered, it seemed best not to. I'd seen how much my master regretted returning to the harbour town of his youth. You can't re-tread old ground without waking up its ghosts. Better to let them lie sleeping, undisturbed.

I was still trying to feel at home in my troupe. It was hard to know where I fit. The others had carved out such strong roles for themselves. Makaydees was our brains, Wally our backbone, Lavern our cautioner, Francis our carer and Rum stoked the fiery passion in us all. I wasn't certain what my own part in the company would be, only that I wished to play it well and for a long time to come.

I didn't know what it meant yet to be the girl of this gang. Those bawds from Bristol had shown me that girls can be more than what men see on their surface. They had woken something in me and not just the usual stirrings of a boy getting his first glimpse of female skin. I was seeing now all that I could become.

I was seeing the girl I might be.

Act Two
Scene One

Pilgrimage

I knew I had to be dreaming.

It could only be a dream because Rum was there but his scars were gone. His dark hair was long once more, tumbling in a wave over his bare shoulders. All his Gwendolyn grace had returned to him. But the curious thing was…I didn't dream of Rum being a girl. Instead he was strutting about the river bank wearing only his breeches. Very much a boy. A roaring boy in the heat of a blazing day.

No, it was me who wore the dress in this dream. The pale blue Mirabelle dress that floated up around me as I struggled in the water, the heaviness of my skirts threatening to drag me under. Rum paced on the shore, watching me flounder, a teasing smile on his lips. Out of nowhere he threw me a line, a rope that coiled around my chest like a snake strangling its prey. He gave it a tug.

"If I save you," he said, "you're *mine*."

I wriggled my legs like I wanted to escape, yet every kick brought me closer to the riverside, closer to Rum and his snatching hands. After fishing me out of the river, he peeled off my dripping frock and hung it on a low branch. His face became serious as he fell to drying me with a rough ragged blanket. I lay back on a grey stretch of stone, letting his fingers graze over my skin. He'd seen me unclothed before, of course. No room for modesty in a band of travelling men. But we'd never been as close as this, nor the two of us so alone.

And I wanted Rum to show me. I wanted him to show me how to be a boy, how to be a girl, and all those things boys and girls could do together. I wanted to be clumsy and slippery with him against the rocks. My skin had to know what it was shivering for.

But then I was waking up and quickly rolling on my side. I tucked my knees into my chest just in case this was to be another of my messy morning dreams. Not quite, but I'd been close. I squeezed my eyes shut, groaning into my armpit. When I dared to raise my head I found, to my abject horror, that Rum was hovering close by, already up and packing our gear. The real Rum. The boy with the scars and sneers. He turned his head towards me, took in my huddled position and then flashed me a knowing smile. A smile that said he knew what I had been dreaming about, even if the *who* might've shocked him.

After a week on the road, Rum's face was healing well. Francis had taken his stitches out and the swelling had gone down. With no sign of infection, it seemed unlikely his cuts would leave him disfigured as first feared. But I still couldn't stand to look at him. I'd been hating Rum this last week. Hating him since he had forced me to leave Doll struggling with the highwayman. I never did find out what'd befallen her. The Madame had left the tea house, hoping to recover her girl and collect the reward for Candle's capture. But Makaydees had insisted on our troupe escaping the town before dawn.

We'd been fleeing on sore feet ever since.

I turned away from Rum's scrutiny, wiping the dew from my face. My ears were drinking in the noises of a new day. Somewhere across the clearing where we'd made our camp, Makaydees and Lavern were in the midst of their customary morning row.

"What else could I do, Makaydees?!" Lavern protested. "When the fighting broke out and the curtain caught fire, you...you told me to get to the stables! When I found our cart gone, I knew someone must've taken advantage of the chaos and robbed us. I thought we were ruined! So, when I slipped back into the tavern and I found Barrentine had left his bar untended, I took my chance...and I..."

"...stole from our host!" Makaydees trumpeted, appalled. "*You*? Our pious Saint Lavern? After all your sermons that we must rise above the level of common rogues. Your insistence that we must be as honest as men can be in this vagabond life. You were the one who disgraced our troupe and swindled my oldest friend!"

We had been a day's walk out of Bristol when Lavern had finally admitted his desperate act of thievery to us. Till that point we believed we'd left the harbour with nothing but the rags that we stood up in and the luggage we dragged along. The rest of us had been laughing with relief to learn that we were not entirely penniless. But for Makaydees it'd been another blow to his pride. This was what Lavern had resorted to after our master's gambles had left us with only losses. The two of them had been squabbling over it ever since.

"That fat landlord had a tidy sum hidden away, Mak..." Lavern argued back. "I didn't take enough to leave him broke. Not even close! He had so much bullion beneath his boards I doubt if he'll even notice the bag that I have pilfered. Do you really think that he built up that fortune by honest means? I for one will not be troubling myself with remorse. He treated us like we were his jester slaves."

"And what if you'd been caught?" our master countered. "Do you realize that you risked every one of us to the noose?"

"It was *you* who wanted to take risks, Makaydees!" Lavern raged. "I plotted us a course on the safer roads. But you had to go back. You had to return to the place where you started your theatre and wallow in memories of what you *think* you once were!"

Makaydees stiffened, his eyes turning to stone. For a moment, I expected his hand to lash out and strike Lavern. I'd have been thrashed black and blue if I'd spoken to Ma that way. Instead both men took a breath, readying themselves for another clash of words.

Francis interrupted before either could speak.

"Aye me. I'd forgotten how these boys could holler when they get in a temper." He gave me a nudge in the arm. "Mark them, Timmy. This is a goodly lesson in hysterics if ever I saw one. How their voices carry on the wind. And with all this yelling, mayhap those watchmen will hear and know just where to come to surround us. We'll make their hunt for our theatre an easy tramp in the sunshine."

A hush fell over our camp, the old man putting us in our place and snapping us back to the present. We had survived this last week in the wilderness, but we had to remind ourselves that we were still wanted men. We were being chased because the highwayman had still not been caught. And all the latest handbills now told that the legendary outlaw was travelling in the company of strolling players. In every village we had passed through, there was a band of watchmen on our tail – a militia of Bristol lads who seemed to have decided that hunting vagabonds was a fine way to spend the rest of their summer.

The Watch hadn't caught up yet but they were never far behind. So, for days now we had been taking the most crooked and thicketed paths, marked only by the footprints of past journeys. Once again, we heaved up our luggage, bracing ourselves for another march, sweating through every hour that the sun would grant us.

"We're close," said Wally from the treeline. "Take heart, lads. We'll soon come to a place we can rest our blisters."

This place that Wally spoke of was a valley in the south where the Farr clan used to meet in the midsummer. It was a gathering spot for many gypsy tribes where they could swell their numbers before making their way to the Buckfast fayre, a little further downstream of the River Dart. This annual meeting was held on the first of August in celebration of Lammastide and the wheat harvest. Wally had been to this festival of fresh loaves and fun pastimes as a boy and he promised its grounds were the safest place for us to blend in with the crowds and do what buying and bartering we could with Lavern's purse.

Wally had really been our troupe's preserver in the last week. He had continued to steer our course, even without a cart to drive, like a bird that knows which way to fly to meet its flock. He was the one member of our company who could offer us a temporary sanctuary right now. Our plan was that we would pose as counterfeit gypsies until we were many miles from Bristol. Wally said that his people wouldn't mind us making a sham of their race. Travelling in crowds too big to cage was how the gypsies protected themselves.

"You realize what'll happen at this fayre?"

It was Rum who asked this. I'd drifted to the tail of our line and he had crept up by my side. I'd been doing my best to avoid him. Now I took a step away and inclined my stare to the ground, wanting to draw an invisible line there and warn him not to cross it.

"We're going to the fayre to get a new wagon, steed and supplies," I trotted out, just reciting what I had been told.

Rum sighed, already exasperated with me.

"And how do you suppose we'll pay for all we need? That purse Lavern snatched will only stretch so far. We can't put on another play with the watchmen searching every town for wandering actors. We'll have to bide our time and find other ways to keep ourselves in pocket. Mak will be looking to trade whatever he can..."

"But…but we've nothing *to* trade."

"They could sell you!" Rum glanced ahead to the other players and then lowered his voice to a whisper. "Think about it, Timmy.

167

Lavern hasn't given you any training since we left Bristol. Francis hasn't been adjusting the dresses to fit you. Nobody's said anything, but they don't seem too concerned over your future with us. And can you blame them? After all the trouble that you've caused?"

I wasn't aware the trouble in Bristol had been exclusively my fault, but Rum spoke as if this was indisputable.

"But I've only been on stage once!"

Rum shrugged. "And you choked. I know how it is, Timmy. Your first show is always your worst show. But a real player doesn't let his nerves get the better of him. Just because you're playing a woman it's no excuse for going weak in the head. You think that we've never faced mobs like that before? When a play falls to rags and ruin you have to do your best to salvage it. You have to improvise."

"I c-c-couldn't!" I stammered. "Lavern told me that I wasn't to s-s-speak any words. He says my voice is still no good."

"We're more than just mouthpieces for Mak's fancy speeches, you know. There are ways to speak with gestures and glances as much as with words. I've seen clowns have more wit than you."

I opened and shut my mouth a few times, realizing Rum was right. The others had held the show together until I broke it apart. Suddenly I felt very rustic and dull, a farm boy again.

168

"I'll be better next time," I vowed.

"And I'm telling you, there may not *be* a next time," said Rum. He tilted his head, seeming sympathetic for my plight. "I'm telling you so you're prepared. Lads our age often get passed from master to master, trade to trade. My Da sold me to a blacksmith in the famine years just to keep himself fed. I might have lived a long life as a stable boy. But my old master could never tame me, not with any amount of whippings. So, he took me to market one day and sold me on like I was a mad colt. Makaydees might do the same with you. Your limbs are all sound and you've no boils on your face. You'd fetch a price."

My breath grew short, my knees almost buckling. "But I *want* to be a player! I would be no use in any other trade."

"Give them a reason to keep you then." Rum left this challenge hanging in the air a moment, then he added. "You really think your old life was so hard? From what I hear your family had their own land and livestock and tis always a goodly harvest in these parts. You should try being born a Murphy from Munster. I was weaned on fear, famine and rebellion. Da said we only survived out of spite."

Speaking of his childhood brought out the brogue in Rum's accent. And I found I couldn't argue. While my family had often deprived me of suppers as a punishment, I was never in real danger of starving, even in the years of our leanest crops. These wars with the Irish and Spanish hadn't touched our quiet little parish either. While I'd always yearned for escape, I'd sacrificed all my security for it.

"Besides," Rum went on, his tone lightening. "You're not the only one tasked with learning a new role. You heard what our master said. He has plans to make a villain player out of me."

"Is that why you were chasing highwayman down dark alleys?" I asked him accusingly. And before Rum could raise any objection, I added – "Will you answer me one thing truly?"

He blinked at me, half offended, half amused.

"Who says that I've told you lies before?"

I kept my face stern, needing an honest answer. "Would you have gone with Candle? If Doll and I hadn't come, would you...?"

"Did you not see the sword he held to my throat?" Rum spluttered. "I went after the highwayman because I wanted to see him caught and hanged. I was playing a confidence trick to win his trust. That's just what acting is!" He fixed me with a haughty glare, his eyebrows giving a sudden hitch. "Now it's your turn to answer *me* one thing truly. Who is the girl, Timmy? Who is the girl in your dreams?"

I felt my cheeks burn. "I don't know what..."

"Is it that little blackamoor girl from the harbour?"

I flinched, remembering only now why I hated him. Yes, Doll had been in my dreams, but not the ones that Rum was crassly alluding to. Dreams of Doll woke me up sweating and trembling for very different reasons. And it was Rum's fault. He was the one we'd gone out looking for. It was him who'd made me leave her behind.

"What do you even care?!" I snapped. "She's just a girl, right? A girl who we left to be killed by that highwayman!"

"I never asked her to pick a fight with him," he said, shrugging off my fury. "And let me tell you something else, Timmy. *Every* time you leave someone, they may be dead the next day. We rarely live to old age on the road. So, we stick to saving only those in our own company. And that's just what I did when I carried you away." Rum fell silent for a moment, looking like he had said more than he'd intended. "You can only have so many people who matter. I'm sorry if she was someone that mattered to you. Was she the first girl you cared for?"

I swallowed. I'd promised to speak true, hadn't I?

"The first girl I cared for was Gwendolyn." I confessed.

I'm sure Rum already knew, but he still smirked to hear me say it.

"Before you knew that I was a boy?" he asked.

"Before I knew that you were awful."

Rum brayed a laugh, insufferably pleased with himself. He looked like he wanted to question me further but he did not get chance. Wally called out from the head of our parade. He was stood on the crest of a down, waving to something beyond its verge.

"They're *here*!" he exulted. "I've found them!"

As we hurried over to the hillside, I was suddenly aware of music. Sounds drifting up the slope, like a fluttering heartbeat that was rising up from the ground itself. As I got closer, this earthy music became a swell of rhythms with voices threading through its ripples, a cacophony of travellers and their tales. Our feet began stumbling down the cant and below us we could see long lines of painted wagons and willow tents stretching through the wide green valley. Boundless crowds of nomads filled up every space in between.

As we came staggering into this camp, a laughing stampede of people rushed towards us. The Farr tribe looked like they were wearing everything they owned – scarves bunched at their waists, furs draping their shoulders and threaded beads dripping from their necks. There were travellers of every age and bearing, their faces a mingling of warm brown shades and their voices a jangling chorus. They flocked around Wally, squeezing his broad arms and standing on tiptoes to stroke the crown of his bald head. Their faces were bright with recognition, but their fingers were busy reading the marks of change on his body. Some remarked on how tall he'd grown or asked how he had lost his hair so young. The scene played out like a family reunion, but surely nobody could have a family so large and sundry.

When Wally began speaking to his clan in a language that I didn't understand my attention drifted to the smells rising from their fires. My fellows pointed their noses the same way.

"Put in a word for us, dear heart..." Makaydees rasped, as he took one of the many handkerchiefs from his jerkin and mopped his brow. "Ask your tribe if they'll spare us a little bread and water. If it turns out they cannot heal our starvation, then *please*...find us a suitable patch of earth where we may make our deathbeds."

At the mention of food, I put all other worries out of my mind. Since I could not speak the gypsy's tongue, I began rubbing my belly in an earnest signal telling them why we had come and what we hoped to receive. Like Rum had said, looks and gestures were a way to speak without words. Wally made what sounded like a flustered apology, but one of the older gypsy women threw back her long mane of hair and bellowed a laugh. She wagged a finger at me but then ushered us to the nearest campfire where the carcass of a deer was being turned on a spit and the only music was the crackle of roasting flesh.

I took my place in the circle, feeling like a dog snuffling beneath a table, begging for scraps of broken meat. To my relief, I was soon handed a bone coated with tough dark flesh. I began to devour it, letting its hot juices trickle over my chin. Lavern passed me a flagon of water, reminding me to drink between mouthfuls, lest I choke myself in this ravenous fit of appetite. I could've eaten this poor creature alive. In the past week we'd survived only on nettle broth, wild berries and the conies Wally caught by reaching his long arms into their burrows and dragging them out by their ears. It had been a lean diet, a nibble of meat each day, most of which had stuck in our teeth.

When we had finished feasting, we were content to slump around the campfire, our bellies stuffed and our feet gently throbbing. The gypsies let us laze. Unlike everyone else we had met so far on this road they didn't demand anything from us in payment. Wally's homecoming was cause enough for the Farr tribe to welcome and feed us as though we were family too. Looking across our circle, I could see Makaydees sucking on his wineskin, his lips a bitter line. This was just the sort of reception he'd promised us at Barrentine's tavern.

The others were in far better spirits. Francis cooed over the gypsy cloths being bundled up for the fayre, reaching out to stroke a hand over the intricate embroidery. Lavern sat with a fortune teller who'd caught him by the wrist and was now reading his destiny in the creases of his hands. If the course of *my* life was written on my palm like a fleshy storybook, then the last thing I would want was someone reading it and ruining its ending. But Lavern was more at ease than I'd ever seen him. Rum meanwhile had taken his tabor from his pack, wandered over to a circle of dancers and was drumming in time.

I had never seen people dancing before, moving and twisting in these wild flurries. As Rum and the fiddlers slowly increased the speed and their accompaniment, so the dancers became fast and frenetic in their movements. Women stretched their arms out wide, shaking their shoulders, bellies and the bells on their skirts. Men stamped their feet and slapped their knees, making drums of their own brawny bodies. I wanted to join them, but it felt more valuable to watch and learn. This performance was stirring as any play I could imagine even though these gypsies weren't dancing for a scattering of coin. This dance was their whim. It belonged to them and the free air.

I glanced about for Wally, wishing to thank him for bringing us to these people and this place. But he was nowhere in sight. I supposed he was busy reuniting with the many long-lost members of the Farr clan. Eventually I grew restless and rose to take a stroll through the vale, hoping to find Wally somewhere in the throngs.

His huge height and dusky complexion usually made him easy to spot, but here the crowds were heaving with tawny-skinned wanderers.

In the end I stumbled on Wally by chance. I'd been heading into the woods fringing the valley to piss behind a tree. And there was Wally sat upon a fallen trunk with a jug of mead in one hand and a cluster of flowers in his lap. I scurried over to his side.

It was only then that I saw he was crying.

"What...why aren't you with your clan?

He stared blankly ahead, tears slipping down his cheeks, wetting his heavy lips. It took him a long moment to answer.

"Gone..." he said at last, his words barely a whisper.

"Gone? You mean they...they left the tribe?"

"No. Gone from the world. It...it happened last summer they tell me. My pa and two brothers. All three taken at once."

My blood turned chill. "Taken? By what?"

"What else? The hangman's knot."

"But...but *why*? What had they...?"

"They strayed too far from the flock. Got caught and lynched by a band of soldiers bound for the Spanish war. They didn't need to have *done* anything. Our kind may be hanged just for wandering this land. Just for who we are and how we live. There's laws against us living on the road. They can't stand us roaming free."

Wally trailed off and I was left struggling in his silence. I hadn't any words of comfort that I could offer. Maybe nobody had words for this. But I trusted that the other players would know better what to say to him than me. I was about to hurry off and fetch them when Wally suddenly caught my sleeve, tugging me back.

"*Don't*. I don't want them to know." His eyes still swam with tears, but his stare had hardened. "They need hope now. Hope we can rebuild and carry on. And I can give them that...my tribe want me to have my pa's old wagon. None of them have liked stepping aboard it since my ma died there of chills and grief last winter. But they believe her spirit will rest easier with me coming home to it."

Wally scrunched the flowers in his fists. His face crumpled and a sob escaped his throat. I tried to put my arms around him but they were too short and scrawny for a proper embrace.

"I should've been there, Timmy. I could have stopped it. I never liked fighting, but I'm built for it. And I know now I can't bear to lose any more of my people. So, we'll use this new wagon to keep our troupe together. To keep our theatre alive. Like Mak says, nothing ever dies on our stage that doesn't get up again to bow."

Scene Two

Behind the Curtain

The gypsy wagon was painted in bright gay colours only just beginning to crack and fade. A little ladder curled from its rear like a tail and led us into a spacious interior that would easily sleep six bodies and leave room to heap our luggage. After a week of tramping on foot, this wagon was a piece of mercy. A trundling home on wheels.

"The best inheritance a traveller could wish for!" Lavern marvelled as he caressed its wheels. "And to think it came without a price."

My eyes darted to Wally in concern. I was the only one who knew how much this carriage had cost him. But he said nothing, standing at a distance, allowing the others bask in his supposed good fortune. The story they'd been told was Wally's eldest brother had won the spring wrestling tournament and therefore been crowned the new Gypsy King. And with this new monarch status, the Farr clan had been able to take their pick of wagons to tour the lands and had left their former transport to be gifted to their prodigal son should he return to the tribe. Given the welcome we had enjoyed in the gypsy camp, the other players happily believed this folktale version of Wally's heirloom.

But the wagon alone wasn't enough to save us from our penury. We still needed a steed to draw it. That morning we'd all had to strain our limbs dragging our new home to the outskirts of the Buckfast fayre where we had secluded it within a brace of trees.

"Well Gentleman!" Makaydees began, seating himself on its rear steps. "You'll be pleased to hear I'm willing to accept the dull duty of watching over our wagon whilst you lads roam the stalls and enjoy a spot of trading. Never fear! I'll have my muses for company. So long as I can rest my bones, I'm prepared to act as our sentry."

Lavern narrowed his eyes on our lazing master, who was presently making himself a pillow with our bundled back curtain.

"This isn't a holiday, Mak," Lavern reminded him. "We need to barter for a new horse before the best ones are sold up. Surely that has to be our first concern now that we're here?"

Makaydees blinked, feigning confusion. "I'm afraid it can be no concern of mine, Lavern." He turned his pockets inside out, displaying their emptiness. "As you can see, I'm an honest pauper without a bean to my name. If you wish to spend any money that you have nefariously acquired then that is business of your own."

"So, you'll have nought to do with it? But I take it that you'll still ride with us once we take to the road again?"

"Lavern, the sooner you have dispersed those slippery coins, the sooner you and I may be friends again. Take the martyred expression off your face, man. I'm sure that you can handle those greasy jugglers by yourself. I dare say you'll do a better job at haggling than I. You've handsome looks to hide your craftier nature."

"My tongue is not so slick as yours. It's your Humbug Mullarkey guise that serves us best when cutting a deal!"

Our master raised his head at the flattery. Then he reached into his breast pocket, producing a handful of parchments.

"Lest you forget...we've only five false passports to share between us." He handed them over to Lavern. "Here. It's your turn to do the humbugging for today, Lavern. Your turn to act as leader to our merry band. Let me know how easy *you* find it."

With that, Makaydees shut his eyes and stretched himself out for a doze. It was a dismissal, but also an assent. For it seemed that he would accept the new horse once it was bought. Lavern seemed to realise this too and so swallowed down his consternation.

"Very well. We shall return by nightfall."

Lavern bestowed one of the forged papers to each of us, then led the way towards the wide open green where the stalls, stages and tents had been raised. On our way we passed a crowd of puritan preachers, who bewailed that we were heading to the Devil's own market and that the fayre was *the shop of Satan*. There were soldiers too who barked demands for all sturdy young men to cease in their revelling and join the fight for our Queen and country over the narrow sea. They hollered that the Spanish would be invading any day now – that they might be here before dusk. We kept our heads low and followed the rear ranks of traders making their way to the checkpoints.

"Remember yourselves, lads," Lavern whispered to us. "We need to blend in here. Do not so much as breathe the word *players*. If any opportune beggar were to learn our true profession, they might sell us to the law. And keep your ears pricked for any news of Candle. He has need to visit this fayre as much as we. Without a horse he's but a lowly footpad. He'll want a steed to hasten his escape."

"Come now, Lavern!" said Francis. "Do you really think it's likely that we'll cross paths with that villain again?"

"Think about it! Rum said he's seeking to board a ship to the New World. If he's been run out of Bristol, then Plymouth is sure to be his next port. This fayre would be his best stop on the way."

I nodded my head vigorously by way of contribution. While the rest of the players seemed to see Lavern a ceaseless worrywart,

I too couldn't shake the feeling that the highwayman might still be on our tail. And besides, if Lavern was our leader for the day then I wanted to impress him. Since my talk with Rum, I'd been trying my best to prove how useful I could be to the troupe. My old family back at the farm would've been staggered. Never in my life had I begun a day *wanting* to work. But as we stepped into the fayre ground, I scurried forth and planted myself before Lavern, bristling in readiness.

"What can I do?" I asked, bouncing on my heels.

Lavern only frowned at me, shaking his head.

"Not now," he muttered, like I'd given him an instant headache. "Rum...I've a task that needs your judgement."

He opened his coin purse and then poured more than half its weight into Rum's cupped palms. Rum's eyes widened.

"I didn't think you'd trust me with a share of the loot," he chirped, quickly stashing the coins deep in his pockets.

Lavern didn't return his smile. "Someone needs to find us a new horse. Since you know the beasts best, I'm putting my faith in you." He narrowed his stare and raised a finger to Rum's nose. "But if you take that money to a gambler's circle, then don't even dare come back to us. No matter how lucky you are in your wagers."

Rum's cheeks flamed like he'd been slapped.

"You've not given me much to shop with."

Lavern held his stare. "But you will make do with shopping. That means no dice, no cards, no cockfights…and no *stealing*."

"You're one to talk about stealing, Saint Lavern!"

Rum turned his back on us and then made towards the long lines of horses being arrayed on the eastern edges of the field. We watched him leave, then pressed on to the rows of merchant tables. The crowds here were thick with peddlers, each with their own fawning spiels for hawking their wares and earning their Lammas bread. They shook new bridles in our faces as we passed. They opened up coats dripping with trinkets. Lavern palmed a few coins to Francis so he might buy some cloth to fashion into new costumes. He asked Wally to seek out any tournaments that he might compete in – wrestling matches, tug-o-wars, anything where his strength might win prizes. Wally, mired in his secret mourning, nodded and slipped away without a word.

"What can I do, Lavern?" I pleaded once more.

"Hush!" he scolded, taking out his lute. "Just try not to trouble me a while. I might earn a few more coins with my music."

I felt sicker every moment, realising Rum had been right. I truly didn't have any role to play. If my fellows found themselves short of coins at the end of this day, I might well be the easiest thing left to sell. After fidgeting at Lavern's side for an hour, he bid me take a walk and stop buzzing around him like a nervous fly. So, I took a tour around the sights and stalls. I breathed in the scent of loaves and gingerbread dolls still warm from the stove. I looked on in envy as other people crammed their cheeks and sprayed crumbs from their lips.

I'd attended market days and summer festivals back in my home parish but I'd never wandered a fayre as rich in entertainments as this one. There were tumblers who could stand on their heads and walk on their hands. There were tiny wars being fought on puppet show stages. There was a dancing bear that almost brought me to tears, for the poor creature was blind and in chains. It only reared up and threw its paws because it couldn't anticipate when its master was sneaking up to jab its side with a sharpened stick. But the crowd just laughed and jeered at the bear in its toils. So, I was forced to flee before any could see my womanly display of weeping and call me a fool.

As the first shadows of evening set in, I made my way to the front of a crowd that was bobbing for apples. This was a game where I could hope to thrive. I took my place in the line and when it was my turn to kneel before the barrel, I sank my teeth into four of the fruits, fishing them from the water before I remembered to breathe. I was treated to a brief and begrudging round of the applause, before I was sent off with my face dripping and apples cradled in my arms.

As I ran stumbling back to our meeting spot, I'd already decided that I wouldn't keep even one of these apples to myself but gift them to my four companions. I'd even let Rum have one. It would be worth a little hunger on my part just to show I'd earned something. But when I returned, I found my fellows in the midst of a row. They were hissing at each other in strained voices, Lavern and Rum had their eyes locked together, their noses almost bumping. Francis was squirming at their side while Wally stood quiet and still as a boulder.

"I got apples," I said with a nervous cheer. I still had water in my ears and my jaw ached from all the dunking, so I was struggling to read the tension of this scene. "Did you get a horse?"

"We're short on coins," said Rum. "Far short."

"We'll find another seller," Lavern insisted.

"And I'm telling you I've already found the best this gaudy fayre has to offer!" Rum snapped back. "Do you know how many of these horses here are sick, lame or in old age? Their owners feed them mint to freshen their foul breath. They shove sneezing powder up their noses to clear out the snot. I know these tricks well! My old master used them all the time to sell horses on their dying legs. We need to get the *best*, Lavern. Otherwise we might as well toss those coins down the nearest well." His eyes flashed with conviction. "You said no gambling, but nothing about driving a bargain. I've found us a colt that will see us through *decades* on the roads…for the added price, that is."

"Makaydees wouldn't agree to it," Lavern protested.

Rum shrugged, undaunted. "Mak's not here."

Before the others could stop him, Rum seized my arm and dragged me over to the shade at the rear of the apothecary tents.

"Are you...?" I shuddered. "Are you selling me?"

The apples slipped out of my palms. I felt like I might faint or scream or punch Rum in the face before he answered.

"No, we're not selling you. At least, not the way you're fearing..." Rum avoided my stare, squatting to collect up the fallen fruit. "The horse courser that I bartered with is willing to trade with us at half the asking price. If – in exchange – we give him a show."

"Lavern said to tell no one we were actors!"

Rum waved a hand. "The play that this fellow is asking for would be a…a private performance. The sort of play that we could only do *off* stage. In the shadows. If you catch my meaning." He narrowed his eyes on me. "You *do* take my meaning, right Timmy?"

My throat constricted. Yes, I knew what he meant. Somewhere at the back of my mind I'd always known this would be part of my new profession. The signs had been there all along – Rum flashing his legs to the crowd in my hometown. The Bristol tavern where men watching had wanted to see my skirts raised high. The mermaid tearooms where Makaydees and Lavern had slipped upstairs with the Madame and her girls, every bit the whores that they were. I knew.

But I'd not let the thought surface till now.

"Lavern doesn't think you're ready," said Rum. "I tried telling him you've been rehearsing every night in your sleep."

If I had any innocence left Rum snuffed it out with that jibe. He slipped his pack from his shoulders, loosened its straps and produced a dark red bundle. He held it up by its neckline and let its skirts unfurl. I realized I was staring at Gwendolyn. It was like I was seeing a ghost. I reached for her now and embraced her to my chest.

"What must I do?" I asked without stuttering.

Rum spoke briskly, keeping a lookout as I slipped the frock over my head and began peeling my boy's clothes off underneath. He told me not to fear. It would just be a show. No 'audience participation' of any sort. He said it was something the horse courser had requested for his brother who, last winter, had caught a hoof in the spine during a gelding gone wrong. The injury had left the man dead from the waist down, no longer able to walk, restricted to a hard wooden chair. The poor cripple just wanted to feel something again, Rum said. Something stirring. Something romantic. Nothing too vulgar.

"Think of it as a dance," he added. "A dance I'll be leading."

"You?" I spluttered. "You'll be...*acting* with me?"

"It has to be me. Lavern will have nought to do with it. But he'll let us play this interlude so long as you're willing. And Wally will be there the whole time, ensuring our spectators behave. I know what I'm doing, Timmy. I've done it before...many nights after curtains. When times are hard, we take whatever crowds we can."

I forced my head to nod, not speaking lest my voice came out as a quiver. Rum reached into his pack again, taking out the wig and setting it on my head. I realized then that he must have planned for this. That he had brought the frock having already thought up this bargain. Still, his hands were gentle as he tucked my fair curls under the skullcap, his fingers combing his old dark tresses forwards to frame my face. Rum had never been so patient with me. Once he was done fussing over my appearance, he wrapped me in a cloak and led me back to the others. Lavern and Wally stood ready, seeming resigned.

"We sent Francis back to the wagon," said Lavern. "He'll let Mak know that we'll be back soon...with the new horse."

We said no more, but let Rum lead the way. The light was fading from the grounds fast, the first stars glittering in a pale purple sky. As we made our way through the lines of stalls being packed up for the day, our path was briefly blocked by a candlelit procession. The late night revellers were marching toward the midnight hour, waiting till the last bells chimed and rang in the dawn of Lammas Day. I stared at their faces in the flickering glow. I thought of Candle still on the run, somewhere in the wilderness. I tried to remember his face that slipped so easily into a crowd. He could be any man in the shadows. You would not know him until his blade was at your throat.

We reached the horse courser's tent and Rum was the first through its flaps. Lavern, Wally and I stood shuffling our feet at the threshold, failing to meet each other's eyes. After some frantic whispering from within, Rum re-emerged and waved first Wally and then Lavern inside. Finally, he came to me and gripped my shoulder.

"Just remember," he said. "Nothing that happens in this tent is real. You don't have to like it. You don't even have to like me. Just play the part. Follow my moves. Pretend you're taking some pleasure in it." He grimaced. "If it makes it easier, close your eyes and think of your dream girl from Bristol. Imagine she's the one you're kissing."

Thoughts flooded my mind. The first thought being that Rum still had no notion *he* had been my dream girl. My dream boy. My constant dream intruder. My head reminded my body very sternly that whatever was about to happen, it wouldn't be real. But a fluttery little voice in my belly still whispered '*Kissing? Did he say kissing?'*

Lavern's lute began playing inside the tent.

"That's our cue, Gwendolyn," Rum said.

He took my hand and we slipped through the tattered folds. An expectant rug had been spread at its centre, a pair of dull lanterns placed on either side. Wally stood to our right, his arms tensed at his sides, while Lavern sat to the left, strumming his instrument. It was too dark to see our audience, but I sensed from the huddled shadows and heavy breathing there was more than one man with his eyes on us. I did not want to see them. I'd rather pretend they weren't there. Instead, I turned to Rum, wondering if he was going to speak any words. His tight smile told me that this was to be a silent performance, a dumb show. It wasn't our speeches these men were gathered here for.

Rum stepped behind me and in a swift movement he loosed my cloak, letting it fall around my feet. We had left our boots outside and the brush of cloth around my toes sent a shiver all the way up to my knees. I closed my eyes, then I felt Rum's hand slip around my waist. He pressed a palm to my stomach, a dancer taking his hold. I felt his breath against my neck, his nose nuzzling into the strands of my wig. Then with his other arm he reached low and snatched up a handful of my skirt, slowly raising it up to my thigh.

He halted there, not exposing any more skin, but leaving our crowd to imagine what lay further up my legs. We wouldn't spoil the illusion by showing the boyish parts of me. Rum's hand left my stomach and stroked up my chest, bunching the material of my bodice to form the bosom that wasn't there. I leaned into him, letting my head loll back to rest against his nape. I felt Rum's rough nails yanking my dress back from my shoulder, then his lips pressing a kiss to my upper arm. And it felt so real. Realer than I'd ever felt before.

I knew what we were pretending in this tent. I'd learned from my brother Flan and his crass descriptions of what he'd be doing with his milkmaid bride once it came time to wed her. I knew these things were not meant to be done between two boys. Not unless you wanted to hang for sodomy and be sent straight to hell. My ma always said my soul was to be damned. Maybe this was what she'd meant? Maybe she had foreseen the sinful acts I would be drawn into? Wasn't this why women were not allowed on the stage?

Because it turned them into temptresses, casting spells of lust over any man watching?

A trembling breath escaped me and I was suddenly aware of a stirring beneath my skirts that threatened to foil our artifice. Rum seemed to realize it too. He spun me around to face him, his palms clasping to my lower back. I opened my eyes in time to see him mouth the words *'not real'*. Then he pressed his lips to mine.

It was a good thing Rum had hold of my waist, else my knees might have buckled beneath me. It was a good thing too that the music of Lavern's lute still played over the leering noises of our audience. I didn't want to hear them. I didn't want to be having my first kiss for their lascivious entertainment. But this was my trade now. My body and soul laid bare on a stage. It wasn't even me. This was *Gwendolyn*. I was the dream girl now. The crowd could steal me into their fantasies and take me to their beds whenever they pleased.

Rum's hands ghosted up my arms before settling on my cheeks. He held my face so only he could see it. I felt the heat of his palms and the throb of his heartbeat through his shirt. And if this wasn't real then Rum truly was the best actor in our troupe. I nodded against his fingers, signalling that I was ready to bring this show to its resolve. His hands fell to my shoulders and we sank slowly onto the rug.

Somewhere in the night, the bells began to ring.

194

Somewhere in the night, the bells began to ring.

Scene Three

The Dumb Show

Scene Three

The Dumb Show

I woke the next morning in the wagon alone. After my scene with Rum in the horse courser's tent, it'd taken hours for my heartbeat to slow, for my blood to stop jumping and for my mind to cease replaying our tender moments together. All that hadn't been *'real'* between us kept me restless. So, I'd been the last of our company to give in to slumber and I seemed to have slept in long past dawn. It looked as though my fellows had all risen early and left me to laze.

Dimly I recalled Makaydees saying that he would be using what remained of our coins to stock up on victuals before we left town. Then we would be making our flight at nightfall and the festival's end. I was back in my breeches now. I stretched and then crawled to the rear door of our wagon and stared out towards the fringes of the farming village. If I just shut my eyes and listened to the early morning market sounds and breathed in the drifting stench of dung, I could almost believe I had come home to another country parish many miles from here. Memories of my childhood hummed in the air around me.

I realized that this was the first time I'd been alone since leaving the farm. This was a chance to indulge in my oldest games, to play pretend while nobody was watching. I ducked back inside the wagon and sank to my knees beside the costume trunk. I raised up its lid and lifted Mirabelle out in my arms. I needed a costume to escape myself. This was no different from stealing rags from the scarecrow. I draped the frock over my elbow and stepped onto the grass. I didn't waste any time. I was wary of being caught. I pulled the dress over my head and tugged it down over my vest and hose.

I let my eyes fall closed and spread my arms wide. I felt the breeze stirring my hair. I began to sway with that breeze, just moving my hips at first, then rolling my shoulders before I started turning in circles. There had been many mornings on the farm when I'd spun myself silly, loving how my head became dizzy and how the world kept on spinning even after I'd collapsed in the grass. Other times when I was alone, I would invent my own dances, making up my own movements and weaving them into a structure of steps, gestures and expressions that I learnt by heart. These silly little jigs were the closest thing I had to my own roles. I remembered their shapes even now.

Before I knew it, I was dancing in the grass with my skirt curling and then unfurling around my knees, the dew soaking my bare feet. The dress had a way of making my movements smooth, graceful and more instinctive than they'd ever been before. I tried to forget the dirty boy's clothes and the scrawny boy's body underneath and I let the dress take over. I started to hum deep in my throat, a wordless music just for me and this moment. I imagined my voice a little higher. I pictured my hair being longer and cleaner, flowing down my back in a wave. I could see my role now. I could see the girl I was meant to play. The girl who was freer and lovelier than my boy-self could ever be.

"What's all this, lad?" asked a voice behind me.

I spun on my heels, my eyes flying open. Francis sat in the shade of the wagon, a bundle of yellow cloth in his lap and a thread spooling from his fingers. My stomach sank as I realized that the old tailor must have been watching me the entire time. Makaydees must have left him behind to guard both me and the new wagon.

I fiddled with my bodice, hardly knowing what to say.

"It's nothing," I muttered. "Just something I do."

"Ah, I see..." Francis nodded his head several times like a hen that was happily clucking to itself. "You do it very nicely."

He returned to his stitching, not seeming to realize how much his intrusion had upset me. I stood mortified a moment longer before he raised his head again, noticing I'd ceased my flourishes.

"Well, carry on," he prompted. "Don't mind me."

"I can't! Not with you watching...laughing at me."

"Come now!" he said, still chuckling. "Folk don't just laugh when they're mocking you. Sometimes they laugh when they're delighting in you." His smile faded as he added —"To be honest, after last night...I'm pleased to see you still have some innocence left. Tis a sorry business when we resort to those manner of performances."

I crossed my arms tight over my chest. I still didn't know what to feel about last night, but I wasn't going to dwell on it.

"It wasn't real, Mr Frank," I said, forcing a shrug.

Sometime during the last week I'd taken to calling our costumer 'Mr Frank'. He'd taken pity on me after hearing how the S sounds in Francis brought on my lisp. So, he had suggested I shorten his name to whatever equivalent I found easier to pronounce. I'd got in the habit of adding the 'Mr' out of respect for his senior years.

"It's realer than you think," Francis warned.

"What are you working on there?" I asked him, shaking off his concern and swiftly changing the subject.

"This?" Francis held the yellow garment like a swaddling child. "I call this one Sonya, my Gypsy Queen. She's the first full dress that I ever made, long before I joined Mak's theatre. I dare say she's older than you are now. I must have darned the holes out of her a hundred times or more. Every few years I'll dye her in dandelion juices again just to keep her colour from fading. Of course, it helps her preservation that she doesn't get worn much. Mak doesn't care for her. He won't say so, but I see it in his sour looks. I suppose yellow is a little too sunny for most of his heroines. He's such a misery."

I drew closer to where Francis sat sewing. He'd bought some new thread in a rare shade of lavender yesterday. Now he was using it to embroider a row of purple flowers on the skirt.

"I like her," I told him, unable to hold back.

"Would you like to try her on?" He smiled knowingly. "Yes, I can see you want to. You'd make a perfect Sonya."

I was already hoisting Mirabelle's skirt up to my knees. But I let it fall suddenly, embarrassed at my own eagerness.

"It's not that I *want* to play the ladies," I argued. "This wasn't ever my choice. But if these are the only costumes I'm given, I have to make the best of them. Any costume would have done."

I pushed out my chin, my cheeks burning.

"You've no need to make excuses to the likes of me, Timony," said Francis. "I'm the queer fellow who spends my days sewing these dainty little frocks. I'm not ashamed of my craft and I won't deny that the dresses are my favourite garment to make. They always have been and I've been tailoring longer than you have been drawing breath. I know there are plenty who might say a man in my trade shouldn't have such a fondness for ribbons and frills. In my pa's old shop, I was trained in making plain simple work clothes for farm fellows tending the lands. I put together my earliest dresses with scraps of stolen cloth left after trimmings. Aye me…it was a hard task to teach myself. Like stitching the petals onto a flower. And I had to keep my ragged beauties hidden under my bed in those days. It's only since I joined Mak's theatre that I've finally been able to show my ladies off."

The quiet sorrow in his voice softened my defences. I sat beside Francis on the log, pulling my knees into my chest.

"I used to do that a lot too," I confessed.

He frowned. "Do what, Timmy?"

I swallowed. "I used to hide things."

"Hide yourself, you mean."

I didn't deny it. I felt like the old tailor could see into my heart with a keener understanding than Makaydees ever had.

"There's worse things than having people laugh at you, Mr Frank. It's when they frown that I really want to hide. When they frown and say you're a loon or maybe just weak in the head. This town…it's like the place where I was raised. It smells the same. My pa stopping taking me to markets at the end of the month. He said he wouldn't risk me making a scene. They don't like *scenes* in towns like this."

Francis tipped his head thoughtfully to the side.

"I don't know about that. We've played country parishes like this one a dozen times or more. I find that most farmers enjoy a little colour and drama passing through their lands. It's something to fill their empty imaginings while they till the earth. Maybe your Pa only thought you strange because you used to sneak around, changing your clothes in shadows, keeping all your dreams inside you?"

I shook my head. "You didn't know my family. Not one of those dull fools ever understood me. If Pa had ever caught me dressed like this, he'd have sent me to Ma for a whipping. They'd beat it out me, beat me bluer than this frock and say that it was for my own good. Say they were saving me from hellfire in the hereafter."

I took a breath, calming my temper before it gave way to tears. Francis stared at me a moment, then leaned close.

"Well, if that isn't the longest and boldest that I've ever heard you speak." He clapped my shoulder, commending me. "So, I suppose you must be speaking to true. I suppose my own Ma and Pa might have dealt with me much the same way if they'd have known of my secret costumes. But I like to believe the best in people, Timmy. It sounds to me like you were judging your family's peasant ways even as they were frowning at you for your oddities. You've got to lose some of your own hardness to give others the chance to know you."

I turned my head and stared into his twinkly blue eyes. For a boy who'd spent so much of his childhood craving attention and making a spectacle of himself, it was still unnerving to have a person finally see me. To see what I'd been trying so long to show.

"You know, Timmy..." said Francis, his voice falling to a whisper, even though there was nobody in earshot. "There were times I used to try on my own dresses. I'd wear them after the shop was closed up and I was alone in my room, just before bedding down. I wore them until I was forced into taking a wife. After I was orphaned and then widowed, I took on Lavern as my apprentice and he became my model. He had to be. My hair was turning grey by then and my face carried more lines than I could ever hope to stitch. So, I suppose I missed my chance at being the maiden." He let out a sigh, his eyes falling back to the yellow dress in his hands.

"If there's something you love doing, lad...or if there is someone who you're yearning to be...then don't hide it away where nobody can see." He stared towards the fayre away yonder. "Have your day in the sun whilst you're young."

I nodded, a lump of resolve rising in my throat.

"Mr Frank...?" I began, still not stuttering.

"Yes, my lad?" he said.

"I think I'd like to try Sonya after all."

The old man smiled. He finished off his flower pattern, bit off the thread and gently passed the yellow frock into my arms.

"Take care of her," he said. "Like I said, she's the most delicate of my wardrobe." He rose to his feet, making for the steps of the wagon. "Now, as you know, I never like to see my dresses worn unless for a performance. So, I'll take myself off for a nap. Just let me know when you're done with...whatever it was you were doing."

I nodded as Francis disappeared into the wagon's interior. Then after checking to be sure I was truly alone this time I removed both Mirabelle and my boy's clothes beneath and pulled Sonya on in her place, letting her yellow cloth spread over me like butter. I stroked my fingers over the wispy embroidery decorating the skirt and bodice. Elsewhere on the dress were ribbons, buttons and patches in a mingling of rainbow shades. This gypsy frock was by far the most colourful and layered of all our costumes. I could see why Francis cherished it and Makaydees loathed it. This girl had no tragedy about her.

I raised my head and looked towards the town of Buckfast and its Lammas festivities. I felt its sounds, smells and market stalls calling to me. Wearing this dress, I wasn't myself anymore. Without thinking, my feet moved at a pace, making for the fayre. Sonya was a girl who was looking for fun. And after my talk with Francis, I wanted her to have it. We needed to get out of the shadows and enjoy a day outdoors. I reached up and ruffled my hair until it felt bigger and bushier. I plucked a few wildflowers from the grass and tucked them behind my ears. As a last touch, I pinched my cheeks, hoping to bring them out in a girlish blush. If the other players were too busy to train me, then it was time I trained myself. Time to master this role.

It was only upon reaching the checkpoints that I remembered I'd need a passport to enter the grounds. Cursing my fool head, I was about to retreat and search the perimeter for a place where I might sneak into the fayre unnoticed. But stewards at the barriers had already clapped eyes on me. To my surprise, they were smiling. They were looking me up and down, seeming to like what they saw. As a boy, I was always considered weedy and peculiar to the point of being unsightly. In a girl's frock and frills, it seemed my waifish looks had become more appealing. So I smiled back at the stewards, resisting the urge to flee. The men strode across the grass to greet me.

"You a minstrel, Miss?" the first fellow asked.

I don't know what compelled me to say it. The spirit of Sonya the Gypsy Queen lived in this dress and had hold of my senses.

"A dancer, sirs! Just looking for my crowd."

My voice came out high and melodic, my rustic accent suppressed. I was hoping that claiming a profession and purpose would hasten my admittance to the fayre, with no papers required.

My ruse worked better than I wanted it to.

"Well, thank the stars!" said the second man, seizing me by the arm. "We're sorely in need of some entertainment at our main stage. The musicians haven't seen their beds yet and are still soused up to the eyeballs. The auctioneers won't arrive till noon."

Before I knew it, the stewards were hurrying me towards the centre of the fayre ground, marching me fast like a prisoner being hauled to a punishment platform. And public humiliation might be just what I was bound towards. I had nothing to perform. My eyes cast about wildly, seeking a way out of this mess. I caught sight of a familiar head of tousled dark hair. Rum was playing football with some stable lads. He dodged and weaved around his fellow players, kicking the pig's bladder towards a goal marked by loadstones. At first, I thought he might be too caught up in his game to notice me. But as he raised his head, throwing up his arms in victory, our eyes locked. He blinked at me, startled to see me here and dressed in my current apparel.

I flashed Rum what I hoped was an expression of overwhelming distress before I was hurried forth through the long clustering lanes of the market where fresh loaves, ripe cheeses and new green apples were quickly passing between hands. I was soon ushered up the steps of a wide wooden platform, raised high enough to offer a view over the entire fayre. Cows and prize pigs were grouped at one side of the stage ready for auction and in the meantime a band of drunk musicians were playing lazy music on battered instruments. After a shove between my shoulders, I stumbled onto the platform, where I stood wide eyed and slack-jawed, with no notion of what I ought to do. This early in the day, there were no other entertainments to compete with. No minstrels, tumblers or conjurers to steal the crowd's attention. There was only me, wearing this dress, standing alone on the stage.

Yellow is a colour that catches the eye and sure enough, all stares slowly turned towards me. An expectant hush fell over the crowd. I stood so rooted and motionless that I feared I would be taken for a life-sized ragdoll brought out for sale. My brow beaded with cold sweat and I wondered if just by holding my breath, I could induce a fainting fit and put an end to this performance before it began. I had the dazzling white sun in my eyes, causing them to squint and water. I looked down at my dress, fearing it would seem dirty and sallow in the full light of day. My cheeks flushed, my nose twitched and I...

I sneezed. I sneezed so hard my whole body shook.

It must have been the wild flowers I'd tucked around my ears that had brought on my summer sniffles so fast. The little convulsion rattled my limbs, causing loose patches and ribbons to fall from my skirts. The crowd laughed at the sight of my leprous costume falling to bits. I tried not to let their laughter shake me. I had to be better than frowns. Their amusement was something I could work with.

I suddenly thought of Doll, the girl who had rescued me from the streets of Bristol. She'd been a funny girl, a girl who thought nothing of making a mockery of her sex, as though her femininity was just a fanciful charade after all. I could still see Doll's face in my mind. I slipped her face over my own like an invisible mask. What would Doll do if she'd let out an explosive sneeze like mine? She would wave for a handkerchief, then flutter that hanky at the nearest man calling his attention to her ticklish beauty. She'd turn her sneezing into something seductive, into something to take delight in.

I snatched up one of the fallen patches from the stage, raising it to my face like a veil. Another sneeze erupted from my nose, a shrieking *achoo* that blew the cloth into mid-air. I reached out for it, twirling my body into a spin. I shook my head, lifting the patch to my mouth again. Another sneeze sent the tissue shooting to the ground. I swept my arm low to catch it, turning the movement into an elegant bow. Once I felt the loosening of my limbs, I began to fall into one of my old routines. At first, I was faltering in my steps, tripping on my skirts or wobbling on unsteady feet. But each time that I stumbled, I would jerk myself upright, fixing my face into an expression of mock surprise, which never failed to raise a laugh from the crowd. This was my dumb show. A dumb show telling the story of this funny girl's first day in the sun. I had found my own way to speak without words.

The band had pulled their wits back together and were strumming a rhythm for me while the crowd clapped along in time. I heard the light clank of coins landing on the stage. Encouraged by this jingling music, I started to make my movements bigger, twisting and folding myself into new shapes that I had never tried before. I suddenly caught sight of Rum and Wally who were watching me in the first row before the stage. Wally was smiling for the first time in days while Rum cackled and slapped his hands on the edge of the boards, looking like he wanted to jump up and join me. Instead he reached and unwound the turban from Wally's head and then tossed it at my feet.

A new piece of costume, a prop to wield. I picked up the scarf and swung it in my hands, coiling it round my shoulders, letting it inspire new poses in me, new steps to my dance. Soon my crowd were hurling more fragments of clothing onto the stage – a glove, a cap, a walking cane, a waistcoat. I rushed over the boards, collecting up each of their gifts. I no longer cared what these people thought of me or if they were dressing me up like a rainbow-clad loon for sport. I'd never been given so many costumes to play with. They were flinging me a whole ragged wardrobe. I pulled on all the clothes at once, making myself a robe of their colour and variety. I was the Scarecrow Queen.

The world was spinning too fast for me now. I felt like I was in danger of taking off from the platform or falling down hard on my face. I feared that I'd become too strange and wild. Something neither a boy, nor a girl, but an imp cast up from the hell where my mother always swore I would be consigned to. I slowed down. I let my breath catch up with me. And I realised that the crowd were not laughing anymore. A blanket of silence had spread over the marketplace. I came to a halt, holding my body still, ready to return their belongings and hoping they'd permit me to leave the stage unpunished.

210

Then I saw that the crowd were not appalled. They were all just *watching* me. I glanced over their faces. I found some were smiling fondly. Some seemed perplexed. Some were blushing like they didn't know where to place their fascination with me. These people, these country folk, the farming men and freckled lads, who looked so much like my own Pa and brother...it didn't seem like they hated me. Far from it. They were looking on me with kindly eyes, even if they didn't fully understand what it was they were seeing.

The silence was terrifying. I'd hushed the traders and brought them to a standstill. I had stopped time and taken these people somewhere else. But the world was not frozen. The crowd were waiting to know what was going to happen next. But there was no next, just as there had been no beginning or no end. There were only the compulsions inside me that could come spilling out at any moment.

Not knowing what else to do I fell into a bow.

The crowd burst out in applause.

Scene Four

A Supper of Vices

By late afternoon I stood facing a very different audience. My master sat on the rear steps of our wagon, knuckles clenched around his knees, his hair in slithery strands about his eyes. His stare held me as fast as any pillory. I'd been stripped of my yellow frock and was back in my shirt and breeches. Taking the dress away felt strangely like it was a part of my punishment. I'm not sure how or when it happened, but I'd come to feel very meek and ungainly as a boy.

Following my interlude at the fayre, Makaydees and Lavern had dragged me back to our camp between them and locked me up in the sweat box of our wagon's interior for the whole humid afternoon. I'd been aware of my fellows arguing at length somewhere beyond the carriage walls but I couldn't make out their words, nor their intentions. It must have been hours later when I was released from my long day of starving and perspiring, wondering what I'd done so wrong. My master wasted no time making my offense clear to me.

"How many people saw you?" Makaydees demanded, grasping his wineskin in his fist like it was a neck he was wringing. "Over a hundred round the main stage alone, I'd wager. And several dozen of those were close enough to see you were no woman. Oh, don't imagine you fooled anyone with that clowning! You were all elbows and knees. A gangling little farmhand in frills. I was hoping that crowd might take you for a lone jester dancing a jig. But alas, this was not the case. Even those dull peasants could see you for what you were."

"We heard them muttering, Timony," said Lavern, his tone rather more nervous than scathing. "They thought that you were performing a prologue. They were expecting other actors and tumblers to join you on stage for a longer spectacle to follow."

"Who in that crowd won't be able to report to the Watch that there are players in town?" Makaydees took a slug of his liquor. "And don't think that just because you made them laugh on a sunny day that any would hesitate to sell you to the law. They'd take as much pleasure in seeing you hanged, burned or whipped to death. For the simpleton folk in these towns it's all part of the festivities!"

I dared not speak. I couldn't deny the danger that I had courted. Makaydees and Lavern had warned us all tenfold that we were not even to breathe the word *players* in this town. But given a costume and a stage to myself I had clean lost my wits.

"I shouldn't be surprised," Makaydees went on. "That day I took you from the farm, I encouraged you to put on a little charade of idiocy. To think I'd been impressed by your ability to take prompts and make a pretence of madness. I thought I had stumbled on a natural talent! I should've realized that you were hardly acting at all. I should've known I had only a mildly diverting fool on my hands."

My jaw fell slack, my breath coming out in offended bursts. But I held my tongue, scared that I would stutter, giving him further reason to mock me. Makaydees snorted at my mute impotent rage.

"You were right, Lavern. I shouldn't have been so hasty hiring us a new leading lady. God's blood! Why did I think I could replace Rum with a lisping farm boy? A bumpkin who can barely string a sentence together, never mind explain his absurd behaviour."

My stomach tied itself in knots so tight they would've brought up vomit if I had eaten. I don't know why this hurt so much. This was a role I should've been accustomed to. I could still remember the nights on the farm I'd been brought to stand before Pa's disappointment. I was well-practised in the slumped posture and shamed expression that all good fathers expect from their errant sons. I just hadn't expected that I would be playing this part for

Makaydees. It made me ache in deep places that Pa's scorn had never touched. It hurt most of all on this day. The first day I'd done anything I might be proud of.

A hand brushed my shoulder and suddenly Francis was there at my side. The other players had been hanging back until now, none of them willing to get in the way of my chastisement. But the tailor cleared his throat now, his apple cheeks flushing red.

"I'm the one who is to blame for the boy's blunder. I got carried away, talking all wistful, telling the lad not to let his talents go to waste. I wasn't expecting him to go showing them off in the instant. But I can see how he took my words the wrong way. So don't go on lashing him with your tongue any longer. Just put it down to a woolly-headed old man who fancied he was sharing his wisdom."

Makaydees hissed through his teeth. "Francis...I trust you meant well, but you must be wary of how your influence..."

"It was *you*!" I blurted out, before my master could say another condescending word to anyone. "You're the one who put me up to this! Ever since you came to the farm, I've been falling over myself trying to please *you*! It was you who made me think I could be an actor. And I just...wanted to believe it! I wanted to prove..."

I stopped abruptly before my tears came.

But I hadn't stuttered. Not one word.

My speech brought my master to his feet, swaying on unsteady legs. He lifted an arm and I flinched, thinking he was raising his fist for a blow. That was before I saw his finger was pointed, ready to launch into another lecture. Before he could start, Wally stepped between us, catching Makaydees by the wrist, holding him back.

"We haven't the time for this," he insisted, his voice weary and solemn. "What we need now is rest. None of us have slept enough since Bristol. Our wits are scattering. We best recover ourselves for the road ahead. Let's to bed early so we may leave this town at dead of night. And let's hope we do not linger long in its memory."

This was the most Wally had spoken since we had passed through the gypsy camp. He wasn't usually the one to give commands, but the others hung their heads in a mutual nod, unwilling to argue and unable to refuse an invitation to sleep. Even Makaydees appeared humbled enough to let Wally take charge of our flight.

So, we packed up our gear, rolled up our maps and climbed aboard the wagon, bedding down on its floorboards. My master didn't spare me another glance. After all my desperate attempts to win this man's favour, I could think of no worse punishment than to simply be ignored by him. Makaydees handed his wineskin to Lavern, Wally and Francis in turn, offering each of them a few sips to settle their nerves so they could sleep through till midnight. Rum was the one they were trusting to take the evening watch. *Rum* who'd been such a helpful boy all day, keeping his mouth shut and tending to the new horse. Rum had kept silent, saying nothing to defend me, nor owning up to how he'd made me fear for my position in the troupe, the traitor.

I lay awake in the woozy shadows of the wagon. It wasn't long before the other four players were snoring around me, grunting through their noses in a way that reminded me of the pigs back on the farm and the many times I was forced to bed with them in the sty. I could never sleep those nights either, not just because of the snorts and the stench, but mostly because my backside would be smarting from Ma's birch rod. Lavern had told me that Makaydees never beat any of his company. The lash was a tool of the correction house and our master had sworn he would never stoop to mimic their methods. But did Makaydees not know how his words struck harder and stung deeper? Did he not care that his disdain would leave me restless far longer?

As I lay there in my toils, I felt sick at the others sleeping, relieved of their cares while I twitched and squirmed. A scream kept bubbling up in my throat, a scream that hurt to swallow. I bit my shirt sleeves till I couldn't stand it any longer. I rose to my feet, tiptoeing around their bodies, towards the wagon steps. I kept expecting one of their hands to snake out and catch me by the ankle, tugging me back to the floor. But I slipped from our carriage without them stirring.

Out in the cool evening air, I threw myself down in the grass, letting its dewy blades muffle my moans as I opened my mouth and let out all the bitter sobs I had been holding back.

"Still playing the woman?" asked a voice.

Rum was the very last person I wanted to see me in this weeping fit. I hadn't been able to look him in the face since our scene in the horse courser's tent. And besides, these weren't tears I wished to share with anyone. This wasn't a tragic spectacle for an audience to savour. It was just me getting red eyed, snotty and pathetic and wishing I could be miles away from the boy crouching by my side.

"T-the heat," I stammered. "Makes my eyes itch and water..."

"Right," Rum scoffed, already tugging at my elbow.

"Get off!" I snapped. "I still hate you! Leave me alone."

"I'm not leaving you. I was just about to wake you. I'm not having my plan go to waste. Hurry now! Else we'll be late."

I blinked in confusion as Rum linked arms with me, hauling me upright and pulling me away from the wagon. He marched me swiftly from the fringes of the treeline and towards the low brick buildings of Buckfast town. The tents and stalls of the fayre were packed up now, leaving only breadcrumbs, dead grass and footprints in the dirt. But the town itself was still rumbling with raucous voices.

"What plan?" I flustered. "Where are you taking me?"

"Can I tell you something, Timmy?" he asked, ignoring my pesky question. "Harken now. This isn't easy for me to say. That funny turn of yours on the stage. The jig you made up on the spot."

I shut my eyes, bracing myself for further derision.

"I loved it," Rum confessed. "The crowd loved it. It's just what we need in our theatre. A little mirth and wonder. So don't pay any mind to Makaydees. He's a crabby old tragedian. He thinks every play has to end with a pile of corpses. You'll never make him care for a heroine who falls down so much and doesn't even die."

I'd no idea how to respond to Rum praising me while deriding our master. I just kept silent and let him go on.

"We'll make an actor of you yet," Rum continued. "I just don't know why you're so bad at playing yourself. I mean, look at you now! You're free of the frock and it's like you've shrunk inside your skin and want to chew off your own tongue. It painful to see. That's why I'm doing something to change it. Tonight, you're going to be a boy. Tonight is for all the terrible things that boys enjoy!" He pulled a tiny drawstring bag from his sleeve and pressed it into my hand. "Here you go, Timony. You're the one who's earned this."

I squeezed the little purse in my palm.

"What is this?" I asked. "Where did you…?"

"It's the coins that we collected from the stage at the fayre," Rum explained. "I swiped it from Lavern's pack. He didn't wake up. That'll be the sleeping draught I slipped into Mak's wineskin. It always puts them into a stupor so they don't hear me sneaking off."

"You…you put something in their drink?!"

"Don't fret! They'll be fine. The rest will do them good. And it's not my usual habit to drug and steal from our companions. But in this case, they were the ones cheating a fellow player. I'm just returning what's rightfully yours. They treat us like we're the little people in this troupe. They're so jealous of our youth and talent. We're the stars who can draw them a crowd and earn them a profit. And we're the ones who can stay up all night to toast our successes!"

"I've never been paid for anything before," I said, overwhelmed. "I've never had any coins I could call my own."

"Ha! I thought as much. That's why I'm taking you to the nearest alehouse to show you the best ways to spend it."

Rum didn't wait for my consent but began steering me through the shadowed streets of the town. I was a little distressed over the prospect of spending an entire evening in his reckless company, but my belly fluttered in anticipation. I was famished after all.

"I...I am in desperate need of a supper," I told him, attempting to claw back control over our funds. "What say you to some bread and pottage with two cups of ale to wash it down?"

Rum screwed up his nose like my suggestion of a pleasant evening meal both embarrassed and repulsed him. He slung an arm around my neck in a gesture that was somewhere between a hug and a headlock. I felt his breath hot and hungry against my ear.

"Listen Timmy. There are ways we can fatten up your little purse. And yes, there's quite a feast waiting for us in town. I just hope you've the stomach for it! You want to hear the special? *Farmer Thorn's prize gamecock.* I saw the beaked barbarian caged at one of the stalls today. That was when I first learned about the fight."

There was a fiendish glint in Rum's eyes now and a sharp edge to his smile that made me tighten my grasp on my purse.

"W-what fight is this?" I asked.

"The cockfight, of course! We'll put your lump sum on Thorn's bird and after the feathers have flown and we've won the early rounds, we'll have enough to buy one of the fallen fowl for our supper. We'll have it plucked, skinned and spitted over a fire before midnight and be back to wake our fellows on full stomachs."

Fear prickled my skin. I had never been to a cockfight before but I had heard enough mutterings from the other players about

Rum's love of gambling and how it often led him to disaster. The scarred rents in his cheeks were a testament to that. I knew that I was being drawn into mischief. But for once I wanted a taste of its lure.

Only one thing gave me reason to hesitate.

"What about the watchmen?" I asked Rum. "After the fayre they are sure to be searching for players in this town."

Rum only laughed at the suggestion. "Don't let Mak and Lav tame you with their paranoid portends. What those two bellyachers seem to forget is that nobody rightly knows what a player looks like. How could they? We never stop changing our appearances. This morning you were a little yellow dancing girl. Tonight, you're a swaggering boy wanting a bit of adventure before you see your bed. So enough chatter, Timony. Let's save our breath for eating up the hot evening air, my friend. The night is young and all the world is ours to win!"

I sighed. It was the word *friend* that got me.

I'd have followed Rum anywhere that night. He could've led me laughing into the jaws of Hell itself. After we'd threaded through the streets, we came to the doors of *The Green Man* inn. Tantalising smells drifted out from its common room, but before I could be drawn into their steamy embrace, Rum tugged my arm, leading me round to the side of the tavern to an uneven tumble of stairs. He sniffed at the air, slinking down the steps like a tomcat seeking out its rightful territory. I stumbled behind him, pawing at the walls. Rum knocked on the door below and it opened up a crack. A squinting eye was pressed to its gape. Rum jerked my arm upright, shaking my wrist so that my purse gave a jingle. This light music was enough to gain us entrance.

It took my eyes a moment to adjust to the gloom. I gagged at the smell of tallow in the close confines, the sickly candle breath stealing away my appetite. But nobody was eating down in the gambling den. A ramshackle bar was set up in a nearby corner, where only a frothy orange ale was being served from an iron pot. Rum bought us a jug of this steaming brew which he said was known as either *mulled scrumpy* or *bonfire juice*. I realised that at some point my purse had ended up in Rum's hands. He really was quick with his fingers.

A man waved us over to the far wall where names and numbers were being daubed in chalk. Rum crossed the cellar to place a bet while I just stood gawping at the men huddled around barrels with their palms locked in arm wrestles, the men hurling balls into the rows of skittles and sending them flying, the men hollering in each other's earholes, their fists flexed and white at the knuckles. There were no women here in this secret cellar. Not even me. Not for tonight.

The cockfight was the bloody beating heart of the den. When Rum returned to my side, he reported that the next bout was just about to commence. So, we elbowed our way through the throng till we came to a low ring of bars, the caging pen that held the fighter birds. The two roosters circled each other in the pit. Their backs were hunched, their necks protruding and their heels scraping at the floor. They held their ground a moment before leaping into the air and meeting in a clash of feathers and squawking. The cock who Rum pointed out to me as Farmer Thorn's champion swiftly got its beak into its opponent's neck, causing the bird to stagger, its head flopping to the side. A second later, the rival collapsed and lay shivering on the stones.

The crowd threw their arms up in the air, whooping as the bird bled out on the cellar floor. A man in the ring slapped the floor three times, before grasping the fallen bird by its limp legs and then handing it back to its owner. The loser wasted no time in clamping his fist around the bird's neck, yanking and twisting till it snapped.

My hand went to my mouth as my stomach lurched.

"None of that!" Rum scolded, elbowing me in the side. "Don't turn maidenly on me now. You're playing a man tonight. And surely you've seen blood split and necks wrung back on the farm?"

I tried to swallow my nausea. "I could never bear to look. Never had to learn either. Pa didn't trust me to handle the knives." I sighed. "It's funny. I played at death every day on the farm. But I couldn't stand the sight of the real thing. I suppose it didn't help that I was fonder of our pigs and chickens than I was my own family."

"That much I understand. I preferred the company of horses when I was a stable lad. Most animals deserve better than the ends we give them. But we all must make the best of our lot. That bird may be dead before this night is out, but we'll remember this last show he gave us. Life's just a little show with a bad ending, Timmy."

Rum pointed back into the ring where Thorn's rooster was flapping its torn wings and puffing out its bloodied plumage. I stared at the proud swell of the cockerel's chest and I was reminded of the bombast that Makaydees used to stuff out his waistcoat. The bird in the ring was like a player strutting on stage before a rapturous crowd.

"Here," said Rum. "Drink this for courage."

He pressed the tankard of scrumpy to my lips and tipped it back. I gulped as the hot brew sluiced down my throat. After that first taste, I clasped the jug to my chest, hugging it close as the fights waged on and the stakes stacked up. My limbs grew loose and clumsy the more that I glugged. I felt myself slumping against Rum's side. He barely seemed aware of me. His stare was fixed upon the match, sweat beading on his brow as he gripped the rails of the ring. With a sinking feeling I realized this night was for Rum, not the two of us together. This gambling habit was an itch he'd been needing to scratch for weeks.

"This bird's good for at least two more rounds," said Rum, talking to himself more than me. "We'll hang on till the time's right."

He turned and kissed me on the cheek, his lips hard as knuckles. If I wasn't so heavy with drink, I'd have slapped him. The felled birds blurred before my eyes. I struggled to focus as yet another dying rooster was scraped from the floor and a new contender placed in the pit. This latest rival was a scraggly creature with bald patches where its feathers had been torn out. It had one eye rolling in its skull and only shreds left of its comb and wattle. A cry from the game master announced that the new fighting cock belonged to a man called Goodfellow.

"He doesn't live up to his name," I muttered into Rum's ear. "That poor thing won't even be worth putting in the pot afterwards."

Rum squeezed my arm. "This is the one."

I swallowed a belch. "The one what?"

"This is when we change our bet."

"No Rum, wait…*wait!*"

226

Before I could stop him Rum dashed across to the wall to change our wager to Goodfellow's bird. I drank down the last of the sour ale and nervously turned my eyes back to the pit. The two cocks faced each other like duelling soldiers. Thorn's bird strode forth, its head raised high, sure that it would prove the hero of this latest bout. The other bird's head was weaving on its neck. It tried to fix its one good eye on its approaching attacker. As their shadows merged in the middle of the ring, Goodfellow's bird let out a piercing shriek that echoed around the cellar and caused the crowd to fall into a hush.

The gamecocks leapt into the air and I caught a flash of silver amid the smashing wings. The other roosters had been fighting bare-heeled, but Goodfellow's cock had a set of barbs affixed to its limping feet. It was using these spurs to slice gashes and holes in Thorn's bird. I raised my head to see if any other spectators had noticed the little knives. But their eye level wasn't as low as my own. Besides, the men were too caught up in the vicious spectacle to realise its trickery.

Thorn's bird leaked blood into its feathers, its strength ebbing away until it toppled and lay vanquished. The gamblers threw up their hands, hissing curses and lamenting the coins they'd lost on this last wager. Rum was the only one cheering. He leapt up and down, tugging my arm like he wanted to yank it off my shoulder. I tried to pull away, but he spun me round, clasping my face in his palms.

"We won!" he rasped. "I needed a win tonight."

For a moment I thought he might kiss me again. And I wanted to slap him. I wanted to kick him sharp between his legs, to scratch his eyes out just for looking at me that way. Because I knew it wasn't real. Because I knew it never could be real. And how I hated Rum for making me wish that I could have something real with him.

He frowned, his face falling. "You're crying."

I scraped my knuckles over my cheeks. "The heat..." I muttered in a choked voice. "It...it's just sweat and my sore eyes."

Rum tipped his head, suddenly wearing the gentle expression he reserved for taming horses. He put his arm round me again.

"Let's take our winnings and go get some air."

He was speaking like a friend again. Like our night together was far from spent and he had so much more still to say to me. And I dearly wanted him to say something that would make amends.

But Rum's words would have to wait. At that moment, the door was thrown wide and a crowd of watchmen burst in.

Scene Five

Outlaws

My cheek was slammed against the cellar wall as a gloved hand seized my neck and the hilt of a sword dug into my spine. From the watering corners of my eyes, I could see that every other man in the gambling den was being restrained in this same rough fashion. My hands were wrenched behind my back and a coarse rope was bound around my wrists. And this was it. We were caught. We had been wondering how close those bounty hunters from Bristol were on our trail. Now we had our answer. They'd been right on top of us.

"Be wise and do not resist us," said a spokesman for the invading watch. "We're not here to trouble you men over your revels. I wager that you have no license for this assembly. But no matter. Let us deal! We'll leave you to your sports if you can cough up any news of the highwayman Robin Candle or that company of players who have been harbouring him. We've heard at least one of the vagabond actors was seen performing a jig at the fayre this morning. Did any of you witness this? Your testimonies will not go unrewarded…"

Some twenty voices in the cellar all began clamouring at once. But none of them were offering up information. Instead they were snarling curses and spitting phlegm at our captors. These men were too drunk and riled over their lost bets for striking bargains.

"Calm yourselves!" the Watch leader yelled above their fury. "We don't want a riot in a cellar filled with flames. If it's a fight you want then we can easily put you in lock up overnight and then ship you off to war with the Spaniards on the morrow!"

It seemed these gamblers had more rage in their blood than sense in their heads. They kept on bellowing and struggling, some of them ripping their hands loose from their bonds and swinging their fists. The watchmen began clearing the cellar, dragging every brawler up onto the streets. I turned to look at Rum, who was pressed against the wall beside me. He nodded for me to lower my gaze. I looked down to see his fingers already loosening the knot at his wrists.

"Be ready to run…" Rum whispered to me.

I was willing to follow whatever escape plan he had in mind since I'd nothing in my own thoughts but blind panic. The drunken gamblers were steadily being hauled up the stairs and out into the night. It was only after the room had been emptied that Rum and I were tugged away from the bricks. I frowned, wondering why we were being kept back and led out last. Perhaps the watchman holding us wished to shield us from the violence out of consideration for our youth.

Our captor marched us across the stone floor that was now smeared with blood, feathers and puddles of scrumpy. It looked like the law had snatched up most of the gamecocks, dead or alive. Only Goodfellow's sorry looking bird was left amidst the carnage. As we drew close to the door, I dragged my feet in last desperate resistance. But our captor did not shove us outside. Instead he slammed the door shut and then pushed Rum and I back so we fell hard on our haunches.

"Well met, friends!" said the man standing over us, his hood still masking his face. "A lucky thing I was the only one to recognise you. Say thank you, won't you? I've just saved your little lives."

He tugged the cowl back from his brow and my blood ran cold. I wouldn't have known the highwayman by his pale indistinct features now covered in a thickening beard. In the gloom of the cellar he hadn't stood out from the crowd in his dull brown livery.

But I knew him now. Hearing his voice, I knew.

"Candle," Rum rasped, slack-jawed on the floor.

"Actually, it's Goodfellow for this evening."

"You've been at the cockfight this whole time?!" Rum spluttered in disbelief. "Then…why didn't the Watch arrest you?"

He shrugged. "Because when they burst in, I copied their actions rather than those of the gambling men. A fine bit of role reversal, I must say! Tis surprising what is missed in the shadows."

The highwayman stepped over us both, licking his fingers and then snuffing out the dwindling tallow sticks with a pinch. He grasped his barely breathing gamecock by its throat, yanked the blades off its feet and then hung the poor creature from his belt by its neck. His jacket was jiggling with the coins that he'd won through the bird's suffering. These were the winnings that should have gone partly to Rum and me before the night took this horrifying turn.

I looked across at Rum now and saw his eyes fixed upon the hilt of Candle's sword, poking from its scabbard. Ever the gambling man, Rum leapt to his feet, the rope falling from his wrists as he reached for the blade. Candle spun on his heels just as fast. As Rum locked his stare with that of the highwayman, his face broke into a smile. He turned his lunge for the sword into a boisterous handshake.

"Well met by whatever name you go by!" Rum exulted, pumping Candle's arm. "And thank you indeed! I dare say that you've spared us from being pressed into child soldiers this night."

"Yes, tis said they're snatching up every man between sixteen and sixty to fight the Spanish. But I see you're a lad like myself who'll not be bound into service" Candle nodded to the heap of rope on the floor. "I made those knots loose on purpose, of course."

I still lay squirming in my own bindings, wondering why slipping free from ropes was so much easier for others.

"Now then, my rascally squire!" Candle said, ruffling Rum's hair and still ignoring my presence. "Am I to take it you have reconsidered my offer? We could sail for the New World from the Plymouth harbour just as easily as we might have from Bristol."

Rum laughed and nodded, playing the part of willing henchman with unsettling ease. "If you will still have me as a first mate on your voyage. So you don't begrudge me fleeing when you were set upon by that little harlot and her lawmen friends then?"

Candle treated Rum to a cuff across his scarred cheek, a slap that landed a little too heavily to be called playful.

"Tis not forgotten, you knave!" he chided, still laughing. "But I'd never trust a fellow outlaw who doesn't save his own skin first. And besides, you were unarmed that night. Do you know how many throats I had to cut before I escaped that alleyway?"

Rum's smiled faded. "I...I don't."

The highwayman stared with glassy eyes, a feverish sweat on his brow and a sickly wheeze to his breathing.

"Nor do I!" Candle sniggered at last, hysteria bubbling up at the back of his hoarse throat. "In truth, I could not count how many my blade struck down in the shadows. But let me tell you, I must've left a very long trail of blood out of that town. Because for the last two weeks I have had every last Bristol watchman hunting me down. Yes, I must have slaughtered the father, brothers or sons of every person living in that wretched harbour! Then there was that little matter of the fire that we started at *The Drunken Boat* tavern. What a way to end a show, hey lads? With the stage itself going up in flames!"

Candle's eyes flashed and he kicked over the nearest barrel table. The last of his tallow sticks were still smouldering there and now they fell straight into the straw of the empty cockerel boxes. The hay caught, swiftly turning black and giving off smoke.

"I wonder how long it'll take before these flames are warming the floorboards?" said Candle, nodding at the ceiling. "This may be another town that we'll leave in ashes. Come, let's away!"

The highwayman seized Rum by his doublet and began to drag him through the door. He seemed content to leave me bound and helpless on the floor, sealing me in a fiery tomb to burn. Which might've been my fate had Rum not stooped down just in time, hooking his arm under my elbow and hoisting me to my feet. I followed them stumbling out into the night. The watchmen had seemingly not realized that they had left three stragglers in the gambling pit. From the sounds of it, they had their hands full with the mob they were sorting through in the square. We slipped passed the militia unnoticed.

Once we reached the outskirts of Buckfast, the highwayman led us in a ragged line over a meadow, his last tallow stick in one hand and the other clutching Rum's collar. Rum in his turn was holding me by my sleeve. At the head of this chain, our captor was laughing into the wind, laughing so hard that it made my head spin.

When my shirt slipped from Rum's grasp, I crumpled onto my knees, my belly cramping like it was being squeezed by invisible hands. The sour apple brew came surging up my throat and I vomited it down my shirtfront, shuddering with every retch. When I'd finished spewing my guts out, I fell to one side, curling myself up like a snail retreating into its shell and finding comfort within its own dank shadows. Candle and Rum stumbled on ahead. I balled up very small, hoping they might leave me behind. But all too soon I heard their footsteps retreating over the grass. Then Candle jabbed me with his boot.

"On your feet, you chicken liver!"

When I didn't move fast enough, Candle drew his sword, tapping it beneath my chin. I struggled back to my feet.

"There that wasn't so hard, was it?" He nudged Rum in the side. "Do you think that he was trying to run away from us? He'd better not try crawling back to those watchmen. The justice would clap a little vagrant like him in irons just for looking at them."

"Don't mind him," said Rum. "He's a milksop who can't hold his ale and has drunk himself sick. Did you see him at the cockfight? He was shaking at the knees and near fainting at the first dash of blood. To think that I fancied I could make a man of him."

I would've been sick a second time if there had been anything left in me to throw up. Even if Rum was playing a confidence trick, he was entirely too convincing in this henchman role. I really had to wonder who it was that he was fooling. Earlier Rum had me believing that we were roaring boys on the town together. But was that just a sly charade so he could use my coins for a stake in the fight?

"You'll never make a man out of this one," sneered Candle. "As I said, he'd be better as a eunuch! Which reminds me…"

I had just planted my feet, my frail legs still trembling beneath me, when Candle lowered his sword and kicked me hard in my crotch. The wind was knocked out of me and flares of pain set a fire in my mind. I crumpled back to my knees as the agonizing ache spread from my groin to my belly, tying me in knots and making me wish I *was* castrated, if only so I'd never have to experience such hurt again. I hated how my boyhood was the easiest part of me to wound.

"I've owed him that injury since he dared inflict the same on me in Bristol," Candle muttered to Rum, who was now shuffling worriedly at the highwayman's side. "But we cannot leave him snivelling here. Never leave a witness breathing, I say! He's your companion, so you decide how you'd like me to dispatch him."

Rum forced out a laugh. "Nay, nay! Don't let's be hasty! What's a pirate voyage without some slaves on board? And if we grow his hair and give him his gelding during our sail, then we can sell him as an opera singer once we reach the New World."

"*Ha*! What a diabolical little mind!" Candle sheathed his sword, forgoing his intention to murder me for the time being. "Speaking of slaves, wait until you see what I'm keeping at my hideaway. Oh yes, I already have one piece of treasure in my hoard."

Rum's mouth fell open, but Candle hissed for silence and harried him to keep moving. The two of them stooped down, grasping me under my armpits and then dragging me between them like a sack of earth. Squinting up ahead, I could see that we were approaching a low cavern in the hillside that edged the woods. Candle halted us at its entrance, shoved me into Rum's arms and then held out his tallow flame over a bundle of tied sticks that he'd pitched in the earth. As the brand began to catch flame, its glow illuminated his hideout.

"I have returned, my Moorish mistress!"

My stomach turned over again at Candle's words. Sure enough at the far side of the cavern, there stood a girl. A girl who had her arms stretched back around a column of stone, chained in place with rusty iron manacles. I knew she must be Doll before she raised her head. I didn't know if I should be glad to see her again. I'd feared her dead. I'd thought she might be just another bleeding corpse left in the backstreets of Bristol. But here she stood breathing before us.

Doll was a skinny shadow of the sugar-fed girl who I'd met in the harbour. Looking at her now I feared she'd become like Mirabelle – a kidnapped maid, every bit as helpless and far from home. Her face was frozen in blankness as she stared right through us.

"You've taken a doxy bride, Candle?" asked Rum.

"Hardly!" he scoffed. "Even a Goblin king wouldn't marry a little monster like this. Do you see these scratches on my cheeks, boy? They were something to compare to your own scars the night I fled from the harbour. This dainty Negress gave me quite a mauling. She's a savage creature like the rest of her race. But I've tamed her since. I've trained her to obey. She's my gentle companion now."

Doll stiffened as the highwayman approached her and brushed a few loose curls from her brow. Candle took a key from his pocket and unlocked her manacles, his eyes creeping over her arms as if counting the goosebumps on her skin. Doll kept her eyes to the ground, her lips a tight line. It made me heartsick to see her this way. I'd been hoping that she'd escaped him and fled back to the perfumed pleasures of her tearooms. But that was only the frailest dream.

"Will you not receive our guests?" said Candle, pouting like a child whose play was being spoilt by slower children.

Doll's expression did not change, save for a tensing of her jaw. In limp movements, she turned to face Rum and I, standing stiff as a maypole before us. I held my breath, waiting for her to recognise me, but her eyes remained vacant. I wondered if the blood and screams of that last night in Bristol were something that Doll had forced herself to forget, along with anyone who'd shared in her ordeal. She offered the barest nod to acknowledge us. The highwayman snorted and reached for the bleeding bird still hanging from his belt.

"Didn't I tell you I could turn this starved rooster into a champion gamecock?" he bragged, throwing the bird down at Doll's feet. "The wretched thing has served me well tonight. Now pluck it, get its guts out and it can serve us again for our supper."

240

Doll said nothing, just sank down and stroked what remained of the bird's plumage. Candle bared his teeth, affronted by the girl's numb silence and desperate for some reaction from her.

"And did I not tell you..." he persisted, slinging an arm around Rum, "...that I'd find a new gang erelong. This scamp with the scars will be my apprentice, my pupil highwayman. The small squeaking one doesn't truly qualify as a man, but he'll make a quaint maid servant, I'll warrant. We'll leave you to the women's work..."

Candle steered Rum towards the cave mouth, but his hungry stare still lingered on Doll. The girl kept her eyes downcast and her back hunched, unwilling to even glance at her captor. Candle marched Rum out onto the meadows, planting the flaming brand in the ground outside the cavern. The highwayman lingered close enough to stand guard over his hideaway but he was at last out of earshot. With Candle gone, Doll gave way to a smile, a whisper of triumph in her eyes. I didn't know how to take her smile. At first, I feared she might have gone mad in her captivity. I approached her slowly, hoping not to startle her, turning sideways to show her my still bound hands.

"Doll? It's me, Timony. Don't be scared, I..."

"Oh, give over!" Doll scoffed, rolling her eyes before striding over to untie me. "I'm far too bored of his bad company to feel afraid. You travel with that highwayman for a few days and you'll soon learn that nothing wears him down worse than silence. If you can kill a man by holding back your words then I might just starve the bastard yet. Who would've thought there would ever be a fellow who could stop me from yammering? Tis good to know I can keep my tongue still in my head if needs be. The Madame would be proud."

I let go a startled breath. Behind her mask of victimhood, Doll was just as bubbly and outspoken as ever before.

"You...you remember me then?"

"Of course!" she said, uncoiling the rope from my chaffed wrists. "The clumsy player boy tripping over his skirts."

"And...you're not hurt?" I asked. Her weight loss aside, she did not seem injured. "He didn't...he hasn't tried to..."

I trailed off, unable to finish the sentence.

"What? Have his wicked way with me?" She shook her head. "You heard him. He won't lower himself to lie with one of my race. Never mind that I was born on this mucky English soil. The colour of my skin has him convinced I have some dark sorcery in my blood. The prattling ass! If you ask me, I don't think he could take any woman to bed right now. The state he's in, I doubt he could perform for a lady between the sheets. I've seen it before with boys like him."

"A man like him, don't you mean?"

"Oh no," she insisted. "Don't let his beard and his bulk fool you. He's younger than he looks. Not yet twenty I'd say. And I'm older than my baby face gives away. I've known boys like him before. Boys so worn down by the road they're losing their wits. He's tired of running, Timmy. But too scared to stop. Too young to die yet he knows he's not long for this world. He has shed too much blood and caused too much trouble now to get away with his life. All this talk of sailing to the New World is just a childish daydream. Deep down, he knows that he has no hope of escaping. That's just what makes him dangerous. Because like a child, he's making a game of how long he can survive."

I swallowed. "So what do we do?"

"We beat him, of course. Are you with me, Timony? If anything happens to me, it'll be your job to see him hanged."

"Shouldn't we just...try to get away?"

Doll gave an amused snort, shaking her head at me again. "Don't make me laugh, boy! I'll lose my nerve if I let myself laugh. You think that I couldn't have escaped him before now? You think I was never taught how to wrestle my hands out of iron cuffs?"

I frowned. "Are you saying you could've..."

"What would I get out of running away, huh? A long lonesome walk back to Bristol. A beggarly Moorish girl on the road, likely to be snatched up by the law before I saw my harbour again. No, he won't reduce me to that. After he's dragged me so far from home, I intend to return with something to show for it. I want that reward on his head. So, I'm sticking with him till I can lead him headfirst into a noose. I owe it to Kit and Ned – those boys he left bleeding in the gutter. And when the Madame sees my face again and my pockets filled with coins, she'll know I'm more than just a nuisance to her house."

Her speech left me breathless. The rasp in Doll's voice suggested she hadn't spoken for days and in her mute spell she'd been surviving on hot dreams of revenge. Having said her piece, she knelt beside the battered gamecock again. The bird lay on its side, its chest wheezing and its one bloodshot eye rolling in its head.

"Still alive, is it?" Doll sighed. "You wouldn't think it could be alive after what it's been put through. It's not like Candle would let me nurse it. There's only one way to make it better now."

Doll's fingers stroked over its bloodied feathers, trying to soothe the suffering creature. I remembered the gibes from the other girls at the tearoom, the way they'd teased Doll for her love of strays brought in from the streets and fed with her milk rations.

Doll's hands encircled the rooster's throat. The bird began to thrash and screech. It had only survived in the cockpit out of blind panic. Doll cursed and closed her eyes tight, refusing to weep. I stared down at the rooster, scrabbling in the dirt. I'd never had the stomach to kill any animal on the farm. But suddenly the task seemed all too simple. It didn't matter if it made me squeamish. It had to be done. Before Doll had to be the one to go through with it, I seized a rock and struck the bird dead.

I fell to my knees, reeling from the swiftness of my action and the strength that I'd found in my arm. The bird lay unmoving while Doll's wet eyelids fluttered open. Her stare flicked between my face and the blood-stained rock in my palm. She seemed to be considering that I might be more than a helpless bystander in her plans.

"It doubles our chances if we're both working against him," she whispered. "I could give you a cut of the reward."

"*Half* the reward," I insisted, holding her stare. "I don't want to go back to my master with nothing to show for it either."

She shrugged. "I can't argue with that." She reached out to shake on it, then hesitated, withdrawing her hand. "What about your friend? The boy with the scars? Is he playing a long con with Candle or does he truly plan on turning highwayman himself?"

I glanced out onto the meadows. Rum was clapping his hands as Candle demonstrated the thrusts and parries of his sword arm.

"I can't tell. He's a better actor than me."

Doll shook her head. "That's the trouble with you players! How can you put your faith in someone who lies for a living?"

"I don't know what game he's playing," I confessed, struggling to meet her eye. "I never know what's real with him."

"Well, you had best learn!" Doll hissed. "Because on our own, we are the girls of this gang. And you might not be stuck playing the girl forever...but for now, you need to learn how to survive as one. And the Madame always taught me that you can't wait around for any boy to rescue you. They're most often the ones that you need saving from. Especially boys like that..." She glared at Candle and Rum beyond the cave mouth. "If your friend is with us, then good. That means we've got the highwayman outnumbered. But if he's with Candle, it means we've another villain to send to the gallows."

Scene Six

Will-o'-the-Wisps

We fled onto the moors before dawn.

In the pale grey light before sunrise we could see smoke rising up from the low buildings of Buckfast. It looked like the fire Candle had set in the Green Man tavern had spread to the upstairs chambers and possibly the neighbouring houses. Dousing out the blaze had likely served to slow the Watch party who'd been hunting the highwayman. But it wouldn't stall their chase much longer.

Candle reckoned it was less than a day's walk between Buckfast and Plymouth, but a day's trek across Dartmoor was far greater toil than any other road that we might have taken. We had not slept and had barely supped as we set out to cross the vast stretch of moorland. The seemingly endless landscape that lay before us was largely featureless with misty distances at every edge of its barren terrain.

After a few hours tramp it still felt like we were stuck in the same place. Still the same rugged hillocks, the same choked streams and clusters of heather, purple as bruises. The grass here sprouted in patchy shades of yellow and green, speckled with little cotton flowers like the trimmings of old men's beards. I'd never been in a place so desolate before. Never been surrounded by so much nowhere.

It soon became clear that the elements themselves were against our escape. After weeks of sweltering weather, the second day of August began sunless and overcast, the sky stuffy with clouds. Not long after first light, the rain came down in a spitting spray that slowly drenched us to our skin. My boy's clothes had been abandoned back at the caves after Candle had complained about the vomit stink hanging on my shirt. I was now dressed in the thin linen smock that Doll had been wearing beneath her ragged green dress. It amused Candle to treat me as another maid in his company. With my fast-growing curls almost touching my shoulders, it would be easy to mistake me for a spindly beggar girl, barefoot, starving and so very far from home.

"Keep your head up," Doll whispered, nudging me as she walked by my side. "We must keep looking for a chance."

My chin had been lolling on my chest, but at Doll's urging I shook myself and stared up ahead, blinking against the rain. Doll and I were walking a few paces behind Candle and Rum, far back enough so we could quietly conspire together and yet close enough to listen to the highwayman and Rum in their ceaseless chatter.

"Make no attempt to fight or flee!" Rum hollered across the moor, as he held the highwayman's mask up to his face. "For you are at the mercy of Robin Candle and his goblin gang!"

"Better," said Candle, slapping his shoulder. "If your voice carries, my legend will soon become a new moorland myth. More fearful than the headless huntsman and his black dogs. Or the old Crockern who comes on stormy nights, riding a skeleton horse."

"This is just tree bark and tallow, yes?" said Rum, stroking a hand over the false face. "With mosses to make it green?"

Candle nodded, proud of his artistry.

"In the autumn when the leaves turn red, I will change its colours so I can go forth disguised as the Devil himself!"

"A villain for every season!" Rum cheered. "Once we've crossed the sea, we'll bring a whole host of monsters to the New World."

Doll drew close, elbowing me in the ribs again.

"You still think your little friend's on our side?"

I winced, struggling to answer. Candle and Rum had been babbling on about their piratical adventures to come for most of the morning. By all appearances they were delighting in each other's company, mutual partners in crime. I hadn't been able to take Rum aside or even catch his eye to be sure this was all an elaborate ruse.

"He's with us," I insisted, forcing down my fears. "He's creating a diversion. Getting Candle to let his guard down."

Doll narrowed her eyes, still sceptical. After all the mud she'd been dragged through these past few weeks, I knew she wouldn't hesitate to send both Candle and Rum to the hangman and even offer to be the one to kick the stools from under their feet. But I couldn't bear to see Rum swing. I was still waiting for a sign, some hint to reassure me that his allegiance to Candle was a piece of trickery. I had to believe Rum was still loyal to our troupe and trade, a player to the bone.

"We'll bide our time and wait for an opportunity," Doll said at last. "Even if we outnumber him three to one, it's Candle who's bigger and carrying a blade. And you best believe that he knows how to wield it! I swear there's some evil spirit possessing his sword arm. He cut down seven men that night in Bristol. But he's tiring now. He hasn't touched a drop of ale, but he's drunk on weariness. I tell you, sooner or later, he'll start to slip. Just keep watching his hand…"

Doll nodded to Candle's fingers twitching by his sword hilt. Our captor didn't seem so fearsome in the frail light of day. His long limbs seemed stretched and taut like they'd been pulled on a rack. His face was pale and skull-like within the folds of his hood. His smile was a leering dispassionate thing with teeth clenched like a man enduring some painful surgery. The longer we marched and the harder the rain lashed down, the more often Candle was stumbling over the uneven ground. He would jerk himself up just as swiftly, turning to make sure nobody had tried to take advantage of his near falls.

"Could you do it?" Doll asked. "If you got chance?"

I knew what she was asking, but couldn't bring myself to answer. What Doll was proposing wasn't as simple as cracking a rock over the head of a suffering rooster. It was asking if I was prepared to blacken my own soul for our escape. It was no small price to pay. Candle was the killer, not us. For now, those were the main terms of our straining truce. But how easily could that line be crossed? If I failed Candle could slice all our throats with one broad sweep of his arm.

"Could you?" I asked, throwing the question back.

Doll flashed me a look then, sharp as a dagger in the dark.

"In my mind...I've done it ten times already."

As if sensing some threat in the sodden air around him, Candle turned on his heels, staring back at Doll and me. His eyes flashed with a bullying mirth. He'd noticed us falling behind and he'd seen our lips moving, swapping words he wasn't privy to. He couldn't have that. He needed to be a leech on our every conversation.

"How is it that a player ends up in the skirted roles?" Candle asked Rum. "Is it a penalty for unmanning himself?"

Lazily he drew his sword. Not to threaten or strike. Just to let the blade swing by his legs, a reminder of the power he held over us.

"I wouldn't know," Rum answered. "I was in britches for all the parts that I ever played in that theatre. Even before my voice cracked, I would never let Makaydees force me into a frock."

My heart gave a leap, knowing that Rum was lying. Knowing that he had loved every one of the languishing maidens he played. Yet here he was denouncing them so he might impress the highwayman with his swagger. And if Rum was lying about this, then it stood to reason that his whole demeanour must be a sycophantic charade.

"Yes, any healthy hot-blooded youth should want to play the hero roles," Candle asserted. And as he spoke, he was no longer looking at Doll and me, but staring over our heads at some sight in the distance. "Those lads a few stretches of land behind us, for example…I'm sure they fancy themselves as knights from the old ballads."

I followed his gaze, looking back behind me.

The rainy moors were shrouded in a thickening fog. But far off on the horizon I could see these *'heroes'* that Candle spoke of. A hazy line of men slowly marching towards us. They looked to be a small army – some forty strong at least. The Watch party from Bristol had seemed to have swelled in number since Candle had spread his flames through a new town. And they looked to be gaining on us. If we were not swift of foot, these hunters could be on us within an hour.

"How long have they been there?!" I blurted.

Candle just laughed, seeming delighted by this close pursuit. It was as if he took pride in having drawn such a crowd for the legendary last stand that he was no doubt envisioning for himself.

"Tis beyond the call of duty for those men to be slogging over this terrain, risking their skin just to catch a small gang of highway thieves. Maybe the price on my head has gone up? Maybe. But I think it would take more than coins to drive them on this arduous quest. These lads are caught up in the thrill of the chase. But we can outrun them. We'll make them sweat to death! Come squire. Set the pace!"

Candle thrust his sword arm into the wind, rain spattering its blade. He nodded for Rum to lead us in our charge. Rum gathered up the last ragged remains of his energy and then set off at a sprint. Candle turned back to Doll and me, motioning for us to follow at the same speed. It seemed he'd force us to run all the way to Plymouth with his sword at our backs, a pirate pushing us to walk the plank.

A short way ahead, we heard a sudden splash.

My head whipped around and I saw that Rum was no longer there. It was like he had just vanished into the fog. But turning my stare to the ground I saw that it was the earth that had swallowed him instead. Now I could only see one muddied arm flailing in the air. The grass around his arm shook and shifted in rippling waves.

"Bog carpet!" Candle exclaimed, taking a tentative step towards the hidden marsh where Rum was now mired. He pressed the blanketed grass with his sword tip. It wobbled and sloshed.

"What sly trick of nature is this?" Candle marvelled.

"Help him!" I yelled, my heart fit to burst.

Rum's head had not yet broken the surface of the peat bog he had been plunged into. Not trusting in Candle to rescue my friend, I rushed forward, reaching for Rum's hand. The flat of Candle's sword swung around to wind me in the stomach and shove me hard onto the ground. I blinked against the tears that sprang into my eyes, still struggling to reach the marsh. Candle snorted at my efforts, then turned his attention back to Rum. He tested the ground close to where he had fallen. After finding a sturdy mound to stand on, he extended his sword so that its blade was in clasping distance of Rum's fingers.

"Grab a hold!" he jeered, revelling in this drama. "Your salvation may sting but it'll be better than drowning in that filthy drink."

I looked across to Doll. The girl was staring at Candle's back, her hands flexing at her sides and her eyes alive with possibilities. This was something that could be called a chance. One well-aimed shove could send the highwayman headfirst into the swamp where his weapon could easily slip and sink into the muddy depths. It would be a risk, of course. We did not know if Candle could swim or not. But I could see Doll was tempted, ready to try. I had to reach out fast to grasp her ankle. She shot me a scowl, but still stopped in her tracks. I pleaded with my eyes, begging her not to attempt drowning our captor just now. Not when he would drag Rum to the bottom of the fens with him.

Rum's head was visible now, his lips gasping above the water and his eyes blindfolded by his roily black hair. With a heave, he threw up his arms and grabbed Candle's sword, letting out a yowl of pain as its blade cut into his palms. I felt sure we could've found a less injurious way to haul Rum to safety, but Candle clearly preferred him to bleed for this rescue. Maybe he didn't trust Rum as much as he pretended. Maybe it suited Candle to have him a little wounded, one less person who might snatch for his sword. Rum soon lay panting and dripping on firmer soil, staring down at the torn skin of his hands.

"I...I thank thee," he said, through gritted teeth.

"It was nothing, lad," said Candle. "And lo! I have added to your already impressive collection of scars! All the better for your new pirate personage." He cackled and strode over to where I still lay sprawled. I flinched as he reached for my arms. With two quick tugs he tore the sleeves from my shift. Candle turned away from me, handing the ripped cloth over to Rum. "Here's bandages for your hurts."

Candle raised his stare to the watchmen crossing the moor towards us. Doll stood staring too, a smile creeping onto her lips.

"Nowhere to run, highwayman," she whispered.

Candle lashed out with his fist, striking her hard across her jaw. Doll didn't cry out and managed to stay on her feet, but she didn't move fast enough to avoid his clutches. Candle seized her elbow, clapped a manacle on her wrist and attached the other to his free hand. He lifted his sword which was still slicked with Rum's blood.

"Remember, my dark doxy," he snarled. "If we're caught, mine will be the last body to fall. I swear that to all of you!"

I looked desperately to Rum, feeling ready to take whatever chance we could, now that Candle was threatening to slaughter all three of us before the watchmen closed in. Rum was already back on his feet, clothes filthy with marsh water, clutching the shreds of my dress in his bleeding fists. He came to stand at Candle's side.

"We'll go slow, testing the ground and picking a path through the mire. This bog carpet will slow them as much as us."

Candle laughed, shaking his head. "We've no need to escape now. All we need's a place to hide. A spot where we can watch the show."

"Show?" I asked, dreading where this was leading.

"Yes, my fairy boy!" said Candle, turning his manic stare upon me. "And you shall take the starring role!" He laughed again, his hysteria mounting. "Nature sets the best snares of all…that is what you learn from a walk across the moors, my little friends. Even the plants that grow here are savage. Have you seen those spiky red flowers that catch flies in their jaws and then drown them in their dew? The very land beneath our feet wants to eat us alive. It'll swallow those men hunting us whole! All we need is some bait for the trap."

The plan came spilling out of Candle in a giddy rush. He handed me a lantern from his pack, along with a tallow stick and tinder box, bidding me to light the lamp. In the wind and rain, this was no easy task. While I struggled to spark a flame, Candle told us the myth of the Will-o'-the-Wisps. The fool's fire that sprung up from marshlands and was known to lead weary travellers to a watery grave. As the story went in these parts, these torches were carried by callous pixies. That was where my role came in. Candle wanted me to cross the moors, to get close to our pursuers and use my lantern to lead them forth, like moths to its flame, luring them straight into the swamps.

"But that would drown me too!" I protested.

Candle waved aside my fears. "Those superstitious bumpkins from Buckfast are more likely to flee back to their homes than follow you. Peasants from these parts truly believe that there are hinkypunks and hobgoblins preying on these moors. Tis a wonder that they have braved it thus far. And if they do give chase...just stay light on your toes and skip over those soft patches of earth. You don't look like you weigh more than a fistful of feathers, little water sprite!"

Candle ruffled my hair in a cajoling friendly fashion, though I had the distinct impression that my drowning would be a pleasing perk to his scheme. My eyes darted between Doll and Rum, but neither of them offered me any excuses in their stares. With my lantern now lit, I could only rise to my feet, shaking myself in readiness.

"Remember," said Candle. "This is a horror show. I want you to fill this moor with ghostly cries and stir up fear in our hunters, enough fear to send them fleeing back to their village watches." He narrowed his eyes on me. "And I warn you now...don't think that you can save yourself by surrendering to those watchmen. If they've a noose ready for me then you best believe it will loop around you too. They strung up every one of my old gang when they couldn't catch me in Bristol. We're all the same outlaw ilk to their minds. Even if the Justice didn't sentence you to the gallows, they would still cart you off to the nearest correction house for being caught in such bad company. I hear tell that new inmates receive a whipping on arrival before being put to hard labour. Often it is a death sentence to the young and frail. Better to stay on the run, player boy. Best you stick with me."

As much as I loathed him, I didn't doubt that Candle spoke true. I was caught between two evils here and I might survive longer with the devil I knew. Candle rubbed a handful of mud into my hair then took the bandages from Rum's hands to add bloody red streaks to my filthy chemise. Holding my lantern aloft, I would appear like a gory spectre on the moors, a ghost girl lost in limbo. Satisfied with my unearthly visage, Candle ordered me to walk to my doom.

Out on the moors the rain had thinned, but the fog hung so thick that it was like the clouds had fallen from the sky. I could no longer see the army of watchmen that I was bound towards. It was dull and murky at midday and the very air felt sick, confused and bad-tempered. A flash of white lit my surroundings and a shriek tore from my throat, echoing over the land. Then just as suddenly the sky darkened again and a loud rumbling filled my ears. I'd seen the weather turn like this before. I'd watched it from the upstairs windows of the old farmhouse as lightning bolts sparked against the night and then disappeared in the blink of an eye. The storm had a way of twisting my voice, so when I screamed again, it sounded like a banshee wail on the wind.

I held my lantern above my head and kept howling until my throat was raw. I felt like I was standing on a very different kind of stage now, a stage with many hidden trapdoors and so many ways that a player could fall to his doom. And if I fell now then nobody would catch my hand and pull me back. I felt a thrill down my spine and a pulse in my blood as I approached the most dangerous crowd that I'd ever faced. A crowd that I couldn't even see. Until slowly, and almost imperceptibly, a shadow emerged through the mist.

I froze in my tracks as the lone figure drew nearer. It looked to be just one man, sent by the Watch to brave my moorland phantom.

And judging by his bearing he was no warrior, being of average height, lean in build and raggedy in apparel. But as he came closer my heart seized with a greater foreboding than if I'd been facing a bear.

"M-Makaydees?" I rasped, my throat full of thorns.

"Afraid, lad?" said the man from the mist, his voice unmistakable. "You're the one terrorizing this moor. Don't let your mask slip."

"What are you doing here?" I asked, still feeling like this must be a waking dream. "Why are you amongst those watchmen?"

"Much like yourself, I have been caught up in the act. Last night, after Lavern and I set off to recover you truants from that den of vice that you'd strayed into, we became entangled with efforts to put out a tavern fire. Then before we knew it we were being swept up in a mob of men chasing a stranger going by the name *Goodfellow*, but believed to be the highway thief, Robin Candle...last seen in the company of vagabond players." Makaydees looked me up and down. "So, are you taking directions from that vile degenerate now?"

I squirmed. "I'm pretending. Just like you."

"Don't remind me! I'm sick of feigning a West Country accent." He nodded over his shoulder. "Lavern's back there with the other men on this merry jaunt, trying to calm their nerves. They were scared enough by the storm before they saw your light and heard you wailing. I've been sent to confront the ghost haunting our passage. It turns out I'm the sole man of reason among these superstitious fools."

The thunder rolled again and I couldn't help flinching.

"Don't jump at the bad weather!" Makaydees chided. "There's no God in that sky who'll either strike you down or save your hide. There's only you and me, standing upon this wretched moor." He sighed. "So tell me. How shall we craft a way out of this mess?"

I floundered for an answer, too tired to think.

"How should I know? You're the playwright!"

"Yes, but the villain of this drama is beyond my reach. Will you be returning to him after this little occult charade?"

I nodded. "Tis my job to scare off the hunt. Either that or lead you into the swamps. There's bog carpet over yonder. Many miles of it perhaps. We'll be slow finding out a safe path." A thought struck me, a chance we might take. "You should lead the Watch back to the road. Even if they take the long way round, tis likely they'll reach Plymouth ahead of the highwayman. They can be lying in wait!"

"Oh, there's already a man lying in wait for him," said Makaydees with a bite to his words. "Wallace has taken our wagon on ahead. He knows these parts better than any of us. He's ready to fight Candle the moment he crosses his path. Look out for his smoke."

"Smoke?" I asked, struggling to follow.

"You'll know when you see it." Makaydees glanced back the way that he had come. "Hence now! You have your messages to deliver and I have mine. We'll both have to do our best to play puppet master over our respective parties, bending them to our will. You must bring Candle to a place where he may be seized and I must try to secure your escape so you aren't gaoled along with him. Take heart. Tis the little people like us who survive these revenge tragedies. Keep your wits about you and hold onto your nerve. Help is on the way."

My master was beginning to retreat in his steps. I wanted to rush after him, to cling to his hand and seek protection in his company. But with Rum hurt and Doll chained I might be the only one left who could offer them an advantage in our confidence trick.

"I...I can't believe you came," I said before he left me. "After what we did. Running away in the night. All the trouble we…"

Makaydees cut me off. "I should not have spoken to you as I did yesterday." He said this swiftly as possible, like it stung him to admit and he was trying to get it over with. "It's one thing to scold you for a foolish blunder. Quite another to talk as if you were worthless to my troupe." His jaw clenched. "A man once spoke to

264

me that way. Same man who raised me, if you wish to know. I wasn't much older than you at the time. And I walked out of his door, never to return, swearing that I'd never live in the shadow of another man's contempt again." He let out a sigh. "I should've known better than to use my words to wound a fellow dreamer. I took you from that farm with good reason, Timony. I never recruit a new member for my troupe on an idle whim. You and Rum are part of my cast. And I will be damned if I'll let that wretched highwayman steal any part of my theatre away from me."

With this oath, Makaydees spat in the mud, puffed out his chest and disappeared back into the swelling mist.

Scene Seven

The Devil's Campfire

"They ran away from me," I told Candle.

He just blinked. "They did what?"

"The hunters who saw my light," I clarified, marching back to the bank of the marshes. "They ran away screaming."

For a moment, Candle was speechless. His mouth twisted into a sneer like he wanted to dismiss my usefulness but was left stumped. The mist had begun to clear and we could see that the watchmen were indeed retreating, moving off westward. It looked like Makaydees had convinced them return to the safer passage of the road. Now I just had to pray I could stall our progress across the moors so that Candle could be caught before we made it to Plymouth dock.

Navigating the swamps was a long hard slog, especially for a band of travellers short on sleep and clumsy with exertion. Candle bid Rum and I to take the lead, using long branches to test the spongy soil that stretched out before us. Many times we were forced to backtrack or take breaks on small islands of firmer ground. The muggy heat had returned by late afternoon and we were ceaselessly swatting away flies that buzzed in our ears and drank up our sweat.

We needed rest, but none dared to take it, fearful that we'd never wake again. We were all watching Candle through the corners of our eyes, waiting for him to falter or flat out collapse in his weariness. The highwayman's head kept on nodding against his chest. He had taken to muttering to himself, like an actor jittery with stage fright, rehearsing his grand final speech, some soliloquy that would justify his terrible actions to come. He made furious gestures, brandishing his sword at the air around him, a mad spluttering shadow of a man. In this state, I almost had sympathy for him. He was lost in his imaginings just as I'd drifted into daydreams so perpetually on the farm.

"We're close now, *so close*," Candle panted, sidling up to me and seizing my nape. "Nearing that same port where Drake, the Dragon of the sea, set sail some twenty years ago. They say he was a murderer, in league with the Devil. Yet he circled the world, sunk fleets of Spanish ships, brought back slaves and riches and was knighted the Queen's own pirate. We can be heroes yet, lad! Our story's far from finished…"

This was the first time that Candle had spoken to me personally, treating me as a comrade. It seemed that my apparent spooking of the watchmen had finally earned me some measure of respect from the outlaw. As he walked alongside me, he still had one hand clutched to his sword hilt, while Doll was still shackled to his wrist. The girl had not spoken since he'd struck her. She just slunk behind him, silent as his own shadow. Rum meanwhile had taken over leading our way, holding the lantern aloft as the broody sky began to darken early. I was left as the sole audience to Candle's rants.

"What if we can't steal a ship?" I asked as his rough nails bit into my neck. "What if we're caught before we reach the harbour?"

He ignored my question. "Do you know where I could be now, lad?" He did not wait for my reply, but threw back his head in reverie. "I could be sat in a little chandler's shop, in a small unremarkable town, making candles and soap with my pa. Providing light and cleanliness to good honest working folk. It would've been a noble trade, yes? But alas...it wasn't right for me. Just as I was never right for the craft. I was too idle and distracted in my chores. I could never seem to focus..." He smiled, his eyes milking over. "When I was a young lad, when they still used to call me Robbie, I had this compulsion for making a spectacle of myself. I would stir up all kinds of trouble at the parish tavern. Dancing and hollering on top of the tables after barely a whiff of ale. A local legend before I had hairs on my chin!"

I stiffened at Candle's words, knowing only too well this lonesome frustration of not being seen for who you are.

"Being remembered...that is the important thing, right?" Candle went on as if he could see into my thoughts. "Being a legend. Leaving your fame and your footprints all over this rotten world. Ah yes, they say that fame brings a swift death to outlaws in these lands. But fame is also the only thing that lives beyond our time."

His eyes grew hazy at the prospect of his own illustrious death, which he seemed to believe would be recalled in folktales throughout the ages. And I knew now that Candle was a man close to his end. This would be the highwayman's last caper. There would be no New World for him...perhaps not even a new dawn.

"Smoke," Candle said softly, almost a whisper.

"What?" I asked, my skin prickling.

"Smoke." He nodded. "Over that hill yonder."

I followed his stare and saw that we were approaching a knoll. In the dusky light of near evening I could see thin tendrils of smoke rising up from just behind the hill. And not just any smoke. This smoke was tinged red. I would have thought that my eyes were playing tricks or that the smoke was catching the glow of sunset, if I hadn't seen Wally cooking up this same crimson mist from our campfire the day that I'd joined the troupe. I stood tensed, remembering my master's instruction and knowing Wally had taken the wagon on ahead.

"We've stumbled on the Devil's own campfire!" Rum exclaimed at the head of our parade. "Should we go sup with him?"

"Keep your voice down!" Candle hissed, beckoning Rum back to his side. "There are only two types of people who travel at nightfall during the midsummer months. The folk at that fire are either very foolish or very dangerous in their own right. Stay close to me all of you! We'll approach this camp with caution. In truth, I'd not expected to find any wayfarers to rob out here on the moors. Methinks we must be nearing the Plymouth road..." He clapped Rum's shoulder. "Perhaps we may begin your apprenticeship after all, squire!"

I threw a look over at Doll, wanting to reassure her with a glance that Rum was not Candle's accomplice, but ours. I hoped she'd believe me. I prayed that I was right to believe it myself. But when I met Doll's stare, her eyes were stony and blank, giving away nothing, giving the impression that she intended to *do* nothing. Doll had told me that she was trying to kill the highwayman with her silence, yet it seemed more like she was trying to disappear. I couldn't see her mind but part of me was wondering if all of Doll's waiting and fading into nothing was some cunning tactic that might just save us all.

We were huddled too close for any kind of conspiring. Candle put on his mask, pulled up his hood and drew out his sword as we came to the hillock and slowly began to climb. It wasn't fully dark yet, just the gloomy end of an overcast day, the light fading quicker than it ought. Candle told Rum to put out the lantern so the four of us were cloaked in shadow as we reached the summit of the knoll.

Down the slope below us, a horse and a wagon were parked on a rough country road. Even in the twilight, I could tell it was our horse and wagon. But strangely, I could see none of my fellows on the scene. Only one person stood before the fire. And that person was a woman. A little crone hunched over a gnarled walking staff.

"What's this?" Rum muttered. "A witch?"

The highwayman shook his head. "Nay. This old basket will be a traveller disguised in myth and magic, just like us. I do not know how she's conjuring the colour from her fire. But no matter. She has a wagon that'll see us the rest of the way to the harbour. You boys take the east slope and secure the horse, see it doesn't bolt. I'll come down the left side and surprise the little hag out of her hoodoo."

With a nod from Candle, we parted ways, Rum and I moving down the rightmost side of the verge, while Candle and Doll approached the wagon and its roadside camp from the rear. We crouched low, walking with ghostly tread. Staging an ambush gave

272

me the same bellyful of nerves as putting on a play. I had to remind myself we weren't meant to be helping this robbery, but foiling it.

"You know who that is, right?" Rum whispered in my ear, nodding to the crone that was walking circles round the fire.

"No, I..." My words dried up on my tongue. Because of course I knew. If Wally had taken the cart ahead and Makaydees and Lavern were caught up with the watchmen, then that left only one member of our company unaccounted for. "Mr Frank?"

"Old Woman Winter we call him when he's in skirts."

"But...but what is he doing out here all alone?"

"He won't be alone. He'll be playing lookout." Rum nudged me in the ribs. "Francis hasn't seen us yet. You need to warn him."

I flustered. "What? What should I...?"

"Scream. Scream at that snake by your foot."

"*SNAKE!*" I shrieked, leaping back.

There was no snake in the grass before me, but I still yelped like one had sunk its poisonous fangs into my ankle. Following my cry, Rum shoved me down, as if in irritation. I looked up from the sodden earth to see that Francis had snapped to attention and was rushing for the wagon. The horse was bucking and whinnying as Francis climbed up into the driver's perch and seized its reins.

"Halt and pay the toll!" Candle bellowed, rushing down the hill with his sword raised, dragging Doll behind him. "Make no attempt to fight or flee! You are at the mercy of Robin Candle and his…"

"Bless me! Robin Candle did you say?"

This question came from Francis in his Old Woman Winter guise. I got to my feet and drew nearer, compelled by the sight of Mr Frank in a frocked role, the part he'd told me he had always yearned to play. He might be too old for the damsels of our tragedies, but with his beard shaved, his head wimpled and his chest stuffed with a matronly bosom, he looked more feminine than my own ma.

"You're the Goblin King?!" he gasped. "God's wounds! I never dreamed I'd live to see you in the flesh, sir…"

Candle removed his mask and stood frowning, confused by this little crone's rapture at being at the mercy of his sword. He'd paid precious little attention to Francis during our last meeting on the road and showed no sign of recognizing him now.

"You…you know me by name?" Candle asked with a yearning in his voice that suggested that fame was the last crutch he was clinging to. "What have you heard about me, crone? What does my reputation mean to a lonely wandering wench in these lands?"

Francis leaned forward on his perch, hands clasped. "They say you were born Robert Chandler, but left that name behind you when you fled your old life as a soldier. They say that you're a devil with a blade and you painted the road red when you fought your way out of Bristol. They say your face turns green under the moon and that you can breathe fire if you're riled into a temper. I'm very much an admirer of yours, Mr Candle – collected every handbill that mentions you, gathered every scrap of gossip, keeping up with your adventures."

Francis rummaged in his apron pockets and took out the pamphlet that Makaydees had shown us back in Bristol, warning us of Candle's crimes and offering a reward for his capture.

"For years now it has been a habit of mine to follow the famous rogues of our times. And you, young Robin, you are by far the most notorious I've heard tell of. I never thought that I'd have the honour of being accosted by a man of your stature and renown, especially so close to the end of your career. Would you do me the honour of signing this, sir? I imagine your written name will soon be valued highly as silver, something to preserve me in my old age...oh, please, sir. Let me see your name set down by your own infamous hand!"

I watched Candle's face as Francis spoke. The flattery had lulled him into a false sense of security, but the fading highwayman hadn't missed the implication that he was close to his demise.

"Hold your tongue!" he snapped, waving his sword. "Else I'll cut it from your mouth and sign those damned pamphlets in your blood! If you're hoping to sell a few souvenirs at my hanging, who is to say you won't be leaving this world ahead of me, hag?"

Francis raised his hands. "Don't be hasty, sir! I've been composing poems and ballads in your honour. Who will sing them if you kill me? It grieves me to say it, but you are not so popular with other folks in these parts. Why I passed two orphaned sisters who'd lost their home and mother to that fire you spread through their town yester eve. Those girls will be left as demanders for glimmer – burning the tips of their hair, rubbing soot into their skirts and knocking upon doors to tell sad stories of how their lives were turned to ash. Tis a tale that tugs at the heartstrings, sir. A fire could happen to anyone."

"What do you know of fire?" he demanded. "By what trickery have you turned the smoke of your campfire red?"

"Oh, I was wondering when you'd ask!" Francis tapped the side of his nose. "Tis a secret mix of dyes and powders that colours it thus. A concoction that I learned from the gypsies. You will find more of their eastern magic in my wagon, sir…if you care to take a look."

An eager smile broke over Candle's face, a smile that seemed to dribble from his lips. Francis might not be a real witch but he'd cast a spell all the same. Candle was seduced by curiosity and quick to trust any complimentary words that came to his ears.

"Well, I wouldn't be any sort of highwayman if I didn't see to the plunder." Candle nudged me with his sword hilt. "Come, fairy boy. I'll have you assist me in testing and tasting these potions."

Francis clapped his hands, still playing the lickspittle, thrilled to have his carriage ransacked by so notorious a rogue. Candle barked orders to Rum to keep a hold of the horse and I followed at his side as we rounded the carriage. And already my heart thundering in my chest. Because I had already guessed the only thing 'gypsy' that Francis had stowed in the wagon was my friend, Wallace Farr.

Sure enough as Candle drew level with the rear wheels, there was a blur of large limbs as Wally burst from the back of the cart, slamming Candle onto the ground. Doll was dragged down with them, still being manacled to the highwayman's arm. I was almost knocked off my feet too as the fighters rolled towards me, grappling to pin each other down. I'd not expected Candle to put up so much resistance, but it seemed that desperation had given him a last burst of vigour.

The highwayman had not let go of his sword.

Slithering free from Wally's grip, Candle sprang back to his feet and pulled Doll in front of his chest, clutching her there like a shield, raising his blade to her neck. Wally got to his feet too, bug-eyed and breathless. Despite his formidable stature, I could see that Wally was no brawler. I could see he would throw all his strength into defending us, into saving his theatre family, so we wouldn't be lost like the gypsy clan he had left behind. But judging by the panic that had seized his face, Wally didn't have the stomach to battle Candle to the death, nor to risk the death of the girl he held hostage. Wally lifted something in his hand. Squinting, I saw it was a sword, albeit a wooden one from our props sack. Candle laughed at the mock weapon.

"What a clash we have here! I'm sure many gamblers would have loved to put money on this bout. What are you prepared to lose, Moon man? How about this girl's head? You know, the law won't even count me leaving two coloured corpses in my wake..."

I stood gasping and helpless, fearing that Candle had defeated us already. I knew that Wally would not risk an attack if an innocent girl's head could roll between them. When I turned to stare at Doll, there was still no hint of terror in her eyes. But I noticed there was something else that had changed. Her hands hung free at her sides. Doll had boasted that she could slip her wrists free from the manacles at need. It looked like she'd waited for the most opportune moment.

Doll threw her head back, her skull cracking Candle hard in the chin, knocking him off balance. In the same burst she rammed an elbow into his ribs. In her starved state, I can't imagine these blows had much strength behind them. But it was enough that Candle had not seen them coming. With her captor stunned and winded, Doll wrenched his sword arm to the side and broke loose from his hold.

"Now!" she cried out. "Take him *now!*"

Wally didn't waste his chance. He lunged forward, smashing his prop sword upon Candle's skull, splitting it in two. The highwayman reeled as blood came streaming from his temples and nose. But still he didn't lose his footing, nor drop his sword. As Wally charged towards him, tackling him to the ground, the deadly blade was lost somewhere between the crush of their bodies. The two men wrestled in the dirt, their knees and elbows slapping in the moorland mud. My thoughts flashed back to the cockfight of the night before. Like those duelling birds, this was a fight with no rules, just a lot of writhing and snarling till one lay vanquished and one rose triumphant. Candle was the smaller man in this struggle, but his reflexes were as quick as a wild cat. There was a flash of steel, like the spurs on the heels of his gamecock. Then Wally collapsed upon his back. Candle's sword was finally out of his hands, its tip now buried in Wally's heaving chest.

"Stop him!" Rum's voice cried out as he rushed towards the fray, Francis close at his heels. "Grab his arm, Timmy!"

The world had been whirling so fast, but now time became slippery and slow. The highwayman had found his feet again. He was reaching for his sword, poised to drive it deeper into Wally's already bleeding body. I threw myself on his arm, wanting to yank it from its socket so he couldn't stab my friend a second time. Candle's free hand whipped across his chest, smacking me hard in the face with the loose manacle cuff. I staggered, dazed from the blow. But I didn't let go. Not even as Candle's gloved hand fastened around my throat, pressing down my windpipe till I choked. I struggled for air, my eyes blurring with tears, blinding me from whatever was coming next.

What came was a blast of flame close to my cheek and Candle's piercing scream in my ear. I felt his fingers loosen from my neck and then his arm was falling away. I wriggled free of him, staggering back and blinking at the sight of Doll holding a burning branch to Candle's hood. She must have seized the stick out of Francis's campfire. Now its flames were scorching the highwayman's cheek and licking into his hair. His mask slipped from his crown and covered his wailing face. Candle crumpled at Doll's feet. He pawed at her skirts like a pleading dog, but she kept the brand thrust against his throat until his ruff was set alight, curling and blackening as it burned.

The highwayman thrashed and slapped at his smouldering clothes. Then suddenly he spluttered out a laugh. For even in his toils it seemed he could appreciate the irony. He had become his own name, a candle man about to be snuffed out. The tallow of his mask was melting and dribbling green wax. In his giddy unravelling state, Candle reached out and grasped for my ankle, trying to pull me to the ground, desperate to drag one other person onto his pyre with him.

But before he could Rum was there at my side. With his palms torn up, he couldn't wield a sword, but that didn't stop him lashing out with his feet. One swift kick to his stomach and Candle's hand fell back onto the muddied ground. The flames were eating through to his skin now. With the last of his crazed strength, Candle rolled on his belly, wetting his burning body in the sodden earth. The flames finally hissed out and the highwayman was left a heap of raw red limbs.

Soon as Candle had stilled, I turned my attention to Wally. Francis reached him first, hoisting up his skirts, his old knees cracking as he sank down at his side. He pulled off his wimple and used it to staunch the blood leaking from Wally's shoulder. The sword was northwest of Wally's heart, but still stuck deep in his flesh. Francis cautioned us not to withdraw it. Wally's eyes were open. He sucked air into his lungs and swallowed the sweat that poured from his brow.

"We best hurry him to the wagon," said Doll, the damsel turned hero of this drama. "We're not far from Plymouth. I know the Madame of one of the brothel houses here. She'll see that his wound is cleaned, dressed and treated with the best poultices she has."

"I'll get him stitched up during the ride," Francis vowed. "I always knew it was worth learning to sew in the dark."

Rum nodded to Candle. "What of him?"

Doll stared at the pile of human ashes she had made of our captor, then looked off into the far distances of the moor.

"Leave him. The Watch are on their way."

I followed her gaze and sure enough I could see the torches of the militia approaching on the southbound road. They were almost on us. Rum curled his lip and kicked Candle again.

"We'll leave him in his own shackles!"

It was only when Rum mentioned the manacles that I felt it. My limbs had been numb till that moment, a tingling shock that'd stopped me from feeling the ring of iron round my ankle. And I knew now why Candle had grabbed me. He had chained me to him, his hand cuffed to my foot. The outlaw would not be caught alone.

Rum looked down and saw it too. His eyes went wide with rage and without any hesitation he pounced on Candle, straddling his body and pummelling him in the chest with his fists.

"Free him!" he snarled. "Now! Or I swear I'll..."

Rum didn't need to finish his threat. I could see in his eyes what he was prepared to do. What he would do with his bare hands if he had to. But I didn't want Rum to make himself a murderer over me. Even if my heart lurched knowing he *would* do that for me.

"Get Wally on the road!" I yelled, yanking Rum to his feet. "Go before it's too late! I'll see the Watch gets their man."

Rum stood breathless for a moment, then he reached for Wally's legs as Francis and Doll carefully lifted his torso between them. It took a straining effort from all three of them to haul Wally into the wagon. Francis stayed beside him, keeping pressure on his wound, while Doll climbed up to the driver's perch and seized hold of the reins. Rum ran to the head of the wagon too, but he didn't jump aboard. He just slapped his hand hard against the horse's hind, sending it off at a gallop. As the wagon rattled up the road, Rum returned to my side.

"Did you think that I'd leave you alone with this piece of smoking dug?" Rum said, before I could scold him for staying. He scowled at the man chained to my foot. "He still breathing?"

I nodded, feeling a wheeze beside my ankle.

"I...I reckon he has passed out from the pain. But he's not dead. Not yet. And it's best we keep him that way. He's worth more to those watchmen alive. And maybe we can still claim the reward on his head? Maybe they'll think us heroes for bringing him in?"

Rum snorted, shaking his head. "Some hero I make. I should have taken my chances and tackled Candle long before now. Before he could stab Wally or try strangling you. I thought that I could play him, Timmy – thought that I could trick him into friendship and get close enough to snatch his sword. I should have saved us all! But every time a chance came, I...I couldn't act. I kept thinking of the last time I found myself at the wrong end of a blade..." He winced, pressing a hand to his cheek. "To think we had to be saved by a *girl*. These scars have made a coward of me. They ought to have made me a man..."

His voice was bitter and tinged with tears. And I wanted to tell Rum that it meant more to hear him cry in this moment than it would have to see him run the highwayman through and become our dashing rescuer. Because this felt like the first time he was being vulnerable with me. The first time that he was letting his mask slip and showing me something real. I wanted to say he was a hero just for staying with me. I wanted to admit how scared I would have been to be left here alone. But I was still shy about being real with him in return. So instead I clasped him by the hand and tugged him close.

"Tis a relief to know you were always on our side. All actors get stage fright sometimes. You're still the best actor I've ever seen. I look forward to acting with you...when we find our next crowd."

"If we're ever *allowed* to put on another play!" said Rum with grim foreboding. "I wouldn't bet any coins on that just yet." We stared out across the moor at the approaching hunt. "I can't make any wagers on where we'll wake tomorrow, Timmy. But right now, I'd say if we live to see a new dawn...I'll count that as a win."

Scene Eight

The Punishment Platform

Rum and I spent the rest of the night in a cell.

After so long on the run, our bodies were thankful for the rest, even if our minds were fraught over what was to come next. Our stuffy little prison was secluded below the floorboards of the Plymouth courthouse and within its walls we could catch up on missed sleep, heal our blisters and cool our sunburn. But this respite wasn't enough to allay our fears that we were now just a trial and short trek away from the gallows. The noose was waiting and now there was no one to fill it.

Candle had died on our journey to the port.

In the end, the legendary highwayman had slipped away quietly, so quiet his death hadn't even been noticed by the watchmen who had bundled all three of us into our shared gaol. I'd had the displeasure of spending the first night of our confinement with my foot chained to a corpse. In our darkened cell, Rum had done his best to calm me down whilst searching Candle's body for what had caused him to expire. One side of his face was mottled with burns that had blanched and swollen his skin. But they didn't look to be fatal wounds.

It wasn't until Rum peeled back the highwayman's sleeve that we found a tiny silver blade lodged in his wrist. It was one of the spurs from his winning gamecock. It'd been used for a self-inflicted death blow that must have been dealt during our ride in the watchmen's cart. We could only conclude that Candle must've cut himself and bled out mutely in the straw, his suicide veiled in shadow.

His death was the final trick that the highwayman played on us. He had escaped from his own cooked flesh and the certain execution he was sure to suffer and left us with the legacy of his last crime spree. I could've sworn when first light crept into our cell and the blacksmith finally arrived to detach his charred carcass from my ankle, it looked like he'd died with a smile on his lips. Because if the lynch mob who had hunted him all the hot summer long were no longer able to see him swing, then we were the only scapegoats left to slake their bloodthirst. Or as Rum put it our second night in the cell –

"They'll still want a show. If Candle's dead, then they're going to demand an understudy. And it's bound to be me."

"W-w-why you alone?" I asked him, my stammer threatening to resurface. "They caught us on the moor together."

"We each have a part to play here, Timmy," he sighed. "When they take us upstairs to the court, you'll be convincing enough as a hostage, whereas I'll look more like a henchman. I suppose that ever since I got these scars I've been destined for the villain's role."

We sat with our backs pressed to the cellar wall. I was close enough to feel Rum shudder. I reached out to clasp his knee.

"I told you to go! Why didn't you go with the wagon?"

"And let you have all the attention to yourself? Not a chance! Can you imagine the crowd that our trial is going to draw?"

I forced a smile, meeting Rum's stare, tears threatening in both our eyes. In truth, I don't think my sanity would have survived that cell if he hadn't been with me. There was so much more I should've liked to say to Rum if we had been alone. But the cells beneath the courthouse were crammed with a revolving rabble of lowlife miscreants. Men who were brought in stinking of ale and bleeding from cudgels. Women who had been hauled in after night-walking and catting around the harbour inns. Our cellmates were never detained for long, but they'd heard tell of who we were and spent their stay pestering us with questions on our adventures with Robin Candle. We gave no answers.

"Fame's no friend to an outlaw," Rum reminded me. "They could be spies sent by the Justice to gather evidence against us."

So to be safe, we kept our lips tight and our whispers only in each other's ears. It wasn't till the third morning that we received a visit from a familiar face. Lavern slipped into our prison costumed in a cassock, disguised as a holy man come to minister to the poor sinners who were awaiting their sentence. With his fair face and saintly manner, it was a role he was well suited to. Rum had to slap a hand to my mouth to stop me blurting Lavern's name and blowing his cover. We let him do the rounds with the other inmates before he came to us.

"Wally...?" Rum began, struggling to ask the question which had been weighing heaviest upon our minds. "Is he...?"

"He's alive," Lavern assured us. "He's a little weak from blood loss and he hasn't got the feeling back in one arm. But there's no sign of infection. Your friend Doll managed to smuggle him into a quiet room of the best brothel house in the harbour. She's been telling tales of his clash with Candle and the ladies are all fawning over his bedside. I dare say their attentions are hastening his recovery! Francis is there with him – hasn't left his side and keeps touching up his stitches like the wound is an embroidered doily. They are in good spirits." A smile rose on Lavern's face and then faltered. "Or at least, they would be…if we weren't worrying ourselves sick over you lads."

"Why are we being kept here so long?" I asked in a jittery whisper. "The other prisoners come and go within hours."

"Have patience. It's taking a bit longer to gather compurgators to speak in your case," Lavern explained. "Witnesses are travelling here from Buckfast and Bristol. But do not despair. We've got people who will speak in your defence. People with influence."

"And others who will want to see us hanged in the highwayman's stead, I warrant," said Rum, slumping despondently.

"It won't come to that!" Lavern insisted. "Everyone knows that Candle was the true villain of this past month's drama. They've hung his body in a gibbet in the main square. That gory spectacle seems to have satisfied the mob for now. Maybe when your trial comes, their rancour will have rotted like the flesh off his bones."

"When *do* we go to court?" asked Rum.

"A few more days. Mak will be prepared by then."

I frowned. "Makaydees? Prepared for what?"

"He's acting as your lawyer, of course," said Lavern.

I sat up with concern. "Is that a safe plan? Won't he risk his own neck if someone guesses he's only pretending to be a…"

"Haven't you told him?" asked Lavern with a look to Rum.

Rum shrugged, sinking a little lower down the wall.

Lavern rolled his eyes and continued. "Our master is no counterfeit lawyer, Timony. He doesn't need a jarkman to provide a false license so he can speak for you in court. Law's the profession he was born into. His father is a London judge. Leastways he was the last time that Mak saw him. That was ten years ago, after Mak finished his schooling and apprenticeship. Not long after earning his license, he fled from the city and headed to the coast. That was when he started his first theatre at Barrentine's tavern. Mak said that he wanted to use his learning tell the stories of outlaws, not to cast judgement upon them."

It was something to finally hear where my master had come from. To know that he had been a runaway like me, albeit one from a higher educated upper-class family. Makaydees tended to keep his personal history as close to his chest like the handkerchiefs he used to stuff his jacket. But I supposed his study of the Poor laws must have kept his troupe out of the correction houses this long.

"So he'll craft a better ending for us?"

"He always does," said Lavern, patting my shoulder. "Don't look so doomed, lads. We'll get you up in the free air."

Lavern didn't linger with us any longer, but moved on to pastor to other prisoners. Rum still seemed unconvinced that we'd be so easily acquitted. He kept scratching at the new scabs on his palms and the old rents in his cheeks, like these scars had marked him out as a criminal and he wished he could somehow rub them away.

It was not until another three days later that Rum and I were finally taken from the cells and led up to the courtroom. By this point we were in no state to make a goodly presentation of ourselves. We'd spent a week sitting unwashed in a cramped cellar. We were pale from lack of sunlight. We had eaten only scraps from the alms basket. We stank of other people's sweat and filth as much as we did our own. I felt faint and breathless just from the walk upstairs. That was before the bailiffs brought us to the bar, standing us on a platform surrounded by ruddy faced men, already hollering out accusations.

"I told you we'd get a crowd, Timmy," Rum whispered, our dire situation bringing out the dark humour in him.

Our trial began with the charges, which seemed to come at us from all sides. Angry voices and their damning words bombarded my ears. My head span as I struggled to take in everything being said about us. The men gathered described Rum as a budding rogue and sneak thief. Some claimed that he had been seen picking pockets at Buckfast fayre while I'd danced to distract their attention. The men called me a 'wild dell'. Others argued that I was a doxy instead. I had heard these terms before. During our gaol time, Rum had explained that dells and doxies were unwedded women on the highway, with the difference being that a doxy was one who'd lost her maidenhead to a footpad like him. And even though Rum and I had shared a sham tryst in the tent of the horse courser, it pained me to think that (if our hearing went ill) I could go to the noose having never experienced a true deflowering.

"So, they think me a girl?" I whispered to Rum.

"*Shush*! It may go in your favour if they think you're one of the fairer sex. Even if you don't look too fair just now."

This was right enough. I was still dressed in the ragged smock, its once white cloth now blemished with dry blood, grass stains and muddy water soaked through its skirts. My hair was a knotted nest, my limbs were covered in scabs, bruises and bug bites and I was itching from some manner of rash. I must have looked the foulest female imaginable. But it gave me some consolation that I had finally become convincing in my role. I was so pleased with this little victory that I could scarcely focus on the recriminations being bandied round the room. Words like *thievery*, *knavery* and *accomplices* filled up the air.

"Will any offer a defence against these charges?"

This question was spoken from the jowly face of the Justice of the Peace, who sat in a raised seat, presiding over our trial. And at his summons, a man stepped up to the bar beside us. And I must've been running a fever, because it took me a moment to recognize this man as Makaydees. My master had swapped his showman's colours for a neat grey suit. His beard was trimmed and his long hair was bound back from his face. But soon as he opened his mouth, he spoke with the same vainglorious mettle I'd come to expect from him.

"Aye sir! Never have I heard so many slanders made against two so undeserving scapegoats!" Makaydees blasted. "As you will shortly learn, your Honour, these plucky urchins who stand before you are not only innocent of any collusion with Robin Candle, but are in fact the chief heroes who brought an end to the highwayman. I speak as one who joined this watch party pursuing Candle over the moors and I am aware that this court room is filled with many a wounded ego. You see, these two daring young paupers succeeded where the men twice their size failed in their long hunt. But you don't have to take my word for it. Let me call forth my witnesses." He turned to the back of the court. "Miss Elizabeth Barrentine and her ward, Dorothy."

Makaydees made a flourishing gesture as two cloaked figures rose and came forward to stand before the judge. As they drew back their hoods, I saw our star witnesses were the women I knew as the Madame and my friend Doll. They were both dressed rather more demurely than when I'd first met them, but their faces were still sultry and enchanting. Our judge sat upright, a lusty gleam in his stare.

"Your Honour," said the Madame. "Let me begin by saying this young Moorish maid you see here is dear to me as a daughter. As you may guess from her complexion, her own poor mother was ravished by a Barbary pirate and later died in childbirth. I've since raised the girl as my own, putting her to work in my humble tea shop."

Doll had told me that it was her own mother or grandmother who had been a pirate queen. But if there was one thing, I'd learnt from my time with the players it was that stories may be twisted to suit the ears that hear them. The judge seemed more willing to listen to women he saw as pretty victims than as warrior women.

"Go on, sweet lady," he said, his eyes glazing.

"In all my days living in the harbour, I've known many an upright man who's sought to steal my little rare bird away from me. Most men lose their heads over her exotic beauty, offering me fat purses for one stroke of her warm brown skin. But I've never let the girl be touched. She's a shy virtuous lass who spends most her evenings at prayer. How I'd hoped to protect her from the evils of this world!"

I wondered how much Makaydees had bribed the Madame for this performance. She was a consummate actress, wringing emotion from every word of her impassioned speech. Even though I'd come to value my role as our troupe's heroine, it had to be said that the laws against women on the stage were a lamentable loss to our craft.

Doll, meanwhile, was biting down hard on her lip, looking like she was struggling not to laugh. She glanced over her shoulder, daring to wink in my direction, revelling in this little charade.

"The night the highwayman snatched my poor lass away I thought I might die of a broken heart. My only hope had been the watchmen of Bristol swearing to return my little Doll to me. But my girl has told me since that it was none of these bold brawny lads who spared her from a life of slavery. No, it was these scruffy waifs at the bar who took on the highwayman and set her free. So, we have come here today to return the favour. Though may I add that these ragged angels deserve more than a pardon, your Honour. They ought to receive that reward on Candle's head for putting out his flames once and for all."

The judge sat back in awe over her testimony.

"Is this all true, Miss?" he asked, turning to Doll.

Doll stepped forward, bobbing in a meek curtsy.

"Every word, sir. Twas them that saved me."

From the trembling of her lips, you would never guess that it was Doll who had saved *us*. That it was she who had burned

Candle till he was begging for mercy. Madame Barrentine thrust out her elegant chin while Makaydees cast her a sly smile. The two of them were wearing matching expressions of triumph. And I could see this was a plot they had hatched, the same bargain I had struck with Doll – to secure the reward then split it between us. I'm sure that there was some measure of sincerity in the Madame's gratitude that Doll had come out of this skirmish with her life. But I was doubly sure that Makaydees was making another theatre out of this courtroom.

Which was why I flinched at what the judge did next.

He began to clap. A slow contemptuous applause.

"You make a strong case, Mr Makaydees," said the Justice of the Peace. "Or should I say...you put on quite the show? Yes, you've done well today, considering it must be some ten years or more since you've stepped inside a courtroom as a lawyer. And from what I've heard – in all that time – you have done well to avoid being brought to the bar yourself...for the contemptible life you've chosen to lead."

My master's face fell, its proud flush draining.

"I'm sorry...do I know you, sir?" he asked haltingly.

"You may not have seen fit to remember me, Arthur," said the judge, a pernicious victory in his own stare now. "But I remember your name and bearing. We were at school together. And even then, you were too lost in your own lofty ideas to pay much mind to those around you. And then you went off to fritter your life away on this failed theatre. Yes, your father told me all about you. Whilst he lived."

Makaydees winced, turning a shade paler.

"I didn't not know that he…when did he pass?"

"Just two years after you left, never to return," said the judge. "You may have driven the poor man to an early grave, abandoning him and your mother with only your ugly unmarriable sister at home. Yes, your father was in the habit of cursing your name in front of his pupil lawyers who were left behind. Loyal apprentices like me..." His smile widened. "How does it feel, Arthur? Staring on what you might have become? It could've been you sitting in my chair this day."

Makaydees, for once, was left speechless. His jaw tightened and his eyes blazed, but he couldn't seem to utter a word. A hush had fallen over the courtroom. Doll and the Madame had drifted to the rear of the chamber, cautiously distancing themselves from our case. Meanwhile the crowd of watchmen who had been so demeaned by the playwright were all looking vengefully eager to hear a verdict.

"Don't look so stricken, Arthur," said the judge with a wave of his hand to trivialize our plight. "I would never seek to abuse my position. I would never sentence a man to hang for vagrancy."

Makaydees stiffened. "I'm not a beggar."

"Oh, so your theatre has a patron then I take it?"

My master's eyes flashed bright with fury.

"This theatre belongs to me! I am its playwright, its courtesy man and I retain sole ownership over all its creations!"

"Ah! So this script we found in Robin Candle's pack..." The judge lifted a small heap of parchments from the desk before him. "*Mirabelle, the Pirate Bride*...this is one of your own works I take it? The hand it is written in matches that on the documents you have submitted to my court today. And yes, I am afraid unlicensed writings are something you will have to take responsibility for. These pages will have to be sent to the Privy Council for closer inspection. In the meantime, *you* Arthur Makaydees stand charged with vagrancy. Our law stipulates that all players performing without proper authority are nought but sturdy beggars. It is therefore my solemn duty to sentence you to sit a day and night in the stocks before you are taken forthwith to the nearest house of correction...to cure you of your idle ways."

My jaw fell open as Makaydees was seized by two constables and marched towards the courtroom doors. There was a commotion among the watchman, who were thrilled with this sentence and the chance to inflict their own punishment on the playwright who had mocked them. For a moment it seemed that Rum and I had been forgotten and our case thrown out. Then the judge raised a quietening hand.

"As for these filthy whelps...even if this tale about them bringing down the highwayman is true, it doesn't change what they are. For I'll wager they're both actors in this unlawful theatre. A troupe so sordid it puts *girls* on its stage going against the conventions of our reputable London playhouses. As they look to be over the age of fourteen, they'll share the penalty of their master. Take them!"

There was no time for words between us. Rum and I were both grabbed from behind, hauled into the streets and swiftly born towards the punishment platform. The first sight to meet my eyes as we reached the Plymouth square was that of a large rusty gibbet hanging above the stage, swinging a little in the light sea breeze. Candle's corpse was still displayed within, but after a week's exhibition in the harbour its skin and organs had largely been eaten away by the gulls, leaving only his festering brown bones still trapped in the cage.

By the time Rum and I were dragged onto the stage, Makaydees was already sat with his ankles encased in the middlemost stocks. There were foot holes either side of him and the constables were only too happy to lock up the legs of two more convicts. We were seated on the bench to the left and right of our master. The wooden board was lifted, brought down and fastened around our feet, trapping us for the rest of the day and night to come. It was a bright morning, which promised to be the prelude to a scorching afternoon. The swollen yellow sun above us would be our tormentor even if all gathered here were willing to let us alone. But it was clear from the spiteful looks of the crowd before us they had no intention of leaving us unharmed.

My mind flashed back to my last morning on the farm when my brother had turned the scarecrow's struts into an improvised pillory then pelted me with rotten eggs and vegetables. From what I could see with my sun-dazed eyes, the rabble in the square had brought harder hitting ammunition with them to this show. I could see sticks, stones and bread so stale that it would bruise like rocks. I threw up my arms, preparing to shield my face, but our guards were already removing the shabby remains of our shoes, offering our bare soles as soft targets for their projectiles. We couldn't avoid what was coming.

When the assault came, most of what was hurled was aimed at Makaydees. He was the biggest target for the mob and the one who had done the most to incur their wrath. My master held himself still, his arms folded tight across his chest and his lips clamped closed. Whilst he was careful to duck any missiles that sailed towards his head, he did not cry out when he was struck anywhere else upon his body. And he was struck again and again. I looked over and saw Rum was following our master's lead, straightening his spine and bracing himself for new scars. I forced myself to mimic their stoic postures. I held firm and tried not to whimper at all the sudden stings that flared over my body. Never in my life had I wanted to cry more than I did right now and never in my life had I been more determined not to.

Then suddenly there was a figure pushing through the crowd to the stage, struggling to move between the sweaty mass of bodies. It was Lavern, out of his cassock, but still just as saintly as he bounded onto the platform and planted himself before Makaydees. He spread his arms wide, preparing to shield us from the tirade.

The crowd stilled, muttering in confusion.

"What's the matter, ye cowards?!" Lavern scolded them. "Will you not throw stones at a man who stands upon his feet?"

For a moment nobody moved. I expected the constables to drag Lavern from the platform for spoiling the crowd's sport. But then a sharp hunk of wood hit Lavern's chin and sent blood gushing from his lip. The guards only shrugged and bid him to stay.

"Lavern, get down!" Makaydees hissed. "Think man! If you stand with us, you'll be bound for the Correction House too!"

Lavern threw a glance over his shoulder, his stare resigned. Ever since I had known them, Makaydees and Lavern seemed to have been locked in some age-old squabble. But as their eyes met now, I saw what lay beneath their bickering. I saw they were a family as well as a troupe. A family who feared for each other's safety and couldn't stand to see one another hurt. Lavern stood rooted, shaking his head.

"If you have a role to play here, master, then so do I. You always give me your epilogues. I'm always the last man standing on your stage. So I'll be staying on these boards till this act is over."

"Lavern," Makaydees began. "Dear heart…"

Lavern smiled and turned his bloodied chin back to the crowd. The crowd who were now slowly lowering their arms.

Scene Nine

The Road to Correction

True to his word, Lavern remained on the platform throughout our spell in the stocks, protectively pacing the stage and sometimes singing in an effort to cheer our spirits. Without his lute, Lavern still had a beautiful voice, even as he sang through split swollen lips.

The mob largely dispersed by midday. Many of the complainants in the Candle case had to head back to their home parishes. By nightfall when it came time for the constables to retire, they chained Lavern to the whipping post, saying he'd be taken to the correction house with the rest of us and threatening that a young gallant like him would soon find himself on a ship bound for the Spanish war.

"We'll run," said Rum, once the square was shadowed and empty. "We've fled from trades we were forced into before."

We nodded with heads that we could barely hold up. In my heart, I was right behind Rum, but my body could only shudder at the prospect of an escape attempt. My soles were so welted and torn that I feared I would collapse after only a few paces. I was battered, sunburnt and sick with thirst. My fellows were in no better shape. And it wasn't until the very darkest quietest time of night that Francis came scurrying into the square, carrying a large jug of water with him. Only then could we cool our throats and wince as the old man stooped down to wash our abused feet. Only then could we start to feel human again.

"Wally will be well enough to travel tomorrow," Francis assured us. "We'll be following you. We'll get you out."

Makaydees snorted. "Bless you for the jest, Francis, but I fear that it will take more than a greying tailor and a wounded gypsy to bring down the walls of a Bridewell. Raids on houses of correction are not unknown. However, I hear they are most often carried out by bands of drunken townsmen and the only inmates liberated are the loose women they wish to take back to their taverns. For myself, I cannot sit around like a helpless maid waiting for a rape and pillaging party. No, I'll come up with an escape plan. You and Wally keep a safe distance, lest you be caught yourselves. Mark me, that's an order."

"If you say so, Mak. But we won't just flee."

"We'll count on it," said Makaydees, clasping Francis by the hand. "We'll need you lying in wait with the wagon. If we do get loose, we won't get far on foot. And who else would offer us a ride?"

"What about Doll?" I asked. "Is she still in town?"

Francis's face crumpled into a sad smile. "Aw, I'm sorry, Timmy. Your little friend left this morning with her mistress. The Madame insisted that they return to Bristol right after your trial went so ill. She could not risk being dragged down with you. A wise woman I'd say. And a fair one to be sure. Both ladies swore if we got out of our current strife then we could stop by their tea house sometime and take our share of their loot. They may not have seen a penny of the reward that the watchmen pocketed, but they kept hold of Candle's sword and mask. Such souvenirs will go for a hefty price in the town where he wrought so much damage. They say they'll be saving our cut."

"Even if I trusted Bess to stick to that bargain..." said Makaydees, "...I know better than to return to that harbour. No, if I get us out of this mess and back on the road, then we won't go begging at the doors of whorehouses. We make our own coin. We'll be our own masters again. Have faith, lads. The curtain's not closed on us yet."

Francis nodded and did not linger any longer for fear that he'd been seen by a night watch patrol and chained up alongside Lavern. There was nothing to do for now but wait until the dawn. In the meantime, Makaydees was willing to suffer Rum and I lying down on our sides and each resting our heads in his lap. Lavern leaned into the whipping post, letting it hold him upright as he rested his eyelids too. It was in this state that the constables found us at first light, waking us with kicks and cuffs before bundling us into a tumbrel. They chained us together by our feet, then set off on the northbound road.

"Forget what I said last night..." Rum moaned, curling up in the cart's straw. "It pains me too much to *stand* let alone run." He threw his head back in the manner of the damsels he'd once played. "Let me sleep or let me die! When we reach the correction house, I'll take my lashes and be put to work. Just let me sleep till..."

"Hush your theatrics so I may hear myself think!" Makaydees snapped. "Tis bad enough that my mind is sun baked and sleep deprived without having to listen to your lamentations. And might I add that if I don't come up with an escape plan, we shall likely suffer worse than a few stripes on our backs and a week's worth of hard labour. It's what comes *after* our correction we must fear. As our guards at the platform said...any able-bodied man will be snatched up and sent to fight the Spaniards. That will mean *you* Rum as well as Lavern. Or you may be shipped the other way to the Irish war. They could make you a kern and pit you against your own countryman! And even *that* fate is a picnic when compared to what they'll have planned for me."

"Why?" I asked. "What are they planning?"

"They've got one of my scripts, lad," said Makaydees. "In our last month of toils, I'd not noticed it missing. Candle must have lifted it that night we gave him and his gang a ride into Bristol. Now my Mirabelle is being delivered to the Privy Council. My play will have a little trial of its own to decide if its words bear any additional offenses. And we all know what the verdict will be. That fat pompous judge knew it too. He was contriving to permanently remove the quill from my fingers. Or rather, to remove my fingers from their fondest compulsion."

"They'll stop you writing again?" I asked.

Makaydees pinched his temples, exasperated. "If my writings are deemed to be seditious or heretical then the punishment will be to sever those parts of my anatomy guilty of inscribing them."

I could only shake my head. "What?"

"They'll hack off my hand, boy."

This doom made my own hands feel numb where they clung to my knees. *No...*this could not happen. I needed my master's plays for my acting craft to flourish. Without his scripts, my own arms would have no reason to gesture. My feet would have no prompts to move them. My throat would have no stories to tell. It would cripple me too. Our theatre would lose too much blood and hope to recover.

"I always said that script went too far," said Lavern. "We really should've cut the Pirate King's lines when he boasts of his nights spent in the bedchamber of our supposedly virgin queen."

"But that speech gets the loudest laugh of our show!" Makaydees protested. "What peasant doesn't enjoy a smirk over good old Queen Bess lusting after her royal sea dogs? And my plays are written for the common folk of the little parishes we tour through. They are not for the gentry who have pet player troupes of their own. But yes, my script makes a few teasing remarks against our sovereign and her humourless officials will surely see fit to misread some treasonous intent into it. They must invent an occasion for another gory spectacle. So they will take my hand to the block and they will slice it off with a red-hot blade. They'll spray the stage with more blood than I have ever spilt in my tragedies. They'll give the crowds what they want."

"We won't let them!" I blurted, already horrified at the thought of a grisly stump at the end of my master's writing wrist. "We won't, Makaydees." I swallowed as the others all turned to me, startled by my outburst. "We'll always need new plays from your hand. To keep us moving forwards. To please our future crowds!"

"Future crowds?" he echoed, a mist in his brown eyes. "Ah yes, my hand still has new stories to tell. Stories to reflect on our changing world. We stand at the dawn of new century, lads. At the tarnished end of a golden age. And theatre is thriving. There's no better craft than ours. Tis too soon to raise a last toast to our dreams. Especially if I'll not have a hand to lift a glass. Which reminds me…"

He reached into his jerkin. The puff of his chest collapsed as he tugged out the wineskin he kept close to his heart. Makaydees put a finger to his lips, instructing us to hush so as not to alert our driver to our early morning libations. Rum scrambled upright in the straw. He was suddenly rather more inclined to stay awake.

"Honestly Makaydees!" Lavern hissed, waving the wineskin away when it was offered to him. "How's that going to help?"

"This is grease to the wheels of my thinking," Makaydees insisted. "Here Timony, you've earned a slug of your own."

I brought the wineskin to my lips, then lowered it again.

"What will they do to me? After correction?"

Rum sniggered. "Well, they think you're a girl. You'll be separated from us as soon as you arrive. Just don't let them marry you off! Else you'll be in a heap of trouble come your wedding night."

"Pay him no mind," Lavern interrupted. "Don't fret, Timony. You have the best chance of all of us. For the women in these places, once their sentence is up, they'll find work as a maid servant in the nearest parish. You could even find yourself on another farm."

"Back to what I was born into?!" I ranted. "Why does this world want to keep you in one place? Stuck in the same station? I...I want to be more than that! I've *been* more than that. I've been something else. I could be many other things besides if they'd let me. How could I have journeyed so far just to land back in the same place?!"

"Hoy! Quiet back there!" yelled our driver. "Lest you want me to halt this cart and give you an early taste of the lash."

I swallowed down any further furious speeches I could make. My fellows had already fallen into a hush, all blinking at me in surprise. It'd been a while since I had really listened to myself. Something had changed. My voice was softer and yet stronger in its tone. I must have been marking my master's pristine enunciations better than I thought, because I'd lost the rough edges of my old country accent. My manners were more refined too. I had cultivated a little feminine grace to my movements to replace my clumsy boyish fumbling. Then of course, there was my appearance. With my smock and my hair brushing my shoulders, it took me little effort to keep up the charade. I was at home in my girlish guise. It lay on me like a second skin.

"Our new apprentice has finally found his voice," Makaydees remarked. "A voice that we can use. But first, quiet it a moment, so I might think up a masterful scheme for our escape."

He snatched back the wineskin, which I'd yet to take a gulp from. Though after my lively gesticulations, there were now little red droplets speckling my hand. Red drops of wine the colour of dark blood. I licked them from my wrist, my mind suddenly whirling.

"Master, may I speak?" I said, raising my head.

"I've told you! I need silence if I am to form a plan..."

"It's just that I...I may already have one."

Scene Ten

The Dying Girl

It wouldn't be the first time I had staged my own death, but if I didn't want it to be the last, then I would have to make it my most horrifying attempt so far. Leastways, that was the plan.

During the remainder of our ride, I described to my fellows how I'd enacted all manner of mock demises during my childhood on the farm. How some had got me out of chores. How some had created a diversion to let me run away. And now I had the notion that if anything could disrupt our internment into the correction house, then it would be a sudden startling death scene. A display of theatrics that our captors wouldn't see coming, nor know how to deal with.

Our driver did not know that we were players. He must not have been told. For when we rode through the busier hamlets, the people living there would come and circle around his cart, asking to know who he was carrying. Common folk love to gawk at the latest convicts and hear their stories of scandal. As Makaydees put it *the unadventurous will always sneer over the misfortunes of the bold'*.

But these peasants, who poked at us through the cart struts, weren't given a true account of our tale. Our driver didn't proclaim that we were the infamous players who'd travelled in the company of Robin Candle. He only snorted that we were 'vagabonds' being sent for hard labour.

This gave us a chance. A chance to use our craft to our advantage. We made our plans and preparations the rest of the way on the road, Makaydees employed his playwright's skill to mould my raw ideas. We sat close as we could, whispering frantically in each other's ears. We were so deep in our devising that we were shocked when the cart came to a sudden halt. Lavern rose and peered over its side.

"We're here!" he reported, nerves rattling in his voice. "We're right at its gates. This is it, lads. Now or never."

We used our last moment of aloneness to squeeze one another's hands. Then Rum, Lavern and Makaydees all reached out to clasp my head, each looking me in the eyes in their turn, silently urging me to hold strong. They knew this show rested on me.

Then men were opening up the cart, removing the chains from our legs and ordering us to dismount. The four of us found ourselves in a small courtyard that seemed to serve as an induction area for the house of correction we'd come to. It looked like we were not the only new inmates arriving today. Already there were two more carts parked in the courtyard and a long line of worn ragged people, lining up before a stage. Upon this platform stood a woman with her arms bound to a flogging frame, her dress torn away from her shoulders and her back laid bare. Her skin was striped with whip weals.

"Harken to me!" said a man pacing the stage, lash in hand. "Once again, for those who are just joining us...this place you've been brought to is no prison. This here is a house of healing, taking in the poor and lawless like you. We'll be curing your idleness with honest work, so that you may be of some useful service once you're fit for release. We get the punishment you have earned out the way early, so your backs can be mending at the same time as your morals."

Following this short speech, the man lifted up his scourge again, striking it against the bound girl's back once more. Her scream rang out over the yard, a scream we'd soon be echoing if my performance failed to convince. Like the warden had said, any outlaw entering into a correction house was treated to no less than five strokes before they set about their labour. Makaydees had sworn that, as our theatre master, he would be taking all twenty for our company. But only if it came to that. Only if I couldn't stop it from happening.

After climbing down from the cart, I stood with Rum's arm coiled round my shoulder, leaning heavy into his side, my hair hanging about my face. For the role I was to play now, I was still wearing the same costume I'd been stuck with all week – the grubby smock covered in old bloodstains. There were a few other garish touches I'd added to my appearance. I'd taken a fistful of straw and rubbed it against my limbs, angering my rash and riddling my skin with scratch marks. I'd dipped each of my fingertips into Makaydees inkwell and smeared black under my eyes and over my cracked lips. I'd also taken a small cake of soap from Lavern's pocket and tucked into my cheek. When the time was ripe, I would suck on this soap and spew bubbles from my mouth. The girl I was playing today wasn't supposed to be beautiful. She was sick, deadly and dying. The scariest girl you could fear coming to your door. I had named her myself – Esther, after my mother.

I glanced to Makaydees, awaiting his direction.

"Hoy! It's not him you need to impress!" Rum reminded me. He nodded to the man on the stage, the warden holding the whip. "He's the one who chooses whether the gate opens or not. I'd wager he's at the end of his working week. The other guards will be feasting and quaffing in other quarters. This fellow won't want any complications. He'll be expected to deal with any trouble by himself."

I nodded, steeling myself. I knew what I had to do, but I was still clinging to Rum's sleeve, reluctant to move.

"Could you go back, Timmy?" Rum asked, seeming to sense my hesitation. "Could you ever go home to your farm again?"

I shook my head. "It never was a home to me. Not really. It wasn't till the night I saw Gwendolyn that I knew a place I might belong."

Rum nodded like he had already guessed my answer. "You were only in the crowd then. Now you're the one who's got to make these people believe. This is your show. Don't squander it."

Rum gave me a gentle shove between the shoulders and my legs fell into motion. This was it. I was making my entrance. I made sure to stagger, moaning beneath my breath, as I moved through the other prisoners in a feverish daze. I started up to the stairs leading onto the platform where the warden still stood. The man was currently barking orders for the whipped girl to be cut down from the frame and a new convict to be put in her place. Once up the stairs, I stumbled towards him and then promptly collapsed onto the boards.

"Please, sir..." I rasped, coughing close to his boots. "Read me my sins. What have I done to deserve this torment?"

The man turned and squinted down at me like I was a diseased dog at his feet. He took a pace backwards, his flogger still gripped in his fist. I watched it warily through the dank hair that hung over my face. I raised a hand, forcing a shudder through my outstretched arm and set my teeth chattering like I was suffering from a chill. Disturbed by my unhealthy little presence in his yard, the warden scanned the courtyard for the driver who had brought us in, only to find that the fellow and his cart were already out of the gate, doubtless in a hurry to get back to the coast before darkness fell upon another day.

"What ails this girl?" he yelled to all present. "Is she weak in the head? If so, she shouldn't be here, but a madhouse."

"The girl is no crank, sir," Makaydees called back. "We shared a cell with her in Plymouth and have travelled here with her today. In all that time she's been showing symptoms of some queer distemper. From what I have observed, this is not any usual kind of summer ague. No, I believe her sickness may be something altogether…new."

The warden frowned. "What are you? A quack?"

Makaydees smiled ingratiatingly and bowed. "Humbug Mullarkey at your service. And yes, I have been sent to correction for doctoring without a proper license. But I tell you, sir, I've seen enough disease in my days to know when a new plague is born."

The man's eyes widened. "Plague?"

This was my cue. The threat of a plague outbreak right here in this courtyard had already stirred fear in the air around me. A fear that erupted in shrieks as I jerked up and threw the hair back from face, revealing my blackened eyes and lips. I also chose this moment to bite down on the soap and start frothing at the mouth. I raised up my hands again, making sure that the crowd saw my dark nails before I began scratching at my cheeks and throat. It was Candle who'd shown me the power of putting on a horror show and now I screamed the same way he had done when his clothes were set aflame.

"Alas, I've made my diagnosis too late," said Makaydees, moving closer to the stage while others staggered back, covering their mouths. "Yes, the girl is showing signs of both Black Death and Scarlet Fever, combined with the convulsions that I've seen with the falling sickness. This may well be some new strain of illness brought over by sailors from the New World. Whatever her malady might be, let us pray she's not beyond cure...for we may all be contaminated."

At this prompt, I unleashed a scream, fell on my back and clawed madly at my clothes. The other prisoners and guards were already in a panic, a few of them now hissing the words *'Get her out! Get her out of here!'* between them. But as Rum had said, it wasn't them I needed to sway. I rolled over and lifted myself up onto my hands, slowly slithering upon my belly towards the warden.

"There's a fire under my skin!" I rasped. "It's burning me from the inside! I beg you, sir…a little water to put out the…"

He cracked his whip. "Back, you witch!"

The leather cord snapped in the air an inch away from my nose. I flinched and scrambled back across the stage. The warden was already stepping forward and raising his lash to strike again, this time looking poised to bring it down hard upon my spine. He would have done so too, if it hadn't been for the boy who bounded on the stage, a blur of heroics before my watering eyes. I blinked to see Rum standing before me. It was Rum who took the whip against his chest.

"*Coward!*" he blasted, the lash bringing him to his knees. "You would use that scourge on a helpless maid who never did any wrong in this world? I won't stand for it, you hear! She may be dying, but I'll not let her perish so friendless and forsaken."

I frowned up at Rum as he slipped an arm beneath my shoulders and cradled me to his now bleeding chest. I frowned because this wasn't supposed to be Rum's part. We had all voted during our tumbrel ride and decided that Lavern would be best suited to playing the hero role. Lavern with his handsome face which he'd used to disperse the mob from the Plymouth stocks. I glanced to see Lavern standing by the lip of the stage. He nodded for me to carry on, even though he plainly hadn't been expecting Rum to jump into his place either. Despite his villainous scars, something in Rum that had compelled him to come to my aid. Something instinctive. Something real.

"Water..." My fingers brushed Rum's cheek as I tried to recall Gwendolyn's death scene. "A little water...or the slightest fall of rain. A tear on my eyelids that I'll not open up again."

"Does anyone have a cup of water?" Rum called to the crowd, who now stood in rapt silence before us. "I must tend to this poor maiden's thirst...even if her affliction takes hold of me too."

I could hardly believe it. This was the scene I'd dreamt up all those weeks back when I first saw Rum on stage. When I'd first imagined it, I'd pictured Rum and I in opposing roles, but admittedly I found that I was more at home performing it this way around. However this moment had come about...it was perfect. And it was ours.

"Here!" Makaydees yelled, reaching into his pocket. "I may have a cure! A tonic I picked up from a miracle doctor on the road. He called this remedy his *Elixir of Life* for it is known to purge sickness from stricken patients, even those who are only a heartbeat away from death. So please, thou noble youth. If you are indeed the bravest man here today…I beg that you administer this medicine."

The inmates watched breathless and hopeful as Rum reached to the edge of the stage and took the bottle out of Makaydees outstretched hand. He did not hesitate a moment but pressed the bottled elixir to my lips. And I was grimly aware of what was coming next. I had been told by now that Makaydees had originally bought this powerful tonic from an apothecary who'd sworn that it would cure the bellyaches brought on by his worst drinking binges. And I knew well from witnessing its effect on others how this *'cure'* came about.

A few moments after this foul medicine sluiced down my throat, I felt my stomach lurch in protest. I jerked upright, still clinging to Rum's jacket, and vomited over both of us. My mouth tasted of the wine I had finished off during the cart journey, but the red stains that spread over our clothes looked more like coughed up blood.

"Keep back! For your lives, *keep back!*" Lavern yelled out as the crowd all reeled in terror once more. "I dare say this girl may be prone to spontaneous combustion, her sickness exploding out of her like a storm wind, dooming all who are touched by it."

"Get her out of here!" the warden was howling himself now. "You boy – take my key and bear her out through that door in the

gates. If you're so keen to play the martyr then pick up your festering maiden and hurry you both far away from this house!"

The warden took his key chain from his belt and hurled it across the stage where it landed inches from Rum's grasp. Rum lifted his head, forcing his face into a valiant grimace. Then he stooped his back and tried to raise me in his arms. I immediately commenced my thrashing, struggling so violently Rum could not lift me.

"May the Devil strike me down!" I shrieked, channelling my ma's infernal fury. "May he damn me straight to HELL!"

"Ah yes, I've heard this can happen," Makaydees said sagely, the only calm voice to be heard in the courtyard. "It is said that when the sufferer's body is in the final throws of its illness it may gain a savage inhuman strength. I fear this brave lad will not be able to save us alone. You'll need more than one man to bear her away."

"Then get to it, man!" the warden snarled, his hysteria rising. "You were the fellows she rode in with. *You* take her!"

If the warden had been in a calmer state, he might have guessed he was being conned. But with the smell of bile in the air, red puddles on the stage and my screams in his ears, our spectacle had worked its dark magic, the only magic that there truly was in this land. The man could only wave a shaking finger at us actors, playing our roles to perfection while he in turn played right into our hands.

"*Go!*" the warden ordered. "Go you filthy vagrants! Carrying your pestilence from town to town. You brought this plague upon us! Now you take it away and don't dare ever come back!"

I could see that Makaydees was struggling not to smile, delighted that he hadn't even needed to make this suggestion himself. This was a trick we had borrowed from the mermaid girls of Bristol who could con their patrons out of their every stitch of clothing and send them away naked, still feeling certain they'd been done a good turn.

"As you wish, sir," our master said with an obliging sigh. "Indeed, tis time we took responsibility for our reckless lives. We have a chance to redeem ourselves with this duty. We'll spare the people of this house by conveying this girl into the woods where she can die with as much dignity as her toils will allow. We can give her a proper burial at least. And not long after her passing, I warrant we will succumb to her same fate. But with the blessing of this kind warden, we'll spend our last days in freedom, recalling our little lives under the sun..."

"Yes, yes!" the warden ranted. "No need to make so many words." He waved his scourge at the gates. "Just go!"

Makaydees and Lavern shared a solemn nod, then came together to take hold of my writhing limbs, lifting me off the stage and bearing me to the gate on their shoulders in the manner of a funeral march. I let my body go limp, my screams fading to a soft melodic moan. I cracked one eye open, twisting my neck to see the prisoners we passed watching us with a breathless awe, some of them offering little bows of gratitude. Either they were taken in by our show, or else they had seen through our sham and had enjoyed our spectacle all the same. I let my eyes fall closed again as I heard Rum turning the key.

What lay beyond the gates of the correction house was a long walk to the shelter of the nearest forest. My fellows carried me until we were out of sight of our almost prison and then lowered me gently onto the grass. Together we trudged on bare broken feet, holding one another up and resisting the urge to collapse for just a little longer. Makaydees took the lead, clinging to Lavern like he was a living crutch. The two of them hurried us forth to the treeline where we were hoping to find Francis, Wally and our wagon secluded in the shade.

"Now *that*..." Rum panted, sidling close to me, "...is what I call a death scene. That death will haunt their dreams for years to come!" He grinned at me. "And it's sure to be the first of many..."

We stared at each other, letting our pace slow and our triumph sink in. I'd just pulled off my first speaking role while Rum had shown his worth as a leading man. More than a playhouse hero, for the line of blood streaking his shirt came from his own lashing.

"A pleasure to die in your arms, sir," I cooed, my voice pretty as a princess, though I looked more like a leprous harpy.

"The pleasure was all mine," Rum returned with a flourishing bow. "I'd kiss you, milady, if your breath didn't smell so foul."

"Coward!" I shot back, slapping his arm. "Your lips would taste just as vile. But what's a little foul air between vagrants?"

Rum raised his eyebrows like he was sensing a challenge. He was never one to back down from a dare. He looked ahead to Makaydees and Lavern, who were several paces ahead of us and not looking back. There was nobody with eyes on us. Nothing here that could be called an audience. Seizing this moment, Rum turned back to me, took my face in his palms and pressed his mouth to mine. Our kiss tasted of sweat and sour wine. It tasted of being young and free.

"There," said Rum, breaking away and haughtily averting his gaze. "That'll give you something to dream about too."

Rum walked alongside me with a roguish swagger but his smile was boyish and tender. I smiled too and I didn't say anything. Not because I was too shy to speak, but because sometimes nothing needs to be said. Sometimes it's enough just to know. Then a voice called out, breaking the hush that had fallen between us.

"Well met, lads!" the voice exclaimed. "You may not be looking your fairest, but I've never been so glad to see you."

We snapped to attention to see Wally standing in the shadow of a tree, one arm in a sling, a smile splitting his face. Francis was there by his side, his crinkled eyes already tearing. And though they both looked every bit as spent as we were, they rushed forth for a round of embraces. We took a long moment just squeezing and staring at each other to be sure we were all here and whole. Following our reunion only Rum had the breath left to regale them with the story of our escape.

The rest of us collapsed down on a damp bed of dew-laced grass. I closed my eyes and soon felt more droplets falling on my face. The water I'd called for in the courtyard had arrived in the form of a rain shower. I lay still and let it soak my skin. I parted my lips and it rolled over my tongue, soothing my scream worn throat. I listened to the slapping it made against the leaves in the trees above.

A sound that was as glorious as applause.

Epilogue

We spent what was left of the summer by the sea.

Since his injury, Wally could no longer make a fist with his right hand, but he could still steer our company in a safe direction. He took us to the secret beaches of north Devon where we sheltered in a cove curtained by grassy cliffs. We spent our days foraging, rock pooling and healing our wounds in the salty lapping waves. In the evening we huddled round campfires, feasting on crabs, clams and seaweed broth. We stayed up late telling stories and we dozed away our dawns. At the time, I asked Lavern why we should ever want to leave.

'No audiences here' was what he told me.

I knew soon enough I'd be craving the road and our next stage. But I'd also been yearning for this – to be among my troupe, to belong with them, to learn my craft from them. Francis taught me how to sew and I stitched new patterns into his old costumes so as to make those frocks my own. Rum, meanwhile, instructed me on how to ride our cart horse, who we'd named 'Dorothy' for its tender brown eyes. When Rum had pointed out that our beast of

burden was a colt and not a mare, I'd only shrugged and said –
'Let it be what it wants'.

It was my time with Makaydees that I cherished the most. It was on those beaches I learned my letters, my first words scrawled with sticks in the sand before the tide swept in to wash them away. I begged my master for a quill and parchment, wishing to make my words stay. But he said I must wait...till I was ready to use them.

This is a story that's come of waiting. That's come from taking the time to learn what I long to be. And like any restless dreamer in this world, I want to be everything. I want to wear many costumes and live many lives, a player to the bone. I want to find those crowds who will care to listen. Who will let my ladies take them by the hand and lead them into other worlds beyond their imaginings.

These are all the words I have for now.

Time for this quill to take a bow of its own.

Till my next stage, dear hearts,

Your Timony

Timony, Makaydees, Rum and the rest will return in

THE PLAYER'S CRAFT

To find out more about our books and authors, be sure to
visit and follow Odd Voice Out Publishing.

www.oddvoiceout.com

twitter.com/oddvoiceout

facebook.com/oddvoiceout

instagram.com/oddvoiceout

About the Author

Chester author Kell Cowley wrote and illustrated her first novel at age eight, telling the story of a runaway radish escaping from a salad bowl to explore the far reaches of the vegetable garden. She has been perplexing her friends and family with her weird stories ever since. She holds a BA in Performance Writing from the wildly experimental Dartington College of Arts, won a novelist's apprenticeship with the Adventures in Fiction development scheme and was a prize winning finalist in the international cli-fi competition for the 'Everything Change' anthology. When she occasionally closes her laptop or latest reading obsession to spend time in the real world, she will likely be found shambolically running a school library, attempting to act in local plays or eco-warrioring her way towards the apocalypse.

THE SUBMERGED SUITE

DRINKING
SEAWATER
IN ALA

By Kate Curtis

One week before the Global Minister... Hibernation and Pica Wheeler will do anything to avoid living winter underground. A claustrophobic climate refugee who has been living rough in the flooded streets of Manchester, Pica dreads the day, she'll be forced into shelter so a geoengineering experiment can attempt to reverse the chaotic effects of global warming. Armed with nothing but her stolen umbrella, Pica is on a mission to stay on the surface and somehow survive the extreme weather.

Shunning Sinking Land is a YA cli-fi story of survival, solidarity and defiance in the face of environmental catastrophe for ages 14 and up.

Copthorne Change Climate Fiction Contest Runner Up (2016)

Suspenseful... sharply well-written... and altogether a success.
Kate Stanley, R. Benson, New York, 2020

By Kell Cowley

One week before the Global Mandatory Hibernation and Flea Wheeler will do anything to avoid a long winter underground. A claustrophobic climate refugee who has been living rough on the flooded streets of Manchester, Flea dreads the day she'll be forced into shelter so a geoengineering experiment can attempt to reverse the chaotic effects of global warming. Armed with nothing but her stolen umbrella, Flea is on a mission to stay on the surface and somehow survive the extreme weather.

'Shrinking Sinking Land' is a YA cli-fi story of survival, solidarity and defiance in the face of environmental catastrophe for ages 14 and up.

Everything Change Climate Fiction Contest Runner Up (2016).

"Suspenseful…sharply well-written…and altogether a success."
Kim Stanley Robinson, *New York 2140*

SHADEBOUND

THE BOOK OF SHADE

By K.C. Finn

Lily Coraline's to-do list for staying unfeasibly life is pretty simple:
1. Make friends.
2. Make it count.
3. Survive her first year in Mouse Harbour.

In the little English town of Piketon this seems more than achievable, so much so that Lily even joins The Illustrious Albion Literary Society, an extra-curricular club that promises a truly unique social experience. What Lily doesn't reckon on are the society's monthly visits to the mysterious Theatre Imaginique at the edge of town, a dark venue that houses the most obscure cavalcade of carnival performers she has ever laid eyes on.

Stranger still is the theatre's enigmatic proprietor, Demariné Noval, a stupendous showman with a broad smile who never seems to smile. How does he levitate with no sign of wires or mirrors? Why do the frightening bolts that shoot from his hands look so real? And why, of all the people in the theatre, do his pale eyes keep looking on Lily?

One decade of the macabre is ushered in heritage and blood. The Book of Shade is opening, and Lily Coraline will read it, whether she wants to or not.

SHADEBORN

THE BOOK OF SHADE

By K.C. Finn

Lily Coltrane's to-do list for starting university life is pretty simple:
1. Make friends
2. Meet a cute guy
3. Survive her first year in Modern History

In the little English town of Piketon this seems more than achievable, so much so that Lily even joins The Illustrious Minds Literary Society, an extra-curricular club that promises a truly unique social experience. What Lily doesn't bank on are the society's monthly visits to the mysterious Theatre Imaginique at the edge of town, a dark venue that houses the most obscure cavalcade of carnival performers she has ever laid eyes on.

Stranger still is the theatre's enigmatic proprietor, Lemarick Novel, a stupendous showman with a frosty wit who never seems to smile. How does he levitate with no sign of wires or mirrors? Why do the lightning bolts that shoot from his hands look so real? And why, of all the people in the theatre, do his pale eyes keep locking on Lily?

The answers to this and more lie buried in heritage and blood. The Book of Shade is opening, and Lily Coltrane will read it, whether she wants to or not.

FALLOW HEART

By K.C. Finn

Fallow Heart is the story of Lori Blake, a sixteen... overweight sixteen-year-old who discovers that a demon has pierced her heart, sparking an incredible transformation. Sleepwalking, fits of rage and impossible strength force Lori to accept that part of her is no longer human...

FALLOW HEART

By K.C. Finn

When a gruesome murder spree leads to the door of a teenage loser, she is forced to face the reality that something demonic is growing inside her.

Fallow Heart is the story of Lorelai Blake, a self-conscious, overweight seventeen-year-old who discovers that a demon has pierced her heart, sparking an incredible transformation. Sleepwalking, fits of rage and impossible strength force Lori to accept that part of her is no longer human. It was hard enough fitting in before, and now that hurtful voice in her head has taken an even more sinister tone. Worse than this, bodies are being discovered. People in Chester are dying and they have only one connection: a nocturnal killer who savages its prey.

Fallow Heart is a tale of strength, suspicion and the supernatural for ages fourteen and up.